She raised her head at a soft sound at the front door.

Ivy cocked her head and listened. Sometimes the wind created odd noises here. The door bell had never worked during her residence, and visitors had to knock.

It came again. Not exactly a knock, but more of a spongy thump. It was too soon for Mac to have made it all the way from Hollywood, but somebody was out there. She got up and went to look.

There were no close neighbors to hear Ivy Hurlbut scream. . . .

CARRION

Fawcett Gold Medal Books
by Gary Brandner:

THE BRAIN EATERS
CAT PEOPLE
HELLBORN
THE HOWLING
THE HOWLING II
THE HOWLING III
QUINTANA ROO
WALKERS

CARRION

Gary Brandner

FAWCETT GOLD MEDAL • NEW YORK

Chapter 1

On a cool Monday evening in February, McAllister Fain pulled heavy crimson draperies across the windows of his second-floor apartment. He put a tape of gutless organ selections on the stereo and lit a stick of jasmine incense. He dimmed the lights and lit candles at strategic locations. Then he stepped to the center of the room to study the effect.

Not too bad, he decided. He walked around, straightening the metaphysical prints he had hung over the Utrillo prints and making small adjustments in the positions of the occult objects he had placed about the room. Outside, a dog could be heard barking, and someone shouted in Spanish for the owner to shut him up or shoot him. Beneath the jasmine swam the peppery aroma of menudo being cooked by the family downstairs. The neighborhood could never be completely shut out.

The neighborhood was the Echo Park district of Los Angeles, a multiethnic backwater in the stream of progress. The architecture of Echo Park was such that it was employed as a locale for motion pictures looking for a 1930s ambience. The movie companies had merely to shoo the locals out of the way, hide the TV antennas, scrub off the graffiti, and they had a reasonable facsimile of Los Angeles fifty years ago.

1

The people who lived in Echo Park included old people who had always lived there, funky artists up in the hills, and young strivers who figured to make a killing when property values went up. By far the majority Echo Park citizens were the down-scale Cubans, Mexicans, Anglos, and Asians who lived in the four-unit apartment buildings and the chopped-up old houses and did not give a damn about the sociological makeup of their community.

Mrs. Viola Trowbridge arrived shortly after Fain had the room arranged to his satisfaction. For her the neighborhood outside the draped windows had no more reality than a stage set. She sat gazing across the table in rapt attention as Fain studied the tarot cards he had laid out in the Keltic Cross. Mrs. Trowbridge's bosom surged up and down beneath the black taffeta dress as she fastened on his every word.

"Very definitely, Mrs. Trowbridge," he said, "there is a gentleman about to become involved in your life. See the King of Cups here in the number-six position?"

"Yes," she said breathily. "Will it be soon, do you think?"

Fain raised his head and looked at her. He had a bony face that looked rather pleasant in the sunlight, but when lit from below, as it was now, it had a mystical, almost satanic cast. His eyes, with irises of pale gray beneath heavy black brows, turned even a casual glance into a piercing gaze.

Fain studied the eager, hopeful face of the woman. "Yes, I would say soon. Possibly he is even in your life now. A substantial man of business. Perhaps connected with the law?"

"Could it be Mr. Inman? He's my accountant."

Fain studied the cards again. "The tarot is not quite that specific, but there does seem to be some connection to figures. To ledgers."

"He does it all on computers."

"Exactly."

"Can I trust him? He won't cheat me, will he? Do the cards tell you that?"

McAllister Fain smiled at her, softening the flat planes of his face. He leaned back, lessening the satanic effect of the underlighting. "My dear Mrs. Trowbridge, I have to remind you that I don't tell fortunes. The Los Angeles police are quite diligent about enforcing the laws against fortune-telling."

Mrs. Trowbridge snorted. "Isn't that always the way. Why don't they use all that energy to catch some of the muggers and rapists who are walking the streets as free as you and me?"

Fain spread his hands and shrugged to show that he did not know the answer.

"Anyway," Mrs. Trowbridge said, "can I trust him?"

Fain returned his attention to the cards. He turned another face up. "Ah, the Ace of Pentacles."

"That's good?"

"In the number-seven position it relates to your fears. Now, considering your question about Mr.—Inman, was it?"

She nodded.

"It would definitely look good. The Ace of Pentacles signifies the onset of a new prosperity. Yes, I would say that you can trust Mr. Inman. At least in financial matters."

"What about . . . in other ways. I mean, say he wants to get romantic with me."

A clock chimed softly across the room. Fain smiled wearily.

"That is another question, Mrs. Trowbridge. We can take that up in detail next time."

She blushed under a layer of powder. "I hope I don't have to get too detailed, if you know what I mean."

"Of course not," he said. "I'm not a therapist. You just tell me whatever you want to, and we'll go from there."

"You are a gem, McAllister," she said.

He waved off the compliment, using his free hand to turn up the lights from a rheostat concealed under the table.

Mrs. Trowbridge pulled a checkbook from her over-sized purse and began writing with a slim gold pen.

"You've given me such good news today, I'm adding a little something to the usual fee."

"That's not necessary. After all, I'm not responsible

for what happens to you. I merely do my best to read what's in the cards."

"That's all right," she said, signing with a flourish. "It makes me happy to do it."

"Well, in that case . . ." Fain accepted the check and made it disappear.

"I was wondering . . ." she said tentatively.

"What's that?"

"You know my William has been gone four years now."

Fain lowered his eyes. "Yes, I know."

"Sometimes I wonder if he would, well, approve of, you know, me and Mr. Inman."

Faint shrugged again. "Why wouldn't he?"

"William was a jealous man when he was alive. Do you ever do those seance things?"

He hesitated before answering. "I have. It's not what you'd call a specialty of mine."

"Do you think you could do one for me? Contact William, wherever he is?"

"Many things are possible, Mrs. Trowbridge. It would take some preparation, mental preparation, on my part."

She stood up, tugging her skirt into place. "No hurry. I just thought I'd mention it."

"I'll give it some thought," he said. "Same time next week?"

She touched her pewter-colored hair. "I might want to make it sooner. Things could happen fast with Mr. Inman."

"Just give me a call," he said.

He walked her to the door and stood outside at the head of the steps, watching as she descended to the street and got into her Cadillac Seville.

Next door his neighbor was swearing in Cuban Spanish at the hulk of a Volkswagen van he was perpetually trying to restore to life. As he worked, he kicked halfheartedly at a chicken that pecked the ground at his feet.

Mrs. Trowbridge leaned over to look up through the window of the Cadillac and wave at Fain as she drove off.

He waved back, then reentered the apartment. He

strolled around the room, yanking open the draperies, dousing the incense. He killed the taped organ mush and replaced it with Kenny Burrell.

He swept up the tarot cards, pausing to make the Queen of Swords vanish, appear in his other hand, vanish again, then rise slowly from his breast pocket. He nodded, satisfied, and put the deck back into a table drawer. In the bedroom he changed from his working clothes—dark blue slacks and black turtleneck—into tan slacks and a soft brown shirt. He went into the kitchen, poured himself a shot of Jose Cuervo, then returned to the living room and sank into his soft vinyl recliner.

Jillian Pappas arrived twenty minutes later. As usual, she sailed in without knocking, dropped her tote bag at the door, and moved ceaselessly about the room as she recited the events of her day. She was a limber five feet seven, with a startling combination of midnight-black hair and electric-blue eyes.

"So I told this guy if he thought I was going to start putting out for a lousy part in some equity-waiver theater, he was out of his freeping mind."

Jillian did not use any of the common obscenities; she substituted her own colorful euphemisms.

"I mean, I'm practically thirty. Well, all right, I *am* thirty, and I'm not about to go for that kind of schmeiss."

"You didn't get the part," said Fain.

"I don't think so. There was some blond babe there with bajoomies out to here. No way was she right for it, but I could tell she was going to get it."

"The bajoomies," Fain said.

"The director couldn't keep his eyes off them. Or wait to get his hands *on* them."

"Speaking of which, are you going to come over here and say hello?"

She skipped across the room and flopped into his lap, knocking the breath out of him. She took hold of his head and kissed him firmly and thoroughly on the mouth. Both of them were breathing a little harder when she finally drew back.

"More like it," he said.

"Oh, I almost forgot." She jumped up and danced

5

across the room. She dived into her tote bag and came out with a copy of the L.A. *Insider*. She carried the tabloid back and handed it to Fain.

"I stopped at the supermarket on the way over and picked it up. Your ad's in this week."

He took the paper from her, glancing briefly at the front page: "I Am Elvis's Son, Claims Downey Teenager" . . . "Born Legless, Mother of Three Enters Marina Marathon." He flipped to the back pages. There a bordered two-inch ad read:

SECRETS OF THE SUPERNATURAL
Seer—Mystic—Oracle
M. Fain, Master of the Occult
Readings by Appointment

His address and telephone number followed.

Jillian put her head close to his as he read. "It doesn't say very much."

"It's not supposed to. Just enough to intrigue a client who is looking for some metaphysical edge in the battle with life."

"I love it when you talk like that."

Fain raised his empty glass. "You want a drink?"

"Got any beer? I'm thirsty as a horse."

"Sure." He walked into the kitchen, with Jillian behind him, and took a frosty can of Coors from the refrigerator and poured it into a mug. Jillian accepted it gratefully and drank a quarter of the beer before pausing.

"Where are we going for dinner?" she said.

"I thought Chez McAllister."

"Again?"

"Business has been slow," he said. "Besides, I found a great new recipe for marinara sauce in *Penthouse*."

"*Penthouse*? What kind of a recipe could you get from *Penthouse*?"

"You'll see."

The linguini with marinara sauce turned out to be more than passable, helped along by a cabernet sauvignon from what McAllister called a small but obscure winery in Mendocino County.

When he raised the bottle to refill their glasses a third time, Jillian said, "Aren't you getting an awful lot of wine out of that one little bottle?"

"I thought you'd never notice," he said.

"Oh, Mac, it's one of your tricks."

"I cannot tell a lie. An ancient illusion called the Sultan's Wine Flask."

"How do you do it?"

"You know magicians never tell."

"Okay."

"Since you coax me so prettily, I will reveal the secret. Observe." He stripped off the light jacket he had put on for dinner to expose a harness and bladder rig with a hose running down one arm to the wrist. "The Sultan's Wine Flask."

"It looks uncomfortable."

He shrugged himself out of the contraption. "A little pain is to be expected for art's sake."

"Art my Adam's apple," Jillian said.

"You're not impressed."

"Sure, Mac, it's a great trick, but aren't you, well, a little beyond that sort of thing?"

"I thought you'd enjoy it."

She came around the table and kissed him, running her fingers up the back of his neck in a way that gave him tingles.

"Honey, I do enjoy you, tricks and all. But tricks are for parties. You do them all day long. You're smart, and you've got talent. You're reasonably young and not bad-looking. You could do a lot of other things, legitimate things, if you put your mind to it. And make a lot more money, too."

"I make all the money I need. And what do you mean *legitimate* things? What I'm doing is perfectly legitimate."

"Fooling old ladies with this fortune-telling and psychic-reading stuff."

"I make them happy."

"And take their money."

"Not much of it, as you point out frequently."

"You could do better, Mac; you know you could. You went to college."

"Oh, sure, a B.A. in psychology. That wouldn't get me a job in a car wash."

"You could go back to school."

"Come on, baby, I'm thirty-six years old. Maybe I could come out with a Ph.D. at forty-two. Then what? Start out as an assistant in some two-bit clinic?"

"Why not?"

"Because it's not what I want to do. I dish out as much solid psychology right here as most of those 'I'm okay—you're okay' guys."

Jillian sighed. "You're probably right. I suppose I wouldn't want you if you were any different. Or you wouldn't want me. I better leave well enough alone." She started to pick up the dishes from the table.

"Leave 'em," he said.

"You don't want me to do the dishes?"

"Not right now."

"If we leave them, they'll get all crusty and hard to wash."

"Are you coming to the bedroom with me, or do I have to carry you?"

She looked up at him through thick sable lashes. "Carry me."

They undressed together in the glow of a soft amber lamp, thoroughly comfortable with each other's body. When they were naked, Fain sat on the edge of the bed and pulled Jill toward him. He pressed his face to her small, yielding breasts, kissing first one, then the other.

"That director was crazy," he said. "You've got the finest pair of bajoomies in Southern California."

"Southern only?"

"You know I never go north of Santa Barbara."

She pushed him down on the bed with little resistance and kissed him lightly on the knee. Her tongue moved slowly up the inside of his thigh.

He groaned.

She raised her head. "A funny thing happened today."

"Jesus, you're not going to tell me a joke!"

"No joke. A funny thing really happened to me. Can I tell you about it?"

8

He groaned again, a different groan.

"You know how a month ago my aunt Rowena died. Well, I was waiting to cross Sunset today, and a bus came by. I happened to look up and saw Aunt Rowena grinning at me from one of the windows. She was as close to me as that picture of an Indian over there. I almost dropped my cookies. I ran after the bus to the next stop, right up to the same window, and what do you think?"

"Tell me," he said.

"There was nobody in that seat. It was empty."

After a pause, he said, "That's it?"

"Isn't that enough, for crumb sake? There's my aunt dead a month, staring at me from the window of a bus."

"Hmm," he said.

"So what do you think?"

"Me?"

"You're the fleeking psychic."

"I think you saw a lady on a bus who resembled your late aunt. I think after the bus passed you, she changed her seat or got up to get off. Or passed out on the floor, for all I know."

"No, really, Mac, couldn't it have been a spiritual experience of some kind?"

He sat up and kissed away the tiny frown line between her brows. "Sweetheart, if there is one thing I have learned, it is never to deny the possibility of anything. All the same, the chances that it was Aunt Rowena's ghost are slim. In all my experience, it has been the tendency of dead people to stay dead."

Jillian was pensive for a moment; then she sighed. "It sure did look like Aunt Rowena. Where was I?"

He lay back down and pointed. "Right here."

Chapter 2

While McAllister Fain slept happily in the arms of his lady, another man sat wearily wakeful across the city. In the moneyed atmosphere of Holmby Hills, Elliot Kruger sat alone in one of the forty rooms of his Spanish-castle home. His head hung forward, supported by his long, bony hands. There were dark purplish smudges under his eyes. A funguslike stubble clung to his cheeks. His white hair hung limp and stringy. Elliot Kruger, who had always looked younger than his years, now looked the full sixty-three, and ten more.

From time to time he glanced off toward the tall French windows that overlooked an expanse of the rear lawn. Beyond that lay the swimming pool and a row of eucalyptus trees that guarded the pool house. Kruger could see only vague outlines in the darkness, but in his mind every line and angle of the pool house was etched forever. In the stillness he fancied he could hear the mutter of the generator idling there. No failure of the lines would cut off power to the pool house.

He sighed and slumped deeper in the high-backed chair that dated to the Spanish Inquisition. Always a robust man, Kruger now seemed shrunken and dried out in the cavernous room and the oversized chair.

At the far wall a log fire was dying slowly in a hearth

built of stones from a Moorish castle. From the high-beamed ceiling an eighteenth-century chandelier provided a subdued light. The three-hundred-year-old Italian harpsichord stood silent, its ornate scrollwork reflecting a dull gleam.

On this night Elliot Kruger was oblivious to his house and his possessions. The wealth his father had amassed and Elliot had increased gave him no pleasure now. With a phone call he could have bought the entire block of Echo Park where McAllister Fain lived without making an appreciable dent in his fortune. Yet at that moment he would gladly have exchanged places.

How different the world had become in just four months. In 120 days his life had crumbled. Kruger's thoughts returned for the thousandth time to the day it began.

October 30, it was. The day before Halloween. Leanne had been busy all morning with arrangements for the party they were giving the next day. Early in the afternoon Kruger came into their bedroom still sweaty after three sets of tennis. Leanne was in front of a full-length mirror, trying on her witch costume; Rosalia knelt beside her, making last-minute adjustments.

Leanne turned and smiled at him. As always, his heart gave a lurch when he looked at her. Not until the seventh decade of his life did Elliot Kruger learn what it was like to be in love. And now he loved to distraction. He loved Leanne's rich brown hair, which she wore long and full, the way he liked it. He loved the big expressive eyes that could look right into his soul. He loved the wide mouth that even in repose seemed ready to smile. He loved the smooth, graceful body that molded itself to his in their bed. He loved her enthusiasm, and he loved her youth.

"How do I look?" she asked.

"Like the most beautiful witch there ever was."

"You don't think it's too revealing?"

"It would be a crime to hide all that."

"Come here and give me a hug."

"I haven't showered."

"Who cares?"

11

She held out her arms, and he came willingly into them. Rosalia stood back and smiled at the shared joy of her people.

Kruger squeezed Leanne, enjoying the firm, resilient feel of her through the satiny witch costume. Suddenly, she tensed under his touch. He released her and stepped back.

"What is it?"

"Nothing. Just my big strong husband."

Kruger raised the costume's short skirt and gently touched a purplish bruise on the inside of her thigh. "Is this still bothering you?"

"No, I hardly know it's there. I'll have to cover it with makeup tomorrow night, won't I. Who ever heard of a witch with a black-and-blue mark?"

"I wish you'd let Auerbach take a look at it. It's been a week now, and the bruise should look better than that."

"How sweet to have a man so concerned about every little bump. Anyway, I'd be embarrassed to tell anybody how it happened. I mean, how many people bang themselves up getting on a horse?"

"All the same—"

"Or I could tell everybody you did it to me in bed. Out of your mind with passion."

Kruger could not keep from laughing. "All right, but if it doesn't look better in a couple of days, I'm going to bring Auerbach over here whether you want me to or not."

Leanne embraced him again. "What a worrier you are. But sweet."

Through the door dashed an animated ball of white fluff. It jumped up and pawed at Kruger and his wife, yapping excitedly.

Kruger released Leanne and looked down. "Damned if I don't think that dog is jealous of me."

"Don't be silly. Pepe loves both of us. You're his daddy now."

Kruger tried to look exasperated but couldn't make it. He relaxed into a grin. "Little did I know I was inheriting a family."

* * *

12

The last log crashed in the hearth with a display of red-orange sparks. Elliot Kruger slowly raised his head and stared at the room's dark walls. The rich Spanish tapestries hanging there did not register. From somewhere in the big house a grandfather clock bonged the hour. The deep note echoed through the silent rooms and corridors, bouncing off the dark walls and rolling through the empty crannies.

Empty. Forty rooms richly decorated and furnished with authentic Spanish antiques. Empty. Half of them closed off now. Still too much for one old man and a handful of servants who walked on silent feet.

Kruger lowered his head again and covered his face. Tears dampened his cheeks, pale now without their accustomed tan. He sobbed silently, thinking of what he had lost.

They had made love that last night before Halloween in the huge bed that Leanne had always laughed about.

"It's much too big for the two of us," she had said. "We could get lost."

"I'll find you," he said.

"You'd better. And don't try slipping out of my reach. I like touching you at night."

He laughed and shook his head.

She gave the bed a mock frown. "It *is* awfully big. We could have another couple in and never know it."

"I intend to keep it just for you and me."

"Well, I certainly hope so."

Their lovemaking that night had been delightful as always. Leanne was inventive, enthusiastic, and passionate. She was as warm and giving as Opal had been cold and selfish. In thirty-nine years of marriage to his first wife, Kruger had not experienced anything like the wild pleasure of his twelve short months with Leanne.

Afterward he lay on his back while she swabbed his body with a moist scented towel.

"God, you make me feel like a boy again. You really do."

She tapped him on the nose with the towel. "Will you stop with that age business?"

"I *am* forty years older than you," he said softly.

"Thirty-nine," she corrected. "I had a birthday, remember?"

"My son Richard could be your father."

"Well, I'm glad he isn't. Richard doesn't approve of me."

"There isn't much Richard does approve of."

Leanne was thoughtful for a moment. "Was your other son very different?"

"Gil was another breed entirely. There was only a year between their ages, with Richard the older, but you would have thought he was the father. Gil had a joy in him, a zest for life, that his brother lacked. It was partly my fault, I guess, for being closer to Gil. I've been trying to make it up to Richard for nineteen years, ever since Gil was killed.

"An accident, wasn't it?"

"Racing. Gil was driving with the Ferrari team in Madrid, and a freak gust of wind caught him. Flipped the car into the air. It exploded when it came down."

"It must have been hard for you."

"A long time ago," Kruger said. "Anyway, I do have Richard. He can be stuffy, but I know he worries about me. Thinks he has to protect me in my dotage."

"Do you need protection?"

"Come here and let's find out."

He pulled her down on top of him and kissed her mouth. He tasted her tongue, warm cinnamon. Her breasts spread against his chest, and the puff of her pubic hair brushed his lower stomach. He felt the beginning of another erection.

"My God, will you look at me!"

"I'll do more than look," she said, reaching down to take him in her cool, busy fingers.

He gasped. "Sometimes I think you *are* a witch."

"Is that a complaint?"

He grasped her smooth buttocks with his hands and let his body give her the answer.

With a groaning effort Kruger pushed himself up out of the chair and crossed the room to the tall window. He stared out into the night. His own ravaged face looked back at him from the dark pane.

14

The pool house and what it held had been the only thing he and Leanne had ever quarreled about. Not a quarrel, really; she just hadn't approved. She hadn't understood.

"I'm sorry, Elliot," she had said when first he took her out there. "It makes me feel creepy. It isn't natural." When she saw the look on his face, she had taken his hand and tried to smile. "Maybe if you explained it to me. The truth is I really don't know much about— What is it, cryogenics?"

"It's called cryonic interment," he said. "The steel cylinder is kept at a temperature of minus a hundred ninety-six degrees Centigrade with liquid nitrogen."

"And that will keep a body from . . . you know?"

"That's right. The blood is pumped out first and preserved separately. It's replaced with a kind of biologic antifreeze solution to protect the tissues. The theory is that sometime in the future medical science will come up with a cure for whatever killed you, so they thaw you out, administer the cure, and bingo, you're back in business."

Kruger's attempt to keep it light fell flat.

"That's the theory," Leanne said. "Have they ever done it?"

"Not yet."

She looked with distaste at the steel cylinder, about the size of an old-fashioned iron lung. "Didn't Walt Disney have it done?"

"That was only a rumor. Disney's relatives had his remains cremated."

"Good for them."

"It's not a crime, you know. Not wanting to die before your time."

"I know, darling," she said softly. "I don't want you to die, either." Thoughtfully, she added, "You don't hear much about it anymore."

"I know. There was a scandal seven or eight years ago when one cryonics outfit went bankrupt. They skipped town, leaving a load of debts."

"What happened to the . . . clients?"

Kruger coughed. "Well, the liquid nitrogen has to be

15

renewed every month, and without the proper mainte- nance they—''

"Rotted." Leanne supplied, and shuddered.

Kruger pulled her to him. "It didn't have to happen. That's why I wanted my cylinder right here, where it can be maintained by my own people. I've made it an absolute requirement in my will."

Leanne shivered, although the temprature outside the cylinder was a comfortable sixty-eight degrees. "Can we go now?" she said.

"Of course."

They left the pool house, Kruger securing the double door after them. As they walked back across the lush green lawn to the main house, Leanne kept her arm around his waist and her body pressed against his.

"Darling," she said softly, "don't you think that when it's time to die, you should . . . let go?"

"Sure," he said. "I'm only hedging against dying before it's my time. My father was younger than I am and just as healthy when he died. He choked to death on a piece of steak. That was before anybody knew about the Heimlich maneuver. My father just turned purple and died while fifty people in the restaurant watched and couldn't do a damn thing."

"You never told me about that," Leanne said.

"It's not something I like to talk about. It's always haunted me how easily my father could have been saved if someone there had just known the proper technique."

His facial muscles relaxed as he pushed away the memory. "If I get torn up in an accident like Gil or eaten away by some disease, that's it, good-bye. Bury me, cremate me; I don't care. But if I feel as good as I do now and I'm still in good shape and some crazy thing or other snuffs me out, I want another chance, that's all."

"It still sounds like something people shouldn't mon- key with. I know I'd hate to be frozen in one of those things."

"Let's call it an eccentric hang-up on my part. I'm entitled to one, am I not?"

"Sure you are." She gave him a playful punch. "Let's play some tennis."

After that day they never again discussed the pool house or its contents. Leanne, however, stopped using the swimming pool. Kruger was sorry about that. He had enjoyed watching her in a bright spandex suit, poised on the board, knifing into the water, crossing the pool in strong, graceful strokes. But he respected her feelings, as she had respected his, and he said nothing.

Leanne Kruger never appeared in the witch costume. The Halloween party was never held. Because on the morning of October 31 Leanne Kruger was dead.

Pulmonary embolism, Dr. Auerbach told Kruger. A blood clot in the internal saphenous vein of her leg, probably a result of the riding injury, broke loose and traveled through the circulatory system. Leanne's heart stopped without warning, and she died silently as Kruger slept by her side.

"Sometimes these things give a warning, sometimes not." Dr. Auerbach spread his hands in a gesture of helplessness.

Kruger stared at him. "She's only twenty-four years old."

"Embolism knows no age," Auerbach said. "Of course, there may be contributing factors that an autopsy will—"

"No autopsy," Kruger said flatly.

"But in a case of this kind, sudden death with no witness—you were asleep—it's customary."

"I don't give a damn what's customary," Kruger told him. "Nobody is going to cut on my wife."

"Elliot, listen to me—"

"Like hell. I'm taking Leanne home with me. Now."

"Be reasonable, Elliot. There are procedures that have to be followed. Papers to be filed."

"Procedures be damned. Get me a telephone."

As Elliot Kruger well knew, there are few obstructions that cannot be overridden by enough money. Within an hour, the body of Leanne Kruger had been signed out of the hospital and returned to the house in Holmby Hills. Under the supervision of a different doctor, the body had been prepared and sealed in the steel cryogenic

17

cylinder. There, in the pool house, watched over by full-time attendants, she had remained through the fall and into the winter while her husband sought a way to bring her back.

At first, Kruger had looked for medical help. From three continents he flew in physicians, surgeons, and specialists in the heart and blood diseases. Some of them were tempted by the huge fees he offered, but when faced with the undeniable fact of Leanne's death and the enormity of what Kruger asked of them, they all backed down.

"Impossible" was their unanimous opinion.

Elliot Kruger would not accept it.

"Why must it be?" he asked. Through the viewing plate of the cylinder Leanne's features remained so perfect, so relaxed and without blemish. Her body was untouched except for the damnable blood clot, no bigger than a dime, that had cut off her life. He would not, he could not, accept it.

After the physicians came the religious practitioners. A noninvolved Protestant himself, Kruger had stood by through endless hours of prayer in strange tongues and finally to strange gods in the hope of seeing his Leanne rise again. Discouraged and exhausted, he had dismissed the last of the self-styled prophets just this week.

Now, as he stared through the dark toward the pool house, Elliot Kruger was ready to break. After so many years, to find happiness and have it capriciously snatched away from him—it was not fair. He would not allow it. There had never been a time when, if he wanted something badly enough, he could not go after it and get it. By God, he would get it this time, too. No matter where he had to go for it.

He went into the study and buzzed the room of Rosalia, Leanne's personal maid. He had kept her on because . . . well, because letting her go would have been like disposing of Leanne's little dog. It would have admitted that his wife was lost to him forever.

"Yes, sir?" a sleepy voice answered him through the small speaker.

"I'd like to see you in the study, Rosalia," he said.

In minutes she was there, her hair tied back, face

innocent of makeup. She wore a quilted robe Leanne had given her for Christmas.

"Rosalia, you, uh, wanted to show me something in one of those supermarket newspapers the other day."

"I'm sorry, Mr. Kruger. I was only trying to help."

"No, *I'm* sorry. I was abrupt with you. I haven't been thinking straight lately. I should have listened."

"That's all right; it was nothing."

"Do you still have the paper?"

"I—I think so."

"Will you get it for me, please? Show me again what you wanted me to see."

Rosalia hesitated a moment, then nodded and left the room.

Alone, Elliot Kruger turned once more to the dark window. Silently, he mouthed the name of his wife. This would be his last try. The final, humiliating step in hopes of accomplishing the only thing that mattered to him. If this failed, it would all be over. If, by some miracle, it succeeded, no price would be too great.

Rosalia returned with the current copy of the L.A. *Insider*. She turned to the back pages and handed the paper to Kruger, pointing to a small ad.

SECRETS OF THE SUPERNATURAL
Seer—Mystic—Oracle
M. Fain, Master of the Occult
Readings by Appointment

Kruger's mouth turned down in distaste, but he folded the paper and tucked it under his arm.

"Thank you, Rosalia," he said. "You may go back to bed now."

Chapter 3

McAllister Fain was definitely a morning man. Oh, he enjoyed it at night well enough, when the darkness outside closed in and made a warm, private space for two people. But sex in the morning had a special kind of urgency and spontaneity that started his juices flowing and set him up for a better-than-average day.

Jillian Pappas was a little slower than Mac to get into the mood once the sun was up. She liked to awaken gradually, letting the bodily functions find their own pace. However, Mac was a patient, knowledgeable man. He took his time exploring her body and making her aware of his own. By the time they came together, both were wide awake and at a trembling pitch of excitement.

At such times it was Jillian's habit to shout whatever came into her head, much to the amusement of Mac's neighbors.

"Oh, you wild man!" she cried this morning at the ultimate moment. "Do it to me!" Her enthusiasm was loud enough to drown out the discreet knock at the door.

As their passion subsided, their bodies wet and cleaved together, the knock came again, more insistent.

"Who the hell is that?" Fain puffed.

"Who's what?" Jillian sighed.

"At the door. I thought I heard somebody."

The knock was repeated. Very authoritative this time.

Fain raised himself on one elbow to look at the glowing red numbers of the clock radio. "Jesus Christ, it's not even eight o'clock."

"Must be important," Jillian said.

"It better be." Fain disentangled himself from Jillian and from the sheets and pulled on a knee-length velour robe.

"I'm hungry," Jillian said.

"Whose turn is it to make breakfast?"

"Yours."

"You sure?"

"I made French toast last time."

"Oh, yeah. I'll scramble some eggs as soon as I get rid of whoever's at the door."

He padded into the living room and took a peek through the fish-eye viewer. His nerves clenched for a moment at the sight of a uniform but relaxed when he saw it was a nonofficial gray color and there was no badge. He shot the dead-bolt lock and opened the door.

"Mr. Fain?" The uniform was that of a chauffeur. The man wearing it was broad-shouldered and dark, with a blue-black shadow on his jaw that no blade would quite remove.

"That's me," Mac admitted.

"My name is Garner. I was sent by Mr. Elliot Kruger." The man paused as though waiting for a reaction to the name. When he got none, he said, "May I come in?"

Mac stepped aside, and the man entered the living room. He glanced around, his cool brown eyes dismissing the apartment and its furnishings as being not worthy of inventory. Jillian came in from the bedroom, wearing Fain's other robe.

"What can I do for you?" Fain said.

"Mr. Kruger would like to see you. He instructed me to drive you to his home."

"What for? I don't even know the man."

"Is that *the* Elliot Kruger?" Jillian asked.

The chauffeur nodded, his eyes flicking over Jillian in

quick appraisal. From his expression, she came off better than the furnishings.

Fain looked at her. "What do you know that I don't?"

"Elliot Kruger is big oil," she said. "Big real estate. Big you-name-it. *Mucho dinero.* I think he invented some kind of a camera lens that the movie companies bought for a bundle."

"That was Mr. Kruger's father," the chauffeur said. "He invented the Kruger Multiflex lens in 1916, and a version of it is still used today."

"Good for him," Mac said. "What does he want with me?"

"A business matter. I'm sure Mr. Kruger would rather talk to you about it himself."

Fain looked down at his robe. "We just got up."

"Mr. Kruger's day begins early," said Garner.

"Does it? Well, Mr. Fain's day begins after breakfast, which he hasn't had yet."

"There are hot coffee and sweet rolls available in the car."

"You're kidding," Fain said. "A car with hot coffee on tap?"

"And color television with VCR," Garner said with a touch of pride. "Also two cellular phones, a refrigerator, a small but complete bar, and chemical toilet facilities."

"Okay, I'm impressed. Just give me a chance to get dressed. I don't suppose this wonder car has a shower."

"Sorry." The chauffeur did not smile.

"Too bad. Keep the coffee hot and we'll be right with you."

"My instructions are to bring only you, Mr. Fain."

"Miss Pappas is my valued assistant," Mac said. "Where I go, she goes."

After a moment's hesitation, the chauffeur touched his cap. "As you wish. I'll be in the car." He turned smartly on his boot heel and left the apartment.

"What's that 'valued assistant' flap?" Jillian said when they were alone. "I don't want to get involved in any of your scams."

"Hey, come on. When will you get another chance to ride in a limo with color television?"

"Who needs it?"

"And a chemical toilet?"

"Well, that's different. Can I have firsts in the shower?"

"You got it."

The car was a customized Rolls-Royce. The color was muted silver, the interior mahogany and burgundy leather. The coffee, as promised, was rich and hot. Fain inspected the bar and found an excellent brand of each variety of liquor. He whistled in appreciation.

Jillian nudged him and raised a questioning eyebrow.

"Just looking, love," he said. "You know I hardly ever indulge before noon. In strong drink, I mean."

"I couldn't care less," she said coolly. "What you do and when you do it is your own business."

"Hey, are you ticked off about something?"

"Me? Ticked off? Heavens, no. If you want to call me your freeping assistant, why should I care?"

"Lighten up, Jill. It's a free ride and free breakfast, and I thought you'd enjoy it."

"Right, boss." She gave him a mock salute.

He worked a hand under her buttock and squeezed. "Be nice to me and I can get you a raise, if you know what I mean, heh-heh."

"Hands off," she said, keeping a stern expression. "What you are doing is known these days as sexual harassment."

Fain shook his head. "Ah, for the good old days, when it was known as copping a feel."

The chauffeur tooled silently northwest on long, ever-changing Sunset Boulevard. The traffic lights seemed magically to turn green as the Rolls approached, as though they, too, responded to the aura of wealth.

Mac and Jillian settled back in the calfskin leather seats to watch the outer world pass through the smoked glass of the side windows. They drove silently through the multiethnic districts of Echo Park and Silver Lake. There the boulevard was lined with taco stands, herb shops, used-furniture stores, and beer joints with names like Sombrero Negro. The exposed walls were covered with amateurish murals and graffiti in the angular script of the street gangs.

As they entered the loosely bounded noncity called Hollywood, the boulevard angled toward the sea. They passed several motels—"Water Beds, Adult Video" —credit dentists' offices, a theater–turned–furniture store, a costume rental company, and assorted fast-food places. At the fabled intersection of Sunset and Vine, the art-deco studios of CBS and NBC in the radio days were long gone, as was Music City, with the revolving record atop its roof. Now high-rise office buildings stood guard on both sides, gleaming and clean and devoid of personality.

On they drove, past Hollywood High and the stretch of sidewalk known as Hookers' Highway. Into the curving Sunset Strip of trendy restaurants and rock clubs dominated by billboards featuring the huge faces of tomorrow's superstars. Or nobodies.

At the end of the Strip the conditioned air inside the limo seemed to change subtly as they eased into Beverly Hills. Money had its own distinctive smell. Sunset Boulevard widened and grew a median strip with well-tended shrubbery. Commercial buildings disappeared. Everyone on the sidewalks wore designer jeans, and everyone on the streets drove a Mercedes. Mac Fain felt the tingle he always got in the area of his shoulder blades when he was in the proximity of riches.

The very street names began to sound like money. Hillcrest Drive, Doheny, Rexford, Rodeo, Roxbury. How could a poor person live on a street called Roxbury Drive?

The Rolls turned off into a hilly section where the streets bore no names. Or if they did, they were so discreetly displayed that Mac Fain could not find them. The homes and estates were screened from the eyes of idle passersby by high walls and dense foliage.

They pulled in at a tall iron gate that opened obediently for the Rolls. A winding drive took them through the trees and up to a side entrance of a mansion that might have been on a Spanish travel poster.

The chauffeur got out and held open the rear door. Off to their right was a garage that had space for six cars. Inside was another Rolls, two Mercedeses, and a Porsche

928. In the driveway stood a three-year-old Buick, looking embarrassed.

A man of fifty or so with a face as smooth as an egg came out to meet them.

"This is Mr. Fain," the chauffeur announced, "and his assistant, Miss . . ."

"Pappas," Jillian supplied, shooting Mac a quick scowl.

"Come this way, please," said the egg-faced man. "Mr. Kruger is waiting for you."

They entered the house. Inside it was cool, and there were shadows in the corners. The air was musty and still, but there was a hint of saucy perfume that seemed to linger from some departed guest. Mac and Jillian were led through a maze of rooms and corridors. The furnishings were old, authentic, and obviously expensive.

They came at last to a high-ceilinged room with tall French windows and a walk-in fireplace. The walls were hung with elaborate tapestries that showed the conquistadores civilizing the Indians. A lean, white-haired man in a loosely knit cardigan sat slumped in a high-backed chair. Beside him stood a portly middle-aged man in a three-piece suit that was too tight for him. The portly man frowned at them through gold-rimmed bifocals.

"Mr. Fain and Miss Pappas," announced their guide.

The white-haired man peered up at them through pale, rheumy eyes. He did not offer to rise but held out a bony, liver-spotted hand.

"I'm Elliot Kruger."

Fain took the hand gingerly. The brittle bones felt as though they might snap if he applied any pressure.

"This is my son, Richard," Kruger said, indicating the man in the suit.

"Pleased to meet you," Fain said.

Richard Kruger sniffed, ignoring the outstretched hand.

"I expected you to come alone," Kruger said, talking to Fain but looking at Jillian.

"Miss Pappas is a valuable, er, associate," said Fain. "We always work together."

"I see. Well, sit down and I'll tell you why I asked you here."

* * *

25

Mac and Jillian sat together on a plush maroon love seat. Elliot Kruger spoke in a subdued monotone for the next twenty minutes while his son stood by, looking alternately embarrassed and hostile. The old man told with suppressed emotion of the death of his wife, the freezing of her body in the cryogenic tank, and his subsequent attempts, medical and spiritual, to bring her back to life. With an effort, McAllister Fain kept his expression noncommittal. However, from time to time he glanced at Jillian and saw her growing look of horror.

When Kruger had finished, Fain coughed politely and said, "Sir, I'm afraid you misread my ad. I do tarot readings, ESP, find lost objects—that sort of thing. Bringing back the dead is not in my line."

"How could I misread . . ." Kruger pulled the L.A. *Insider* from a brass magazine rack beside his chair. He read from the page to which it was folded. ". . .'Secrets of the Supernatural'?"

Fain smiled apologetically. The old man did not respond. Richard Kruger leaned forward, his eyes narrowed behind the bifocal lenses.

"It *is* only a newspaper ad," said Fain.

The old man slapped the tabloid with the back of a skeletal hand. "Are you or are you not an 'occult authority,' as you represent yourself here?"

Fain cleared his throat. "That's a fairly loose term. I admit I'm not exactly a stranger to the field. I have a pretty good library on the subject and I—"

"Never mind the sales talk. I am prepared to hire you and let you prove it."

"Mr. Kruger, as I said a minute ago—"

"Don't turn me down until you've had a chance to consider my proposition. I never ask a service from anyone that I can't pay for."

Fain looked around the richly furnished room. "I don't question your ability to pay, Mr. Kruger."

"Then let's talk business. If you succeed in returning my wife to me as she was, I am prepared to be . . . extremely generous."

Fain studied the old man and decided he was serious. He felt the prickling at the shoulder blades again. Very strong. "That's an interesting proposition, but as I told you, it's not the kind of thing I do."

Kruger went on as though he had not spoken. "Let me be specific. I am prepared to pay you an immediate retainer of ten thousand dollars. That's in addition to any and all expenses, which I will cover. For merely making the attempt, even if you should fail, I'll add another ten thousand dollars at the conclusion of your efforts. Should you succeed, I will double the final payment."

Fain swallowed hard at the mention of the figures.

Kruger watched him intently. "Perhaps it would help you decide if you came with me to see my wife."

"Well . . . it couldn't hurt to look."

Jillian snapped her head around. "Mac!"

He gave her a quick gray-eyed stare. "It couldn't hurt to look."

Kruger levered himself out of the chair and led them across the thick carpet to the tall windows. Fain followed, ignoring Jillian's attempts to get his attention. Richard Kruger, with unconcealed distaste, brought up the rear. They left the house and walked in single file across an expanse of lush lawn, past the swimming pool—sparkling blue and empty—through the tall eucalyptus hedge, to a small building beyond. From inside the building Fain heard a soft, rhythmic throb like a muffled pulse.

A crew-cut young man in a white laboratory coat let them in. The small building contained pumping and filter machinery for the swimming pool, and one corner was fitted out as an office for the attendant. But the room was dominated by the dark steel cylinder that lay in a bed of pipes, tubes, and gauges. The young man stood by, watchfully respectful, as Elliot Kruger led his guests inside.

Fain moved up to stand beside the old man as he gazed down through the shatterproof viewing window set into the upper end of the cylinder. Richard Kruger and Jillian stayed back by the door.

"Here she is," said Kruger unevenly. "This is my Leanne."

The glass was faintly misted, but the lovely face of the

woman inside could be clearly seen. Her eyes were closed. The rich brown hair, showing highlights even through the dull glass, lay softly on her shoulders. The mouth quirked up faintly at the corners as though she enjoyed some secret joke. Except for the ivory pallor of the skin and the absence of any breathing movement, the young woman might have been asleep.

"Beautiful, isn't she."

Fain started and looked up. "Yes," he agreed. "Very beautiful."

The old man started to speak, then made a strangled sound and turned away. "Excuse me," he said.

The white-coated attendant hurried to his side and helped him out of the pool house. Richard Kruger came over to Fain.

"I won't let you get away with it, you know," he said in a strained voice.

"What are you talking about?"

"This con game you're pulling on my father. He's not in good shape mentally, and he's liable to agree to anything. But I'm here to see that he's not victimized by people like you. I can make it very uncomfortable for you."

Fain turned to face him squarely. "Maybe you'd better get specific."

"As you may imagine, my father's name carries considerable weight with state and local authorities. That disgusting ad of yours in the scandal sheet may well be in violation of a number of laws."

"Oh, I don't think so," Fain said.

"Think again. There are people in high places who owe my father favors. I could make a couple of phone calls that would have you behind bars by nightfall."

Fain drew himself up to emphasize his three-inch height advantage over Richard Kruger. His expression has hardened, and the pale gray eyes smoldered. When he spoke, his voice carried a new ring of authority.

"Now you listen up, friend. Your father sent for me. I didn't come looking for him. I haven't asked him for a damn thing. I've made no promises. If he wants to make me a business proposition, I'll listen. And his name may carry all the weight you say it does, but that's his name, not yours. Don't threaten me again. I don't like it, and I don't think your father would, either."

Richard Kruger sucked in a lungful of air through his nose. He puffed out his cheeks. Before he could speak, his father and the attendant reentered the pool house.

"Forgive me," said the old man. "I don't do that often. It's just that . . . you're my last hope. A small hope, I admit, but you're all I have. Please"—the word did not come out easily—"Mr. Fain. If the retainer isn't enough—"

"The retainer is fine," Mac said quickly. He looked down again at the lovely, pallid face beneath the glass. "Can I let you know? There are certain arrangements I'll have to make."

Fain was acutely aware of the hostile glare from the younger Kruger and a look of disbelief from Jillian, but he kept his eyes on the old man.

"How soon?" asked the old man.

"Tomorrow."

"That's acceptable. My man will give you a number where I can be reached directly as soon as you have reached a decision."

They returned to the main house and exchanged brief good-byes. Not until they were in the backseat of the Rolls, sealed off from the chauffeur and heading back east on Sunset, did Jillian speak.

"Mac Fain, are you crazy?"

He brushed his hand across the buttery leather upholstery. From the bar he took a bottle of Hennessy V.S.O.P. and held it to the light. He selected a fist-sized snifter from the rack of glasses. "This is good stuff. Care to join me?"

Jillian watched him soberly from the opposite side of the car. "You *are* crazy," she said.

Chapter 4

When they were back in the Echo Park apartment, McAllister Fain opened a can of beer for each of them. Jillian sat sipping hers thoughtfully in his big recliner while Mac paced from one end of the living room to the other, clutching his like a hand grenade.

"Are you going to talk to me?" she said finally.

"Twenty thousand dollars," Fain said. "Do you know how much money that is?"

"Yes," Jillian said quietly.

"It's more money than I cleared in the last two years."

"Uh-huh."

"Combined."

"Gotcha."

He paced some more and swallowed some of the beer. "What do you suppose it's like to have as much money as Elliot Kruger?"

"It can't buy happiness," she said, waiting for him to pick up on the cliché.

It went right past him. "Imagine living like that. Did you see that house? That car?"

"Yeah, toilet and all."

Fain went on pacing and talking as though she had not spoken. "And servants! A chauffeur, at least one maid, and whatever that guy was who took us into the house.

My God, I didn't think people had real servants anymore. That's out of thirties movies. And what about that old piano with all the gold on it?"

"That was a harpsichord, and it was gold leaf."

"Right. I'll bet it's worth more than this whole building."

"I get the idea," Jillian said. "You're impressed."

"Aren't you?"

"Sure. I'm also impressed by Yosemite Falls, but I'm not tempted to ride over it in a barrel."

Fain drained half his can of beer. He sat down on the sofa, got up, sat down again. He drummed a rapid tattoo on his knees and grinned at Jillian. Then her words seemed to filter through to him. "What's that about a barrel?"

"You're going to do it, aren't you."

"Do what?"

"Take Elliot Kruger's money."

"It's a business proposition."

"Trying to bring a dead woman back to life?"

Fain did a sitting-down tap dance. "Why not?"

"*Why not?* Mac Fain, you are out of your mind."

"What the hell, you heard the man. Ten thousand retainer, unlimited expenses, and ten more big ones just for giving it the old college try. I can't lose even if I fail."

"What do you mean *if* you fail? You know, you're talking as though you might actually do it."

Fain crossed to where Jillian was sitting. He took her hands and pulled her up, then hugged her tightly.

"Hey, I haven't completely flipped out," he said.

"I'm beginning to wonder."

"I'm the same old levelheaded, lovable Mac Fain."

"Then you don't think you can raise the dead."

"Of course not."

She relaxed in his arms. "You had me going there for a while."

"But Elliot Kruger thinks I can."

She drew back and stared at him. "So what?"

"Twenty thousand dollars' worth he thinks so."

"You would actually take the poor man's money?"

"Poor man? Hell, twenty thousand dollars is parking-meter change to people in his bracket."

"What difference does that make? You'd be cheating him."

"Who says so? You heard him say he'd pay even if I couldn't deliver. He knows the odds, honey. God knows how much he's already shelled out to doctors and Bible thumpers. Now he says I'm his last chance. He'll pay for a good try, and that's what I'll give him."

Jillian stepped back and stared at him. "Mac, this is not telling fortunes for little old ladies. This is messing around with life and death and a man's grief."

"Think of it as putting on a show."

"It's *not* putting on a show," Jillian insisted. "That old man is going to pay you to make his wife get up out of that flipping freezer and walk into his arms. If he thinks there's even one chance in a million you can do it, you'll be cheating him. The whole idea is crazy."

Fain looked at her. The pale gray eyes glowed under the dark brows. "Is that so? Who can say for sure that I can't do it?"

"Aagh!" Jillian spun away from him and stalked into the bedroom.

He followed her and stood in the doorway as she moved briskly about, rearranging objects on the bureau, adjusting the shades, smoothing the bedspread, kicking at a loose corner of the carpet.

"Something's bothering you," he said. "I can sense it."

"Oh, sure. Mister Mystic. Master of the Occult. Sometimes you make me so fleeping mad, Mac Fain. . . ."

"Hey, lighten up, kid. What I do for a living isn't all that different from what you do. You get up on a stage and pretend to be somebody you're not, right?"

"It's not the same at all. People know a stage performance is just make-believe. They know we're actors. They come to be entertained."

"Why do you think people come to me?"

"To have their fortunes told. Hear you predict a great love life for them. Find their lucky number." Jillian took a moment to regain control. "Or, God help me, to bring back a dead wife."

"That's not it at all," Fain said. "People come to me for hope. That ocean voyage they've always dreamed of, the tall, dark stranger they wish would walk into their lives. The sudden fortune they know in their hearts they're never going to have. I give them the possibility that it just might happen. Nobody gets hurt; nobody gets lied to. I never tell anybody their future is guaranteed."

"Not since the plainclothes policewoman nailed you for telling her to beware of a large blond man."

"Okay, I was careless once. Anyway, I read a month later where she was shot in the foot by a freaked-out junkie. He was blond and weighed damn near three hundred pounds."

"You're telling me you really saw that in her future?"

Fain grew serious. "Sometimes I don't know what I see. I open my mouth, and things come out. Most of the time I'm careful to keep to generalities, but there are times . . ."

His voice trailed off, and Jillian came over to stand close to him. "What times, Mac?"

"I was just thinking about when I was a little boy."

"You've never told me about your childhood."

"There wasn't that much to it. I was born and grew up in Michigan. Dad was a civil engineer, worked for the state. My mother was . . . just a mother, I guess. Housewife, a now-and-then churchgoer. The whole thing was very Midwest."

"Were your parents happy?"

"Not really, now that I look back on it. The folks never had a lot to say to each other. Dad tried. Sometimes, when he'd had a couple, he would start clowning around, but my mother would always turn chilly and give him a look. I don't mean they were miserable, but now I don't think there was a whole lot of love between them."

"Poor little Mac," Jillian said.

"Hey, not me. I was treated just fine by both of them. No lack of love there. Like I said, all this is hindsight. At the time, I figured all families were like mine. And then we had Darcia."

"Who was Darcia?"

"An Indian girl who worked for us for a while. People

said she was strange and had spells. I figured out later that she was an epileptic. I didn't know at the time, and it wouldn't have mattered. Darcia took about as much responsibility for raising me as either of my parents."

"What happened to her?"

"I don't know. After my mother died, she just went away. I used to ask Dad about her, but he never really answered."

"How old were you? When your mother died, I mean."

"I was seven. That's what I started to tell you about. I saw my mother dead before the fact."

"What happened?" Jillian said softly.

"It was the damnedest thing. I was in the house playing, or watching TV or something, and all of a sudden I had this sick feeling about my parents' bedroom. Something terrible was in there, I just knew it, but I had to go and see. I ran back and opened the door, and my mother was lying there on the bed all broken and covered with blood."

"How awful for you," Jillian said.

"More awful than you think. You see, my mother was out shopping at the time. She came home when she was supposed to, just like nothing had happened. I was too embarrassed to say anything about what I saw, but I couldn't forget it.

"Then, three days later, my mother was out in the front yard working in her flower garden. We lived at the bottom of a hill. Up at the top a truck was parked. Somebody didn't set the brakes properly. My mother never saw it coming. She never knew what hit her. The neighbors rushed out and carried her inside. I heard all the commotion, and Darcia tried to keep me from going into the bedroom. I broke away from her and ran in where they had laid her down, and I saw my mother lying there dead for the second time."

Jillian was silent for a long moment. "How come you never told me about that before?"

"I never told anybody."

"Did anything like that ever happen again?"

"Nothing that dramatic. Sometimes I would have a feeling about where to look for something that was lost.

Or I'd know somebody was going to call just before the phone rang. That kind of stuff happens to everybody."

"Then that's how you do the fortune-telling—I mean card readings—and all that stuff?"

"Nah, that's a performance. I tell the people something that will make them happy. Like I said, give them hope. If it happens the way I tell them, they think I read the future. If not, they can't blame me, and at least they had the fun of thinking about it."

"You make it sound so harmless, yet I can't lose the feeling that you're doing something wrong."

"You're not going to go moral on me now, are you?"

"But, Mac, all that stuff—the tarot cards, the palm reading—is small potatoes compared to this business with Elliot Kruger. I mean, that woman is dead."

"No doubt about that," he agreed.

"You said yourself the dead don't come back. Like my aunt Rowena, remember?"

"Yeah, that's what I said, and as far as I know, they don't. But who really knows for sure?"

"You're beginning to scare me."

Slowly he relaxed. The feverish look went out of the pale eyes. "Don't worry about it, honey. I'll give Elliot Kruger the performance of my life. It's not likely that his wife is going to get up and walk, but if the man wants to pay twenty thousand dollars for the attempt, I'm not about to turn it down."

"You're going through with it, then."

"Sure. And you can help me."

She eyed him suspiciously. "Help you how?"

"You're my assistant, remember? And a darn good actress."

"Forget it," she said. "I don't want any part of fooling that sad old man."

"I wish you'd stop thinking of it that way."

"How am I supposed to think of it?"

"Try twenty thousand dollars. That's not hard to think about."

"I liked you better when you were poor."

"You'll come with me, won't you? When I do the scene? You don't have to do anything, but I'd really like to have you there."

"I don't know. When are you going to hold the . . . ceremony?"

He became thoughtful. "Not right away. I'll have a lot of research to do. There are things I'll need—material, equipment."

"It sounds like you're planning a space shot."

"I can't just rush into this. The man is paying twenty thousand dollars; he'll expect more than a pot of incense and some mumbo jumbo."

"What he expects," Jillian said, "is that his wife will come back to life."

"Besides, there's that unlimited expense account. It would look funny if I didn't have a few expenses."

"Oh, sure." Jillian looked at her watch. "I've gotta go. I'm having new pictures taken at one o'clock. Will I see you tonight?"

"I don't think so. I've got a lot of reading to do about bringing back the dead."

Jillian shivered. "I wish you didn't sound so serious about it."

"Honey, I *am* serious. Twenty thousand dollars' worth of serious."

She kissed him quickly and headed for the door. There she turned. "There's no chance you'll change your mind?"

Fain was already prowling along his bookshelf. "Um, what's that?"

"Never mind," Jillian said. She shook her head and went out the door.

Fain let his finger trail along the row of books until it stopped on a black-covered volume with the title stamped in gold. *The Holy Bible*.

What better a place could there be to start? he thought. He carried the Bible back to his recliner, adjusted the reading lamp, and opened the New Testament to John 11 and 12.

The raising of Lazarus.

Chapter 5

After a few minutes Mac Fain closed the Bible with a sigh and returned it to the shelf. John 11 and 12 had been a disappointment. There were no useful details given as to how Jesus raised Lazarus from the dead.

Not that Fain had expected a how-to manual, but he was hoping for some hints he could adapt for his own use. It turned out to be one of those unexplained "miracles" like walking on water and such that Jesus pulled off occasionally to impress the populace. As a boy in Sunday school, Fain had wondered why, if Jesus was so handy with the miracles, he let himself get nailed to the cross.

But there was no time now for theological musing. He started over with the occult books, noting every reference he could find to raising the dead. An hour or so of this left him more discouraged than before. The major concern of the books in the resuscitation field was bringing back the spirit of the departed to deliver some message from the other side. Ghosts were no help. Elliot Kruger wanted a flesh-and-blood woman returned to him. Nothing less would be acceptable. Scratch the seance.

Back to the bookshelf. Fain continued down the row

of titles. Witchcraft, astrology, the magician's handbook, numerology, fortune-telling, voodoo.

Voodoo?

Weren't those people famous for revivifying corpses?

He flipped through the pages to the section he wanted. Uh-oh, zombies. That didn't sound good. Elliot Kruger wasn't shelling out twenty thou to have some blank-eyed hunk of meat shuffling around the house.

Fain looked up suddenly from the book. What the hell was he thinking of? He wasn't actually going to *do* anything. Elliot Kruger didn't have to know it, but all he was buying was a performance of mystical mumbo jumbo. Ghosts, zombies, what difference did it make? At least the voodoo book gave him some impressive-sounding French-Creole expressions he could drop to give the old man the impression that something was going on. It was a start, but he would need more details about the actual ceremonies to be convincing, and Fain thought he knew where he could get them.

But first, he might as well make it official. He scribbled some notes from the voodoo book, laid it aside, and picked up the telephone.

He dialed the number Elliot Kruger had given him that morning. The old man answered on the first ring. His voice quivered with a pathetic note of eagerness. Mac had a brief pang of conscience, but he quickly swallowed it.

"Mr. Kruger, I've decided to accept your proposition."

"Thank you. I suppose you'd like a copy of our agreement in writing."

"That's not necessary, sir. I have your word." It would do no harm to boost the idea of trusting each other.

"Fine," Kruger said. "I'll have my check for your retainer delivered to you by messenger. Will tomorrow morning be soon enough?"

"Oh, definitely," Fain said, hoping his voice wouldn't crack.

"The expenses will be covered in any manner you choose."

"Plenty of time for that."

"Time," Kruger said thoughtfully. "How soon will you . . . do it?"

"Well, now, I'll have to make preparations."

"Mr. Fain, I don't like to rush you, but I'm sure you understand the urgency of this matter to me. Every day I spend without Leanne is like a year off my life."

"Well, I, uh, suppose we can speed things up. Shall we say two weeks?"

"Suppose we say this Friday." A hard note of the driving businessman returned to Elliot Kruger's voice.

Fain rubbed his jaw. Three days wasn't much, but how much could he need? "I suppose I can manage it by then."

"Good. Is there anything I should do in advance?"

"I'll let you know."

Fain hung up, checked his voodoo notes again, and left the apartment. He walked down the flight of stairs to the street, turned left, and headed up the walk to his neighbor's house.

The house next door to Fain's stucco apartment building was a clapboard bungalo dating to the 1920s, when Echo Park was a somnolent small town within the exploding city of Los Angeles. The house had survived storms, earthquakes, a flu epidemic, smog, uncounted tenants of varied ethnic backgrounds, and twenty or so amateur paint jobs. The current color was a pastel blue found only on certain birds' eggs and buildings in the Caribbean.

Fain strolled up onto the lawn where his neighbor Xavier Cruz was engrossed in his ongoing battle with the wreck of a Volkswagen van. A pair of chickens flapped out of his way, clucking wildly.

"Hey, Xavier, *cómo está*?"

Cruz looked up from the engine cavity where his head had been buried. He wore a black T-shirt with sleeves rolled to his shoulders, displaying a tattooed eagle on his brown biceps.

"Talk English, man. Your Spanish sucks."

"Yeah, well, I'm working on it."

"Work harder."

Xavier dived back into the engine compartment. Fain

39

picked up a loose spark plug and played with it idly. He made it vanish from his left hand and plucked it out of the air with his right.

"Say, neighbor, I wonder if you could help me."

Xavier emerged and squinted at him suspiciously. "Help you do what?"

"Not *do* anything, actually. I need a little information."

"I thought you knew everything. Ain't you a college man?"

"Ha-ha. Seriously, though, you could do me a favor."

"How?"

"What can you tell me about voodoo?"

Cruz stared at him. "You crazy, man? I'm Cuban. I don't know nothing about that stuff."

"Hey, I'm your neighbor, remember? I live right up there. Once a month I see twenty, thirty people coming to your place all dressed in white with bandannas around their heads. I hear chanting inside the house. I see the chicken population drop to nothing."

"So we have a barbecue."

"I don't smell any cooking."

Cruz hefted the crescent wrench he was working with. He slapped it several times against the callused palm of his left hand. "Why you asking me this shit, man?"

Mac produced a neighborly chuckle. "Well, I'm in sort of a bind. I promised to put on a little show for some people, and it would help put it over if I threw in a little voodoo shtick."

"Voodoo is not a show, man. It's like a religion, you know? Heavy stuff. You stick to card tricks."

"Then it *is* voodoo that goes on over here," Fain said.

The Cuban did a noncommittal flip-flop of one hand. "Something like that."

"So fill me in."

"Listen, man, I don't really believe in that stuff, but a lot of people do. They wouldn't like me talkin' about them. I let 'em use my house, okay? I can't tell you nothing."

"Ever see this trick?" Fain said. He made a pass and slowly drew a twenty-dollar bill from the Cuban's ear.

"Pretty good," said Cruz, pocketing the twenty. "If

40

you got to hear about voodoo, what you want to do is talk to the Haitian. He's the *houngan*. The priest.''

"Has he got a name?''

"All I know is they call him Le Docteur.''

"Where can I find him?''

"I don't know where he lives, but he's down at the clinic a lot.''

"The place next to Big Mary's on Sunset?''

"Yeah, that one.''

"Thanks, Xavier.''

"Hey, man, you di'n' hear nothin' from me.''

"Right. Gotcha.''

Fain walked back up to his apartment, humming to himself. He mentally entered the twenty dollars under expenses, then mentally raised it to fifty. What the hell.

The People's Sunshine Clinic was located between Big Mary's lesbian bar and a motorcycle repair shop on one of the sadder blocks of Sunset Boulevard. The clinic existed as though in a time capsule from the sixties. The face of the cinder-block building was painted with rainbows and flowers and the swirling paisley colors of the psychedelic generation. The people who hung out in front of the place looked like a road company of *Hair*.

In the unpainted waiting room young people with beards and beads and headbands and granny dresses sat around on thrift-shop furniture. KRTH, the Golden Oldie station, played Led Zeppelin on somebody's portable.

Mac Fain, in his clean Levi's and Arnold Palmer jacket, felt decidedly overdressed. He edged past a young woman reciting Kahlil Gibran and pushed through a door at the rear labeled NO ADMITTANCE.

A Latin woman with enormous dark eyes intercepted him. "You're supposed to wait out there. Somebody will come and help you.''

"I'm not a patient,'' Fain said. "I want to see Le Docteur.''

The woman took a step back and looked him over. "Wait out there. A doctor will come.''

"No, no, I don't need a doctor. I want to talk to Le Docteur. The Haitian.''

The woman's eyes clouded. She pointed down a short

hallway with curtained doorways on both sides. "Find an empty room and wait."

Fain started to protest, but the woman had turned away. He shrugged and wandered down the hallway. The first cubicle he looked into was occupied by a youth with ghastly sores over most of his body. Fain quickly zipped the curtain closed and looked into the next. There an old man lay on the floor in a pool of vomit. He was relieved to find the third cubicle unoccupied.

The side walls were plywood. There was no window, and old linoleum on the floor. The furnishings consisted of a waist-high padded table, a white-enameled stool, a locked metal cabinet, an empty Kleenex box, a cotton-ball dispenser. Fain peeked into a trash can filled with tongue depressors, wadded tissues, used bandages, and other items he didn't want to think about. His nostrils stung with the smell of disinfectant.

Fain hoisted himself to a perch on the edge of the examination table, thought better of it, and moved to the stool. Across the hall someone groaned without letup.

He started as the curtain was slashed aside and two men entered. One was a totally bald Anglo with the mashed-in face of a professional wrestler. Biceps the size of cantaloupes bulged from the sleeves of his T-shirt. The other was a whip-thin Latin with a Zapata mustache. They eyed Fain with icy suspicion.

Mac rose from the stool and tried to look friendly. "Hi. Is one of you men called Le Docteur?"

An uncomfortable pause went by, and Fain's smile grew strained. Finally, the Latin spoke. "You a cop?"

"Me? No way," Fain said hastily. "I live in the neighborhood." That wasn't going to make them all brothers, he thought, but it couldn't hurt.

"What you want with Le Docteur?"

"It's . . . a business matter."

The Latin looked to the wrestler. The muscular man wore studded leather wrist bands. His hands were balled into fists like boulders.

"What kinda business?" the wrestler growled.

Sweat dampened the shirt under Fain's armpits. He swallowed hard and said, "Personal business."

The Latin and the wrestler exchanged a look. The

42

Latin put his face very close to Fain's and said, "You gotta do better than that, man, or they gonna have to put you back together out front."

Clearly, evasiveness would get him nowhere here. Fain leaned even closer to the swarthy man and said through his teeth, "It's about magic. Want to make something out of that?"

The others backed off a little. "Who sent you here?"

"Xavier Cruz."

"That name don't mean nothing to me."

"He didn't send me to see you."

"Let's crack him a little," said the wrestler. The muscles in his upper body strained to burst through the tight T-shirt.

"Look, it's not really all that important," Fain said. He made a tentative move toward the doorway. "If you're busy here, I'll just run along and try another time."

The two men stepped closer together, blocking his path.

"I knew he was a cop," said the wrestler.

Oh, shit, Fain thought. Then he saw the glint of a steel scalpel in the Latin's hand and groaned aloud.

The curtain whipped open again, and an enormously fat black man pushed himself into the room. The other two stepped back deferentially. The fat man's eyes, glittering from deep in the folds of dark flesh, looked into Fain's soul. He made a small motion with one pudgy hand, and the other two slipped silently out, closing the curtain behind them.

"You have business with Le Docteur?" The man's voice seemed to belong to another body. It was clear, high-pitched. He spoke in a lilting Caribbean accent.

"Y-yes," Fain said, improvising frantically. "I'm a screenwriter, and I'm researching for a movie that has to do with black magic."

"Do you mean voodoo?"

"Well, uh, yes, but it's no big thing. The movie will probably never be produced. But I got your name from a friend and thought maybe, if you had the time—"

"All that is bullshit," the huge man said. "You have been lying from the moment you came in here. That is very dangerous with these people. You came very close to dying just now."

"Well, I'm sure glad you came in when you did," Fain said.

The black man held up a hand the size of a catcher's mitt. "You have not walked out of here yet. So I say again, state your business with me."

"Right." Fain dug into his wallet for a bent business card. He straightened it out and handed it to Le Docteur.

The black man read the card carefully and looked again at Fain. The smooth, round face was unreadable. "You represent yourself as a 'master of the occult'?"

Mac attempted a chuckle. "That's just advertising. Got to make a living. You know how it is."

"Yes, I do know," the Haitian said. "But I do not think you do. Come with me."

He heaved his bulk around like a tugboat in a snug harbor and pushed back out past the curtain. Fain looked after him for a moment, then followed.

In the hallway stood the two men who had first confronted him. Their eyes were still cold, but to Fain's relief the scalpel was nowhere in sight.

Le Docteur marched on to the end of the hallway and out a back door, with Fain hurrying to keep up. They crossed a small yard choked with weeds and trash barrels to a windowless shed of corrugated steel. The black man keyed open a padlock on the door, and they went inside.

He motioned Fain into one of two chairs on opposite sides of a battered card table. Then he lit a fat yellow candle. The flame sputtered and gave off the smell of rancid fat. The Haitian pulled the metal door shut and sat down across from Fain.

The flickering light of the candle illuminated their faces and little else. Fain looked around and got a shadowy impression of things hanging from the walls. The hanging things seemed to writhe and twist with the wavering flame. He looked away quickly.

"You have come to ask something of me," said the Haitian. "It is not my function to give answers. Do you know why I am spending this time talking to you?"

"No," Fain said.

"Because of what I see in your eyes. They are the eyes of a *gangan*. Do you know what that is?"

"No."

"I thought not." He made a rumbling, wheezing sound that might have been a laugh. Or a growl. "A *gangan* is a man born to special powers. Not, certainly, a 'master of the occult,' but a man with a gift, all the same. Do you know what a *houngan* is?"

"A voodoo priest," Fain said, remembering Xavier's description of the Haitian.

"Good. You are not totally ignorant. I am a *houngan*. It is a level a *gangan* like you could not attain in a hundred lifetimes. Do you understand?"

Fain nodded. The air in the steel shed was stale and damp. He shivered with a sudden chill.

"Since you do have the gift—from where, I cannot guess—and even though you are unaware of what you have, I am required to answer you. What is it you want?"

Fain worked his mouth to relieve the dryness. "I want to know the ritual for raising the dead."

For a long time the only sound was the whistling breath of the black man and the thudding of Fain's heart. Finally, Le Docteur said flatly, "You do not want to know that."

"Not for real, of course not. It's just for a . . . kind of a show I'm putting on. I want to make it look authentic."

"You are a greater fool than I thought. A show!" The Haitian rolled his eyes up until all that showed in the candlelight were the yellowed whites.

"You said you would tell me," Fain reminded him.

"So I did, and so I must. If you were less a fool, you would know how much more valuable is the secret of returning the spirits of the dead once they are risen."

"Thanks, but I don't need that one."

"It is well. You would find it much more costly."

Fain was growing dizzy and claustrophobic in the airless shed. He held his wallet up to the candle and thumbed out several bills. "Naturally, I'll pay you for the information."

The Haitian spat on the table. "I have no use for your money. If you must know the ritual of the dead, I will give it to you. I do this only because you have the eyes of a *gangan* and I am bound by my oath."

"I appreciate the trouble you're going to," Fain said. "I'd really like to thank you in some way."

The Haitian shook his massive head. "You owe me no thanks, as you will soon see. Let us begin."

Chapter 6

A rooster was crowing.

McAllister Fain pried his eyes open and saw nothing but darkness. The rooster crowed again, splitting the silence of the night. Fain coughed and licked his lips. They were dry and tasted salty.

Damn bird, he thought. If the Cuban next door had to keep those suckers, why couldn't he teach them to crow when the sun came up the way roosters were supposed to?

His mind began to function, slow and balky like a cold engine on a winter morning. He had a growing feeling of unease. Things were not as they should be.

In the first place, he was not in his bed. He was not in anybody's bed. He was sitting in the reclining chair in his living room. He had not fallen asleep watching television, because the screen was dark. And the heat was turned off. He felt cold and cramped. He groped beside him for the switch to the table lamp and snapped it on.

It took a minute for his eyes to adjust to the sudden light. He looked down and saw that he was fully dressed. There was a faint rancid smell that seemed to come from his clothing.

Beside him, on the lamp table and the floor beneath it, was a collection of jars, bottles, scraps of paper, bits of fur, and feathers. There was also a bundle of oddly shaped candles in assorted colors.

He sat back in the chair, closed his eyes again, and slowly began to remember. He had talked to Cruz next door about the voodoo business; then he had gone to the People's Sunshine Clinic on Sunset. There he had met the big black man called Le Docteur and followed him into that metal shed out behind the clinic. That was where his memory became jumbled. He had no conception of how much time the two of them had spent in the shed. His digital wristwatch told him it was now 4:35. That would be A.M., Wednesday, unless he had lost a day somewhere.

Fain stood up and stretched. His muscles and joints ached as though he had come through a vigorous physical workout. He turned on more lights and went into the kitchen, where he drank two glasses of cold water. A sudden chill made him shiver and raised gooseflesh on his arms. He went back out to the living room then and shoved the thermostat lever forward until the gas wall heater came on with a soft *whump*.

He took time then to examine the objects on the lamp table and on the floor. He had a vague memory of Le Docteur loading him down and explaining in rapid accents what each was for. What the hell *were* they all for?

The jars contained powders and ashes in many colors and consistencies. On the bits of papers were scrawled barely readable passages in some language that was not English and not quite French. On others were sketched inticate designs. These Fain recognized as *vévés* from his reading of the voodoo book. They were diagrams to be drawn on the floor with the powders to call up desired spirits, or *loa*.

He picked up one of the candles, thick as a man's wrist. This one was an unhealthy gray-green and gave under his touch like the body of a snake. The wax, or whatever it was, gave off an unpleasant odor. Fain put it down quickly.

He was even less anxious to handle the little shriveled bits of fur and feathers. They reminded him of the shadowy hanging things on the wall of the voodoo shed. He

48

resolved that whatever use he made of the other things, these he would do without.

Bits and fragments of the time he had spent in the stifling shed with Le Docteur began to come back. He saw again the huge face like a black jack-o'-lantern in the candlelight, eyes glowing deep in their fleshy pockets. He heard in his mind the voice of the *houngan,* sometimes high and piping, at other times dropping to a hoarse rumble. The words were partly in English, partly in French, and partly in a Creole dialect, which Fain could not understand.

The acrid smoke from the sputtering candle, the heat, and the lack of oxygen in the shed had numbed his brain, distorting the memories. Sometime during the night he must have left and returned to his apartment, but of that he remembered nothing.

On a sudden impulse he grabbed for his wallet. He counted the bills inside. All there. So were his Visa and his Mobil credit cards. At least he had not been rolled. And apparently he had not paid anything for the material he had brought home. Mentally he added a hundred dollars to his expense account. What the hell.

Suddenly he was very tired. Without bothering to turn off the lights or the heater, he stumbled into the bedroom, stripped off his clothes, and collapsed on the bed. The rooster crowed several more times before dawn, but Mac Fain did not hear.

At nine o'clock he was awakened by a persistent knocking at the door. Still groggy, he stumbled out to find a uniformed messenger there with an envelope for him from Elliot Kruger. He signed the man's book, took the envelope inside, and ripped it open. The amount written on the check snapped him wide awake. He sat down and spent a full five minutes savoring the beautiful symmetry of the figures.

One-oh-comma-oh-oh-oh. Ten thousand dollars. It was easily the largest check Mac Fain had ever seen. He hummed softly to himself and petted the slip of paper as though it were a small, lovable animal.

He was still carrying the check when he went into the bathroom. There he leaned across the sink and studied his face in the clouded mirror. There were dark smudges on his cheeks and forehead. Grease or ashes, or something. His hair was matted, and he needed a shave.

"So what?" he said to the reflection. "You don't have to look good; you're rich. Anyway, a lot richer than you were yesterday."

He cocked his head and stared into the eyes of his image. The whites were clear, the irises pale gray, almost silvery. What was it Le Docteur had said? Eyes of a *gangan*. Whatever that meant. Fain had no objection, since it seemed to be his ticket to the club. He leaned closer. There did seem to be something different about his eyes today. A cold spark in the gray depths that he had not noticed before.

Fain turned away from the mirror with a little snort. Power of suggestion. The fat old fraud had hypnotized him. No matter, he had gotten what he wanted: a little information and the raw materials to put together a ten-thousand-dollar—no, make that twenty thousand—performance for Elliot Kruger.

He got into the shower and turned it on steaming hot. Feeling great, he started to sing at the top of his voice, then stopped suddenly. What the hell was that he was singing? Something in a monotonous minor key that he had never heard before. And words he did not understand—nonsense syllables. More of the old *houngan*'s doing, he supposed. He finished the shower silently, but the echo of the strange chanting song lingered in his mind.

He was shaved and brushed and feeling quite healthy and wise when Jillian Pappas arrived.

"Where the heck were you last night?" she asked, dropping her tote bag at the door. "I tried to call you three times."

"I was taking witch-doctor lessons," he said.

"Very funny." Jillian stood looking at the paraphernalia on the end table and the floor beside the recliner. "What's all this junk?"

"That junk, my love, is what is going to make you and me a bundle of money."

"No kidding."

"Absolutely."

"How?"

"Trust me."

"Where have I heard that before?" She picked up the book he had left lying there the previous afternoon. "*Voodoo Practices of the Caribbean*. Oh, no, Mac, you're not going to try to do this stuff."

"No, of course not. But I needed something for a convincer. This sort of thing is not part of my routine."

"I thought you were going to fake it."

"Well, sure, but I want to look like I might know what I'm doing. I can't pull coins out of Leanne Kruger's ear and tell her husband that's how we bring people back to life."

"I wish you wouldn't do this," Jillian said. "I don't feel good about it."

Fain skipped into the bedroom and hurried out with the check. "Take a look at this and see if you feel any better."

Jillian examined the check and handed it back to him. "Is it good?"

"People like Elliot Kruger do not write bum checks. And this is only the first installment. After the job there'll be another just like it."

"Jeez, he must really believe you can do it. Bring his wife back to life."

"Let's say he's betting I can do it. If he wins, he's got his loving young wife back. If he loses, it's only money."

Jillian put out a hand to slow him down. "Wait a minute; did you say, 'If he wins'?"

Fain gave her a disarming grin. "Just psyching myself up, babe. If I don't act like I believe, nobody else will."

"You scare me sometimes."

"Why not?" He gave her a wide-eyed stare. "I've got the eyes of a *gangan*."

"Don't do that."

"Just practicing."

"The eyes of a what, did you say?"

"Never mind. It's an old voodoo expression."

Jillian shivered. "Got any coffee?"

"No, I just got up."

"I'll make some." She went into the kitchen and started a kettle of water heating while she spooned Hills

Bros. into the funnel of a stove-top drip coffee maker. She moved among his kitchen things with easy familiarity.

"I've got some news, too," she said. "I got a job."

"You got the equity-waiver thing?" Mac said, coming into the kitchen.

"No, that went to Miss Bajoomies, like I figured."

"What, then?"

"It's more modeling, really, than acting. But it's three days' work, and the pay isn't bad. . . ."

"Not the RV show out at the Rose Bowl?"

"Well, yes, as a matter of fact." She turned to face him. "What's wrong with that?"

"It's wrong because you've got too much talent to be spieling Winnebagos to a bunch of shitkickers from Saugus."

"I agree with you, but while I'm waiting for Aaron Spelling to call, I can be picking up a few bucks."

Fain flourished the check. "Hey, you've got a job, remember. My valued associate."

"Bolshoi."

He put an arm around her and pulled her close. "I'm serious, honey. With twenty thou I can put a down payment on a condo in the Valley or Orange County or somewhere. Put down some roots. We can move in together, and you can work on your classes and hang tough till something good comes along. You won't have to take these Mickey Mouse gigs with a bunch of yokels grabbing at you."

"Wait a minute. You're not talking marriage, are you?"

"Lord, no."

"For a minute there you *really* had me scared."

"So how about it? Will you tell the Winnebago people to stuff it and come help me with the Kruger business?"

Jillian relaxed against him and sighed. "I suppose somebody ought to be there to keep those people from drowning you in the pool when you make a big fool of yourself."

"That's my girl. Confidence."

"Ha."

"Tomorrow we can work out a routine. Tonight we'll celebrate."

Chapter 7

To make the scene perfect, McAllister Fain thought, there should be a spectacular electrical storm with brilliant slashes of lightning and thunder that boomed like giant kettle drums. Working with him should be a manic hunchback who called him "master." And they should now be clattering to their laboratory over cobblestones in a closed carriage drawn by a team of angry black horses.

Reality was hardly ever perfect. Instead of a storm, they had a drizzly February night. In place of the hunchback, a quiet Jillian Pappas sat at his side. And Elliot Kruger's custom Rolls tooling west on Sunset stood in for the clattering carriage. Close enough, he decided.

Fain leaned back to study his reflection in the tinted side window. He was wearing a black turtleneck under a conservative gray silk jacket, purchased yesterday at Silverwood's especially for the occasion. The effect, he thought, was properly mystical.

Jillian wore a silky gown of midnight blue that was unadorned and modestly cut but did not hide the smooth contours of her body. This, too, had been purchased the day before, chosen by Fain for the dramatic effect.

As though she sensed his scrutiny, Jillian turned toward him. He gave her a smile that she did not return.

"Cheer up," he told her. "You look like you're going to a funeral."

Jillian gave him a long look from under her finely arched brows. "Is that supposed to be funny?"

"Just making conversation."

She turned away from him again. They rode on in silence through the garish lights of the Strip and into the moneyed hush of Beverly Hills.

Still watching Jillian, Fain reached into an inside pocket and brought out a flat package gift-wrapped in silvery paper. He let it rest gently on Jillian's silken knee.

"I was going to save this until afterward," he said, "but maybe if you open it now it will lighten the mood in here."

She studied him for a long moment, then slowly unwrapped the package. Under the paper was a plush black jewelry case. Jillian gave Mac another look, then raised the hinged cover. A slim, elegant bracelet lay inside on a bed of pale satin. Even in the dim light the diamonds seemed to glow with inner fire.

"My God, Mac, it's beautiful."

"It ought to be, considering what it cost."

"How much?"

"Who cares? When you got it, spend it, right?"

"You know you shouldn't have done it."

"I don't know any such thing. In three years I haven't given you much in the way of presents. I'm going to start making up for it."

"I don't care about presents," she said.

"Well, *I* do. It boosts my ego to give things to people I like."

"You need an ego boost like Rome needs Catholics."

"I'll ignore that," he said.

She leaned over in the seat and gave him a kiss. "It was sweet, Mac, even though it was dumb. Thank you." She fitted the bracelet around her wrist and closed the clasp. "Look how nicely this dress sets it off."

He rubbed the back of his neck. "Uh, you're not going to wear it tonight, are you?"

"Why not?"

"It's just that it kind of detracts from the effect I wanted from the dress."

54

She let a beat go by before she spoke. "Oh, right, I'm the Mistress of the Occult. Almost forgot."

"You know what I mean," he said.

"Sure, I know." She took off the bracelet, returned it to the jeweler's box, and handed it to Fain. "Take care of it for me."

He held the box for a moment, then sighed and slipped it back into his pocket.

They rode in silence for another five minutes through the rain-wet streets. When Jillian spoke again, she did not turn from the window to look at him. "You know, Mac, I can't believe you're going through with this."

"Hey, come on . . ." he began.

"And even more, I can't believe I'm helping you."

Fain took her hand and held it until she turned toward him. "Jill, we've been over and over this. I did not make the man any promises. We are not breaking any laws. It's just make-believe. Like when you go on a stage and play a part."

"When I'm on the stage, the audience knows it's make-believe."

Fain nodded toward the back of the chauffeur's head, visible behind the glass partition. "We can discuss the ethics later. Remember, there's another ten thousand when we finish tonight."

"Is that supposed to make it all right?"

"Would you rather be right and hungry or wrong and rich?"

Jillian sighed and slumped lower in the seat.

They turned up into the hills and drove through the tall gates and along the wooded drive to Kruger's house. Every light in the mansion blazed, haloed by the misting rain. The smooth-faced man who had met them before hurried out with an umbrella. Garner, the chauffeur, opened the rear door, and the other man held the umbrella above Fain and Jillian as they walked between the car and the side entrance to the house. Garner retrieved Fain's satchel of equipment from the trunk and followed them in.

Elliot Kruger was waiting for them in the same high-ceilinged room where he had received them the first time. He had aged noticeably in three days. A fat log burned in the closet-size fireplace, but the room held a deep chill. Outside the French windows, the lighted pool shimmered blue and cold in the fine rain.

The old man rose with difficulty from his chair to greet them. His son, Richard, stood against the far wall, arms folded, a disapproving frown on his round face.

"I don't suppose there is any reason to delay," Kruger said when the greetings were out of the way.

"I don't suppose so," Fain agreed. "We might as well get started. He turned toward the French windows that overlooked the lawn and the pool.

"She's not there," Kruger said.

Fain turned to look at him.

"Leanne is upstairs," the old man said. "In our bedroom."

"Bedroom," Fain said, digesting the information.

"Naturally, I assumed you would want to work with her in a natural state, so I ordered her temperature carefully raised and the blood restored to her veins."

"Oh . . . naturally," Fain said through a tightening throat.

Richard moved in and thrust his jowly face close to Fain. "You do understand," he said heavily, "that the body cannot be refrozen. It will begin to decompose in a matter of hours."

"Well, I, uh . . ."

"Please, Richard," Kruger interrupted, "I do not want Mr. Fain to think I am putting added pressure on him. We both accept the fact that this is my last attempt at bringing Leanne back. The cryogenic tank is shut down for good. If we do not succeed tonight, that will be the end of it. I will have her interred in the usual manner."

Fain cleared his throat. He deliberately did not look at Jillian, who was pale-faced and staring at him. "Let's get on with it," he said. Belatedly, he remembered those were the final words of Gary Gilmore before the Utah firing squad blew him away.

The master bedroom on the second floor was as large as Mac Fain's entire apartment. The bed alone was the size of his bedroom. When they entered, there were pale gold draperies drawn across the floor-to-ceiling windows.

56

The subdued lighting was provided by a crystal chandelier and a table lamp on either side of the bed.

Fain saw that the others hung back at the doorway, waiting for him to take the lead. Elliot Kruger's face was skeletal in the deep shadows. Jillian stood rigidly, carrying the satchel. Richard stood apart from the others, watchful.

Drawing a deep breath, Fain walked slowly over the springy beige carpet and across a cool expanse of parquet floor. When he reached the bedside, Rosalia and the young medical attendant from the pool house stepped aside to make room for him.

Fain looked down at the huge bed with its satiny chocolate cover, and everything else in the room vanished. Resting there with her head on the gold pillow, chestnut hair brushed to glowing life, arms relaxed at her sides, lay Leanne Kruger. She was dressed chastely to the throat in pale blue silk that clung lovingly to the mounds and hollows of her body. A pair of tubes inserted into the veins of her arms were connected to a softly muttering pump at bedside. The infusion of blood had returned some of the color to the pallid face Fain had seen three days before through the glass plate in the tank.

But forget the brushed hair, the carefully arranged pose, the false blush of the cheeks. McAllister Fain reminded himself that this woman was unmistakably, undeniably, irretrievably dead.

He became aware of a heavy silence in the room and realized he had been standing for over a minute gazing down at the dead woman. He turned and looked at the three people who still waited at the door. Along with Rosalia and the young medical attendant, they tacitly acknowledged that he was in charge. Even Richard Kruger, whose skeptical frown was softened by the presence of death, looked to him for the next move.

Fain gave them a small nod, hoping Jillian would remember her part and not get carried away now with moral questions about what they were doing. To his relief, she seemed to gather herself and slip into character. She brought the satchel across the room and knelt at his side to open it.

Jillian began laying out the contents of the satchel. She placed the candles in neat rows on the floor and arranged the jars of varicolored powders on the bedside table. She kept her eyes on what she was doing and refused to look at Fain.

When the satchel was emptied, Fain made his selection from the rows of candles. He chose them in assorted shapes and colors, more for the aesthetic effect than for any special properties each might have. The night before last, Le Docteur had explained at length the different purposes for each type of candle, but now the whole evening in the shed with the *houngan* was a smoky blur in Fain's memory.

As before, the texture of the candles was somehow unpleasant to the touch, but Fain tried not to think about it as he placed them in strategic locations about the huge bedroom. As he lit the candles, he motioned to Jillian, and one by one she snapped off the bedside lamps and doused the chandelier. When he had finished, the scene was lit only by the flickering flames of twenty pungent candles.

He returned then to the bedside and looked down at the dead face of Leanne Kruger. Something cold prodded the region of his groin. In the three heady days since Elliot Kruger had made his outlandish offer, the main thought in the mind of Mac Fain was the money. Now, for the first time, he saw clearly the whole eerie tableau.

What the hell am I doing here? his mind cried. He had a wild impulse to grab Jillian and run out of that house of death and back to the noisy, tacky, comfortable apartment in Echo Park. But once again the thought of ten thousand dollars, and ten thousand more, pushed him onward. He peeled off the new silk jacket and handed it to Jillian. She folded it carefully over a chair.

He beckoned Rosalia over and told her by gesture to remove the furry rugs that surrounded the bed. She obeyed, watching him with huge frightened eyes, leaving a bare patch of parquetry all around the bed.

Fain turned his attention next to the jars of colored sands and powders arranged on the table. Jillian turned to face the window, looking neither at Fain nor at the woman who lay on the bed. He could not blame her.

The candlelight gave the illusion that muscles fluttered just beneath the smooth dead skin.

He cupped a handful of glittery blue sand and began spilling it in a curving line as he walked around the bed. He next took a handful of red and retraced his steps. He was interested to see that the two paths of dribbled sand twisted in and out together in the beginnings of some intricate design. It made no sense to Fain; he was making it up as he went along. Still, he was pleased with the way it looked. For the hell of it he threw in a little hand magic and made the powders appear to spill from mid-air. A little showmanship never hurt.

He did not even try to remember the complicated patterns the fat *houngan* had shown him there in the shed. There was a different cryptic pattern to go along with each phase of the voodoo ritual, but Fain had neither copied the designs nor made any effort to memorize them. The effect was all he wanted. He felt a surge of exhilaration now as the sand patterns grew, seemingly of their own volition, under his moving hand. Hell, this was easy.

Jillian, meanwhile, had stepped back away from the bed and the body of Leanne Kruger. The way they had planned it, she was supposed to be supplying a chanting background now—just something that would sound vaguely Middle Eastern to heighten the atmosphere. Fain glanced over and saw her standing transfixed. Even without the chanting she looked impressive standing there, straight and silent in her long gown of midnight blue. Fain felt a twinge of pride in his costuming.

The air in the bedroom became smoky and hard to breathe as the candles sputtered and popped, emitting their peculiar rancid odor. Once Richard Kruger moved to open the window, but Fain motioned him back. He felt he was on a roll now and did not want anything intruding, not even fresh air.

The sweat ran down his face and soaked the black turtleneck, pasting it to his body. Fain lost track of the passage of time. The multicolored diagrams on the parquet floor grew ever more convoluted. He used both hands now, letting the fine streams of color spill freely to trace their own designs. He had no idea what he was drawing, had no time to think about it.

Gradually he became aware of a humming in his ears. It grew louder and modulated into a chant consisting of strange unworldly sounds. Fain glanced over to see if Jillian had remembered her part but saw her standing silent, her mouth grimly closed. He realized then that the chanting came from his own throat. There were no words as such that he recognized, but the sound had an oddly soothing effect on him, so he made no effort to stop.

Finally, he was finished. An area six feet wide all the way around the bed was completely overdrawn with the arabesque markings of blue and red and black and green and yellow powders. Fain had somehow managed to move nimbly about the bed without smudging one of the delicate lines. The muscles of his back and upper arms cried out with the tension of the hours, yet a powerful exhilaration coursed through his body like a hit of pure cocaine.

The others stood or sat in various attitudes of exhaustion. Rosalia and the young medical attendant slumped in chairs against one wall. Richard Kruger, his suit coat discarded and tie pulled loose, sprawled on a couch at the far side of the room. Elliot Kruger had pulled a chair to a position just outside the border of Fain's mystical diagrams. He sat there, leaning forward, the candlelight accentuating deep shadows on his face. Jillian had maintained her rigid stance, her dark eyes watchful.

It was time, Mac sensed, to close the show. He had used the last of the powders he had brought along; several of the candles were sputtering. His throat was dry, and his muscles ached.

He stepped carefully around to the side of the bed, away from his audience. He spread his arms, forming a huge black cross. In the strongest voice he could muster, he repeated the one powerful incantation Le Docteur had given him that he remembered clearly and verbatim.

"Ralé. Méné. Vini." Call. Bring. Come.

The guttering flames of the candles seemed to flare, giving the room a sudden unnatural brightness.

"Ralé. Méné. Vini."

A loud *bang* from the window. Rosalia awoke and screamed, cutting it off instantly with a hand over her mouth. The medical attendant started so violently his chair clattered to the floor. Elliot Kruger gasped and stood up. Richard rose from the couch and took one step toward the bed before he froze. Jillian's hand went out in reflex toward the window, where the sash swung free of the casement, letting in a cold, wet wind. Only Fain held his position—arms outstretched, head high, eyes cast down now on the inert body of the woman on the bed.

"Ralé. Méné. Vini."

For an agonized ten seconds there was not a sound, not a breath, not a blink, in the candle-lit bedroom.

Then the dead woman opened her eyes.

Chapter 8

Hallucination.

It had to be. A trick of the lighting, combined with his exhaustion and the lack of oxygen in the room. It had to be. Thus spoke McAllister Fain's weary brain. What he had just seen happen could not have happened. A dead woman does not open her eyes and look around.

But this one did. Leanne Kruger's eyes, a clear, pale green, had snapped open and looked directly into his for one terrible moment. Then her head shifted on the pillow, and she found her husband.

"Elliot," she said, "it's cold in here."

The voice was whispery and dry from disuse, but the words were clear. The woman on the bed tried to raise herself to a sitting position but fell back.

"I feel so weak," she said. Then, looking around, she asked, "Who are these people?"

Elliot Kruger moved swiftly to his wife's side, while the others remained frozen where they stood. Rosalia began to whimper. Richard Kruger made inarticulate sounds in his throat. Jillian Pappas seemed to emerge from a trance and turn her gaze for the first time fully on Mac Fain.

To Mac's eyes the scene shifted and blurred then as though the room had been submerged in murky water.

62

His stomach lurched, and there was a buzzing in his head. Darkness leaked in at the edges of his vision.

The next thing he saw was the face of Jillian Pappas looking down at him. Behind her was the young medical attendant. Mac looked around and saw he was lying on a couch in a bedroom much smaller than the one where Leanne Kruger had lain. From the damp darkness at the uncurtained window Fain could tell that it was still night and still raining.

Jillian looked at him with a mixture of concern and awe in her dark eyes. She spoke in a hushed sickroom tone.

"Are you okay, Mac?"

"I guess so." He looked past her at the white-coated attendant. "Am I?"

The young man wore the same odd expression as Jillian. He bobbed his head up and down and said, "I think you just fainted."

Through an open door Fain could see people moving about in the hallway.

"What's going on?" he said.

Before anyone could answer, an angry-looking man with a cropped gray beard and tiny glasses came into the room.

"I'm Dr. Auerbach," he said, glaring down at Fain. "I want to know what went on here tonight."

Mac pulled himself to a sitting position. "I was just asking the same thing."

"Your name is McAllister Fain?"

A nod.

"I've just come from the Krugers' bedroom," said Auerbach, "and I don't believe what I saw there."

It all came back to Fain then. Those pale green eyes, bright and searching and unmistakably alive. The woman moving, speaking. Jesus, he thought, if that's what the good Dr. Auerbach saw, no wonder he didn't believe it.

He stood up and massaged his arms. His brain raced ahead, seeking the best path to take, the best way to deflect trouble and capitalize on this remarkable event.

"What, specifically, did you want to know?" he asked the doctor.

Dr. Auerbach's mouth opened and closed several times before any words would come. Finally, he got out, "How could you have known that Mrs. Kruger was not really dead?"

"I didn't know anything of the sort," Fain said, beginning to feel more like himself.

"You had to," snapped Auerbach. "It was suspended animation of some sort. Catatonia. Hypnosis, maybe."

"Is that your diagnosis?" Fain said.

"No, certainly not. I'd have to do a complete examination to tell exactly what has occurred here medically."

"Well, then?"

"Mr. Kruger refuses to allow it."

"I wonder why."

"Sir?"

Fain studied him. "Wasn't it you, doctor, who examined Leanne Kruger at the time of her death?" He let the faintest emphasis fall on the last word.

"I was her doctor," Auerbach said, his face reddening under the beard.

"Ah, well."

"I assure you that my examination at the time was complete and the records are in perfect order."

"I have no doubt of that," Fain said.

After a pause Auerbach said, "I'd like to see your credentials, sir."

"Sure." Fain slipped a business card from his wallet and passed it to the doctor.

Auerbach read the card, looked up at Fain, read it again, looked back again. Finally he said in a slow, strangled voice, " 'Master of the Occult'?"

Fain shrugged modestly.

The doctor's neck swelled as he breathed rapidly in and out. "And how much did you charge Mr. Kruger for this . . . this . . ." Words failed him, and he gestured helplessly in the direction from which he had come.

Fain answered him coolly. "Do you want to tell me what your fee was for pronouncing her dead?"

"You're being insulting."

"Good, I was trying to be. Now maybe you get the message that the financial arrangements between Mr. Kruger and me are confidential."

"Well, what I want to know is—"

Fain stabbed a forefinger, surprising the doctor to silence. "Hold it. I've had enough of your cross-examination, doctor. Four months ago you signed Leanne Kruger's death certificate. Now it looks like your diagnosis was, to put it kindly, premature."

"Now just a minute—" Auerbach sputtered.

"I'm not through yet," Fain said, holding him with the gray-eyed stare. "If you made a damn fool of yourself, that's tough, but it's not my problem. What I am saying to you, Dr. Auerbach, is get off my case. Now."

Auerbach glared until his glasses began to cloud over. His face reddened as he forced the words out. "You'll be hearing from me, Fain."

"I'm in the book," Mac told him.

Auerbach stormed out into the hallway. When he was gone, Jillian came over and stood close to Fain. "Weren't you a little rough on him?"

"He was beginning to piss me off. I never have liked doctors much."

"Do you think he'll make trouble?"

"What kind of trouble can he make?" Fain snaked an arm around her waist and squeezed. "He'll be too busy checking his malpractice insurance to give me any static."

Fain let go of Jillian and turned toward the medical attendant, who had watched the exchange, wide-eyed, and stood now as though paralyzed.

"Are you okay?"

"Oh, yes, sir," the young man said. "May I say that I've never, ever, seen anything like that before."

"I don't suppose too many people have," Mac said.

He turned back toward the door as Elliot Kruger entered. It was a younger, more buoyant Elliot Kruger than the old man who had sat hunched forward in the chair at his wife's bedside, dying himself by inches. He came toward Fain, his eyes shining with renewed vigor.

"Mr. Fain, I don't know how you did it. I don't think I want to know. But I have no words to express my gratitude. You have restored my wife to me."

Mac Fain knew when to keep quiet. This was one of those times. He dropped his eyes modestly.

"I told you what I was willing to pay," Kruger continued. "I stand by that. You have given me back the most important part of my life. However you want the payment to be made—"

"No need to discuss that tonight," Fain said. "There will be time."

Dr. Auerbach came back into the room. He had his bag in one hand and a raincoat over his arm. "Elliot," he said, "I have to talk to you."

"Not now," Kruger said brusquely.

"As long as I am your doctor, I feel it's my duty to warn you—"

"You are not my doctor. Not anymore."

Auerbach stared at him. "What do you mean?"

"I mean you're dismissed. I no longer want you treating me or my wife. I've already called someone else in."

"Elliot, are you sure you know what you're doing?"

"Perfectly. Now, please excuse us."

The two men faced each other until Auerbach dropped his gaze. He turned away and left the room.

"Sorry about the scene," Kruger said.

Mac waved off the apology.

Kruger's expression softened. He said, "Leanne would like to see you."

"Of course."

Kruger led the way out into the hallway and back to the huge master bedroom. The window was closed again. The candles had been extinguished and the lights turned up. The colored powders on the floor around the bed had been swept into a neat brownish mound.

On the bed under a silk coverlet, her face pale but tinged with pink, her hair soft and vibrant at her shoulders, lay Leanne Kruger. The tubes had been removed from her arms, the pump wheeled away from the bed. She raised a delicate hand and held it out toward Fain.

He crossed the room toward the bed. Rosalia edged past him as he approached. As they passed, she made the sign of the cross on her breast.

At the edge of the bed, Mac reached down and took Leanne Kruger's hand. He was surprised by the strength of her grip.

"Mr. Fain," she said, "I understand I owe you a good deal."

He smiled down at her, saying nothing.

"I have no idea what's happened to me," she said. "In my mind, this should be Halloween, but they tell me it's the end of February. I seem to have misplaced several months."

Mac found his voice. "You remember nothing from all that time?"

"Nothing. Not even a dream. Usually I'm a good dreamer. And I always remember them. This time, nothing."

"Maybe it's better that way."

Their eyes locked for a long moment. Mac had the uncomfortable feeling that the woman was looking into his soul.

"Maybe so," she said. With a smile she released his hand. He turned at a sound from the doorway and saw that Rosalia had returned. She was carrying something white and furry that wriggled in her arms.

The smile of the woman on the bed brightened. She held out her arms toward the maid.

"Pepe! Oh, Rosalia, you brought my little Pepe. Come here to your mommy."

Rosalia carried the squirming poodle to the bed and set it down on the coverlet. As Leanne reached for the dog, it jumped back and bared its little teeth in a growl.

"What's the matter, baby?" Leanne said. "You know Mommy won't hurt you."

Stiff-legged, the little dog backed out of her reach, the fur bristling at its clipped neck. It continued to growl menacingly until Rosalia moved in and scooped it off the bed.

Leanne looked after Rosalia with wide, hurt eyes as the maid carried the poodle from the room.

Elliot Kruger hurried to her side. "I wouldn't worry about it," he said. "This has been quite a trauma for all of us. Give the dog a chance to get used to having you back and he'll be all over you just like before."

"I've never seem him act like that to anybody," Leanne said, looking toward the door.

Kruger forced a laugh. "You can't blame him too much. Matter of fact, I'll probably need some time myself to get used to the idea."

Leanne turned back toward her husband, and her face relaxed into a smile. "We'll see about that," she said.

Fain eased out of the bedroom and returned to where Jillian waited for him. "Are you ready to go?" he said, then added, "Our work here is done." He meant it to be comically overdramatic, but somehow the humor was lost.

"What was wrong with the dog?" Jillian asked. "The maid came past here, chasing it down the hall."

"Who knows? Wouldn't you be upset to see somebody you thought was dead sit up and talk to you?"

"I would, and I am."

Elliot Kruger came back in and cleared his throat for attention. Mac and Jillian turned toward him.

He held out a check to Fain. "I'm sorry this is only made out for half of what I owe you now. To tell the truth, I, well, I wasn't anticipating such spectacular results."

"That's understandable," said Fain.

"I'll have the balance delivered to you by messenger as soon as my son draws up the draft."

"No hurry," Fain said.

He slipped the check casually into a side pocket without reading it. Jillian watched him curiously.

Kruger looked eager to get back to his wife, but he hesitated. "Is there anything at all I can get you now?"

"Maybe a ride home," Fain said. "I'm a little tired."

"Of course. I'll have Garner outside with the car right away." He hurried out.

When Kruger had gone, Fain turned to grin at Jillian. "How about that? A multimillionaire falls all over himself to do things for me. Gives a man a whole new perspective."

"I can see that," Jillian said.

Rosalia came in carrying Fain's satchel. "Mr. Kruger said I should give you this," she said. "I put the candles in—what was left—and the powders I put in a plastic bag. They're all mixed together now. I couldn't help it."

"That's all right," Fain said, taking the bag from her. "Thank you."

Rosalia led them downstairs to the main entrance.

Richard Kruger stood at the door, watching them. He stepped in front of Fain and spoke through tight lips.

"I don't know how you did what you did in there tonight, but if you're pulling some kind of con on my father, I swear to God I'll make you pay for it."

Fain gave him the intense gray stare until the other man backed off, seeming to shrink under the scrutiny.

"If you think I have done anything illegal or dishonest, you go ahead and prove it. In the meantime, stay out of my way. Tonight you only saw a sample of what I can do."

When they were seated in the back of the Rolls, heading east on Sunset, Jillian said, "What did you mean by that?"

"What?"

"That stuff you told Richard about he ain't seen nothing yet."

"Just shaking him up a little bit. I don't have to take crap anymore from people like him and that society doctor. And you know what? It feels good. Damn good."

He took Kruger's check from his pocket and held it up so he could read in in the light of the passing traffic. He whistled softly.

"The whole ten thousand?" Jillian asked.

"One-zero-zero-zero-zero," Fain read aloud. "And more to come. Honey, this is only the beginning. No more cheap seats for McAllister Fain. From here on it's first-class all the way."

"Terrific," Jillian said. She huddled against the opposite door.

"That's it?" he said. "No applause? No hugs? No flowers strewn at my feet?"

She did not respond to his bantering tone. "Mac, what happened there tonight?"

"I became a rich man, that's what happened."

"That woman was dead."

He waved it off. "What the hell is dead, anyway? You heard that doctor. Suspended animation or something. Medical science still has a lot to learn."

"That's bolshoi, and you know it. Leanne Kruger was as dead as President Lincoln. We both saw her in that tank thing. Then you pulled that funny stuff with the colored sand and the candles and that weird humming, and she came back to life. What did you do, Mac?"

"Got lucky, I guess."

She punched him in the shoulder, not lightly. "Cut it out. You don't want to face it. A dead woman sat up and talked. God knows what she's doing now. You made it happen. Was it that voodoo stuff?"

"Nah. I didn't pay attention to what that old witch doctor told me. All I wanted from him was some atmosphere."

"You had that, all right."

He grinned into the darkness. "It was a pretty good show, wasn't it. Too bad we had to close it after one performance."

Jillian shuddered. "God, don't even think about doing it again."

"No way," he said. "I could never top tonight. And hey, I'm not forgetting that you helped."

"*I* want to forget it," Jillian said. "It's not right."

"Who says?"

"Mac, stop and think. You didn't just read somebody's tea leaves tonight. How can you be so casual about it?"

He made a pass and plucked Elliot Kruger's check from the air. He waved it gently under Jillian's nose. "This helps."

She turned angrily away. After a minute she said, "Mac, I don't want to stay over at your place tonight."

"Why not?"

"I just don't feel like it, that's all."

"Maybe it's just as well," he said. "I am pretty tired, and I've got lots to think about tomorrow. I'll have Garner run you out to your place after he drops me off."

"Thanks," she said softly. She was looking at him in a strange new way.

Chapter 9

The exhilaration of the night's events carried McAllister Fain from the limousine up the stairs and into his apartment without letting his feet touch the ground. Or so it seemed. Friday night at Elliot Kruger's Holmby Hills mansion had been a turning point in his life, and he knew it.

Fain was not yet ready to examine exactly what had happened in that oversized bedroom, or how it happened. The important thing was his success, and he was not going to question it.

Once inside, he fitted a Herbie Hancock album onto the turntable, poured himself a stiff Jose Cuervo, and settled into his recliner to savor the sudden upturn in his fortunes.

Instantly he was exhausted beyond words. The music faded to a background hum. The glass of tequila slipped and almost fell from his hand before he caught it. He had just enough energy to hoist himself out of the chair, tuck Kruger's check safely into his nightstand, and fall into bed.

The dreams followed one another without a break. Elliot Kruger was in most of them. Usually he was surrounded by the trappings of wealth—greenbacks, gold coins, jewels.

Fain wandered through a dreamscape filled with limousines and castles, swimming pools and squads of servants. Sometimes Jillian Pappas was there, but always at the edge of things, almost out of sight. She was trying to say something to him. Her mouth moved, but Fain could never make out her words. Too many other things were going on.

Once his parents showed up—his mother in an apron, hands floury from baking, his father with his usual distracted expression, the slide-rule badge of his profession peeping from a shirt pocket. Then, disconcertingly, his father had turned into Elliot Kruger and was handing him money. Worse, his mother became Leanne Kruger, reaching for him seductively from a huge bed. While her hands writhed and clutched at him, the beautiful face was pale and frozen, as he had seen it through the window of the cryogenic tank.

Fain woke up tangled in the sheets and sweating. He had a fierce thirst. He stumbled into the kitchen, broke loose an ice tray, and filled a glass with cubes and water from the tap. He drank it down, filled another, drank that.

Feeling a little better, he checked the time. It was still dark outside, so he figured he could not have slept long. The clock said 8:15. What the hell? It took a minute to get his brain into gear and realize that it was 8:15 P.M. Saturday. He had slept away the entire day. The knowledge made him suddenly hungry. He had not eaten for more than twenty-four hours.

He took a brisk shower and called Jillian's number in Studio City.

"Hi," said the answering machine in a friendly tone, "this is Jillian Pappas. I can't take your call personally right now, but when you hear the beep—"

Mac dropped the phone back into its cradle, cutting off the recorded voice. He hated talking to machines. At least Jill's message was straightforward. Worse were the cute ones. Still, he felt like a fool talking into somebody's recorder for playback at a later time.

And where the hell was Jillian on Saturday night, anyway? Then again, was it any of his business? He had made a big point of avoiding commitments, so he could

72

hardly object if she had something else going. Still, it would have been nice to see her, have an intimate dinner someplace, slip into bed naked together afterward.

Ah, the hell with it. He walked up to the corner of Sunset and Alvarado, bought a green chili burrito at the Burrito King, and took it home for a solo dinner washed down with cold Heineken. Then, to his surprise, he found he was tired again, so he changed the sheets, went back to bed, and slept, this time without dreams.

On Sunday, Mac Fain awoke shortly before noon, feeling like a million dollars, or a good portion thereof. A brilliant sun erased all memory of the recent rain. He scrubbed his teeth, shaved, and showered. Then he sat down on the edge of the bed and took Elliot Kruger's check from the nightstand and read it again. The figures had not changed. The signature was still there. He passed the slip of paper under his nose and inhaled, imagining he could detect the aroma of riches. This was the way a man's life ought to smell. Rich leathers and five-dollar cigars, corks from dusty wine bottles and the heady perfume of expensive women.

He tucked the check into his wallet and strolled out to greet the day, tossing the bulky Sunday *Times* inside. In the yard next door Xavier Cruz continued his never-ending battle with the rusting van. Fain went over to join him.

"Buenos Dios, amigo."

Cruz looked up wearily and wiped his face with a grease-stained kerchief. "Man, why don' you just talk English. You know what you just say to me? You say 'Good God.' Hello goes *Buenas días. Comprende?"*

"Whatever," Fain said cheerfully. "I wanted to thank you for sending me to the man over at the clinic."

"Forget it. You got nothing to thank me for," Cruz said, leaning back into the engine compartment.

"The guy was full of baloney, sure, but he gave me some good ideas," Fain said.

Cruz straightened up again to look at him. The coffee-brown eyes showed no glint of humor. "Man, if you think what he tol' you was baloney, you keep thinking that. Now you seen Le Docteur, you take my advice;

73

you stay far away. Don' press him, and don' ever make him mad."

"No problem, *amigo*. I got all I wanted from the old boy. He wouldn't even take any money. Maybe I'll make a donation to the clinic. Think he'd like that?"

Cruz shrugged. "Who knows?"

Fain stood for a moment shifting his weight from one foot to the other. "Hey, you feel like a beer? I've got cold Heinekens in the fridge."

"No, man, I got things to do."

"Yeah, well, maybe later." He waited for Cruz to say more, but the Cuban was occupied again with the battered works of the Volkswagen. They had been neighbors now for what, four years? There was a wall between them that was never going to come down.

"Adiós," he muttered, and walked back out to the sidewalk and up the steps to his apartment.

Here he was newly rich, driven around in a limousine, catered to by millionaires, and he couldn't even get his semiliterate Cuban neighbor to have a beer with him. Damn, he thought, it's lonely at the top.

He resolved not to spend Sunday alone. He went inside and dialed Jillian's number, mentally preparing a flippant message to leave on her answering machine this time.

"Hello?" It was Jillian's live voice that answered.

"Hi. What you doing?"

"Eating lunch." Very cool. Warning flags went up in Fain's head.

"Want to do something?"

"I am doing something."

"I mean later. Dinner. A movie. A few chuckles. Whatever."

"I can't. I've got a reading."

"Are you mad about something?"

"Mad? Why should I be mad?"

"You sound mad."

"I told you, I've got a reading."

"A job?"

"Just some friends. One of the boys is a playwright. I've told you about him. We get together sometimes and read his work in progress."

"Oh, sure. Well . . . I'll talk to you later."

"Fine. See you."

A click and a dial tone and that was it. Served him right for getting mixed up with an actress. Jillian was all right, but her friends were a bunch of fringies. Boys with long lashes and tight jeans, girls who didn't shave their legs, poets who couldn't rhyme, writers who didn't write. Mac had gone to a couple of parties with her and felt like an alien. Jillian, with all her eccentricities, was as straight as Marie Osmond compared to the rest of that crowd.

He went into the kitchen and uncorked a beer. Back in the living room he shuffled through the Sunday *Times* for the sports section. Not much doing this time of year unless you were a hockey or basketball fan, and Mac Fain was neither. One game had a bunch of Canadians skating aimlessly and endlessly back and forth. The other involved ten glandular cases stuffing a ball in a basket from above.

Baseball, there was a real sport. A man could get comfortable over the length of a season with the rhythms and drama of baseball. However, this time of year the teams were just opening spring training. There would be no real news until the season started, in six weeks.

Fain tossed the paper aside and sat gloomily pulling on his beer. Sunday night alone with television. Maybe there would be a good movie on cable. Whoopee.

He got out of the chair and smacked one hand into the other. This simply was not right. He was thirty-six years old, a not-bad-looking college graduate with a nice record collection and newly acquired riches. And here he was sitting home alone with a beer and the Sunday paper. Maybe that was all right for the Mac Fain of a week ago, but last Friday night should have yanked his life around and sent it in a new, exciting direction. He was on a different level now—a level where important things happened, where the beautiful people lived. McAllister Fain should not have to depend on the vagaries of cable television for companionship.

The telephone rang.

Fain let it ring four times. No use letting Jillian think he was poised by the phone, just waiting for her to decide that he was more fun than that flock of weirdos she ran around with. As the fifth ring began, he picked it up.

The female voice that spoke to him was not Jillian's. This voice was younger, more nasal, without Jillian's stage-trained modulation.

"McAllister Fain?"

"That's me."

"I'm Ivy Hurlbut. I'd like to come over and do an interview if you've got the time."

"An interview? What about?"

"About what you did Friday night for Elliot Kruger's wife. That was pretty sensational, you know."

"Where did you hear about that?"

"We have our sources."

"And who is 'we'?"

"The interview would be for the L.A. *Insider*. You know the paper?"

"Yeah, I know it. You work for them?"

"I'm a free-lancer, actually, but I've done stuff for the *Insider* before. I've got a photographer lined up, if you can spare the time this afternoon."

Fain hesitated. The L.A. *Insider* was not exactly *People* magazine. He was not thrilled to be included with women who had sex with space creatures and two-headed bushmen and babies who survived falls from the roof. But it was better than nothing. And face it, *People* hadn't called. Besides, Ivy Hurlbut might help him fill what looked like a tedious Sunday.

"I guess this afternoon is all right," he said.

"Neato. Want to give me directions to your place?"

Neato? Oh, well, it was somebody to talk to. He told Ivy Hurlbut how to get to Echo Park from Santa Monica, where she was calling from, and hung up feeling a little better.

She arrived about three o'clock. Mac's mental image of the girl reporter, picked up from television and old movies, was given a rude jolt. He figured she was twenty-two at the outside. Ivy stood about five-two with long, frizzy blond hair and an opulent body that was packed into stretch jeans and a baby-blue T-shirt that advertised the Minnesota Twins. A look at the thimble-size nipples pushing against the taut blue cotton erased any idea that she was a baseball fan.

"Hi," she said brightly, and poked him in the solar plexus. "Hey, you're in good shape. You work out?"

"I, uh, play a little tennis," he said, staring at the huge young breasts.

"Good for you. I like a man keeps himself in shape." She walked by Fain into the apartment and left him standing in the doorway, facing a tall, sleepy-looking black man with camera equipment hung all over him.

"I'm Olney Zeno," the black man said. "I take pictures."

"Yeah. Right. Come on in."

Ivy dropped her tight-jeaned bottom on his tweed couch and patted the cushion next to her. She took out a pocket-size notebook and ballpoint pen. "Should we get started?"

Zeno prowled about the room, his sleepy eyes missing nothing. A couple of times he checked a light meter and muttered something under his breath.

"Can I . . . get you anything?" Fain said.

"No, thanks," Ivy said. "After, maybe."

"You got any beer?" Zeno said.

Fain brought him a Heineken, half of which the photographer chugalugged, and sat down next to Ivy. Her round, plump thigh touched his, and he could feel the heat of her.

They quickly dispensed with his early life—born in the Middle West, B.A. in psych from Western Michigan, unmarried, ten-year resident of Los Angeles.

"Okay, now the good stuff," Ivy said. "When did you first learn you could bring dead people back to life?"

He chuckled as though they shared a joke. "Well, that isn't really my business. I just happened to fall into that. What I do is more like character readings and like that . . ." His voice trailed off as he saw he was losing his audience. Ivy had stopped writing. She moved her thigh a fraction of an inch away from his. He picked up the pace, deepening his voice and giving her the gray-eyed stare. "But I guess it's in the blood. The gift of power. Down through the generations, every so often one of my family will have the eyes of a *gangan*."

Ivy scribbled in her notebook. Her thigh pressed again against his. "Neato. What is that, exactly? A *gangan*?"

"In the ancient religions brought to Haiti by the African slaves," he improvised, "there is a hierarchy of the priesthood—those who have the dark power. *Gangan* is second only to the *houngan*."

"Wow, great stuff," Ivy said, staring at him in open admiration.

Her eyes were blue and guileless, and for a moment he felt guilty about giving her all this bullshit. Then she reached over and touched him on the leg, and the guilt pang went away.

While Fain spun out fanciful tales of his occult adventures and described the resurrection of Leanne Kruger, Zeno moved about the room, snapping pictures from different angles. The *click-whir* of his camera had a lulling effect, like cicadas in a summer meadow.

At one point the photographer interrupted. He pointed to a satanic poster Fain had mounted near the door to his bedroom. "How about one of you standing by this?"

"Oh, that, ha-ha. Picked it up at a swap meet."

"Yeah, it's cool. How about standing to one side of it."

Feeling foolish, Mac walked over and stood in the position the photographer indicated. "This okay? Is there enough light?"

"Plenty of light." *Click-whir.* "One more standing on the other side." *Click-whir.*

Zeno packed up his equipment. "Got all I need," he told Ivy. "I'll have 'em for you tomorrow morning." With a sleepy nod to Fain he went out.

Mac started back toward the couch and Ivy. "I wouldn't mind a glass of white wine if you've got some," she said.

"Sure."

He veered off toward the kitchen and poured two glasses from a chilled jug of Gallo chablis.

"Would it bother you if I smoke?" Ivy called from the living room.

"No, heck no. Ashtray right there on the table."

He screwed the cap back on the wine jug, returned it to the refrigerator, and started back with a glass in each hand. A whiff of acrid smoke from the other room told him Ivy was not smoking Virginia Slims.

She was holding her breath, eyes half closed, when he returned and set the wineglasses down on the coffee table. She let the smoke out in a long gray streamer.

"Thai stick," she told him. "Good shit." She offered him the tightly rolled joint. "Want a hit?"

Fain hesitated. Heineken was his drug of choice, or Jose Cuervo for something heavier. But he did not want the plump little free-lancer to think he was a square. He accepted the joint and took a medium drag. He pulled the smoke deep into his lungs and held it. Little colored lights danced between him and Ivy's round, smiling face. A nice relaxed feeling spread outward from the region of his navel.

"Good shit," he agreed.

"I told you."

They drank some wine and smoked the rest of the joint. Ivy asked some more questions, and Fain gave whatever wild answer popped into his head. They got hungry, and he brought out some gouda cheese and Ritz crackers and more wine. He put on a Randy Newman album, and they both marveled at the insights of the ragged lyrics.

After a while Ivy said, "Are we going to go to bed or what?"

"Right," he said. "Bed. Good idea." He rose from the couch, swaying slightly, and led her by the hand into the bedroom. They undressed each other, and Fain marveled at the way the girl was constructed of a series of globes varying in size but all with a nice resilient texture.

In bed, flesh on flesh, he thought briefly about Jillian. She was firm and supple and lean. Ivy's body was very different—rounder, bouncier, more generous. In a few years she would probably be fat, but right now all the globes stayed nicely in place. So much for Jillian Pappas. She could go ahead and spend the evening reading her fag playwright's latest piece of crap. Other people had things to do, too.

"Tell me what you like," Ivy said. She was looking

down at him, her arms braced on either side of his head. The Minnesota Twins hovered above him, bobbling like gelatinous moons. "What do you want me to do?"

He licked at one big pink nipple.

"That's what I thought," she said, and damn near smothered him with the things.

Fain awoke Monday morning alone in the bed. He vaguely remembered Ivy getting up and leaving some-time during the night. The sheets were gummy from their lovemaking, and his mouth was dry from the Thai stick, but overall he felt great. It was time, he decided, to call Elliot Kruger and talk about collecting his fee.

Chapter 10

Elliot Kruger was genuinely surprised when McAllister Fain did not try to raise the price they had agreed upon. Considering the results, Kruger was prepared to pay several times the agreed-upon thirty thousand dollars. But as a businessman he was not about to argue when Fain seemed satisfied with the original terms. The Kruger fortune was not built by giving money away.

It was not, he reminded himself, that he was in any way cheating the young man. Thirty thousand dollars was nobody's pocket change. And to a man in McAllister Fain's position it probably looked like a good deal of money. These things were all relative.

And Fain would never have to know that Kruger had been prepared to pay, if necessary, up to a million dollars. Hell, make that two million. No price could be put on what Fain had accomplished. It was not Kruger's fault if the young man did not know his true value.

Richard was already stalling, looking for loopholes in the final payment of ten thousand dollars, but Kruger would not stand for that. He had told his son not to fool around with the figures, but he could not expect Richard to change the habits of a lifetime. Richard was not Gil—dashing, handsome . . . and dead at twenty-three—but he was damn good at what he did. He could be a pain in the ass, but he guarded the Kruger money with the zeal of a pit bull protecting its supper. Richard had taken a dislike to Fain, and hated to see any of the Kruger money go to him, but there was nothing he could do about it.

Of greater concern to Elliot Kruger was his son's continuing hostility toward Leanne. It had been a sore point between them ever since Kruger announced his intention to marry the young woman. Richard sulked at the time, but Kruger was sure he would get over it. However, in the last few days, since Leanne's—*return* was the only word Kruger was comfortable with—Richard had turned grim and silent. An irritating crack in the surface of Kruger's newfound happiness.

Kruger had spent little time pondering the how of his wife's return. She had been restored to him whole and alive, and that was all that mattered. Magic, a miracle, suspended animation—he did not care and refused to think about it.

Now, after three full days of having her back, he was still a little afraid to believe it. He paced nervously in the billiard room, bouncing the balls idly off the green felt cushions, and waited for Leanne to come out of the adjoining bathroom. He hated to allow her out of his sight even for a minute. He had a nagging, irrational fear that the miracle that had given her back to him might be somehow reversed by a higher authority and she would be snatched away again.

He heard the bathroom door open, and in a moment Leanne came in. Kruger felt the tension ease as he rose and crossed the room to meet her.

Leanne was wearing a flowered-print jumpsuit with a skimpy halter top. The roundness of her breasts bulged nicely at the sides of the halter. She smiled as she walked toward him.

Kruger took her into his arms and held her tightly.

"Boy," she said, "what a welcome."

He said, "I don't know if I'll ever be able to let you walk into a room again without holding you."

She said, "Can I have that in writing?"

"In blood if you want."

"How gallant."

With his arms still holding her, Kruger leaned back and looked down at his wife. The pink tip of her tongue ran over her lips. He drank in the look of her, the smell of her. Scented soap, shampoo, minty mouthwash, a touch of musky perfume. Leanne had always been fastidious about her person, but even more so since her return. It was as though she were trying to wash away the months she spent sealed in the icy cylinder.

"Ready for lunch?" he said. "Wendell has whipped up something special. A soufflé of some kind."

Her eyes clouded for a moment. "I'm sorry, darling. I'm still not very hungry."

"Well, that's all right. Soufflés are really not his best dish. Is there something else you'd like?"

"I really don't feel like eating," she said. "But I do hate to disappoint Wendell."

"Don't worry about him. You just decide what you want when you feel up to it."

She leaned against him, letting him feel her body. "You spoil me, Elliot."

"That's my pleasure," he said.

His hands slid down over the dip of her back to the firm rounds of her buttocks. Leanne moved under his hands. She slipped a long leg in between his and worked it against his groin.

Kruger felt his erection growing. Leanne's restored sexuality had come as a bonus. He had been prepared to wait as long as it took for her to feel like having sex again. Just having her back was reward enough.

Then, to his surprise, she was immediately eager and hungry for his body. The first night, when all the others had finally gone, she had insisted he come into bed with her. When he had held back, trying to be gentle, she had dug her nails into his flesh and pulled him forcefully into her. Her passion made him forget all about restraint, and their reunion was a thing of violence and explosive orgasm.

When he was thoroughly drained, Leanne lay curled beside him. Her body was damp and feverish, her breath shallow. Alarmed, Kruger had tried to get up and call for the doctor, but Leanne had held him there with her.

"Honestly, darling," she said, "I never felt better in my life."

Reluctantly, he stayed beside her. In time, her temperature returned to normal, and she slept.

Over the next three days, while she had little interest in food, Leanne's sexual appetite had shown no signs of abating. Always a vigorous man, proud of his virility, Kruger found it difficult to keep up with her. This, too, he assumed, was somehow connected to her months of deprivation. It was certainly not something he was going to worry about.

Someone in the doorway of the billiard room coughed politely, and Kruger stepped away from his wife, feeling foolishly embarrassed.

"E'scuse me," Rosalia said. She held out a silk jacket toward Leanne. "You better wear this. You don't want to catch cold."

"Really," Leanne said, "you people have got to stop treating me like an invalid. I don't feel a bit different than I did before."

Rosalia gave her a reproving look. Leanne smiled and took the jacket from her. "But I must admit it is nice to be fussed over. Thank you, Rosalia. If you think I ought to wear the jacket, I'll wear it."

The maid nodded, satisfied. To Kruger she said, "Wendell, he want to know if you will eat lunch here or in the dining room."

Kruger glanced at his wife. "Tell him we won't—"

Leanne took his hand. "I think maybe I could eat something, after all, darling."

"Wonderful," he said. "Do you have a preference as to where it's served?"

"Could we have it out on the patio? It looks like such a nice day."

"Of course. Please see to it, Rosalia."

"Yes, sir," the maid said, and hurried off.

Kruger said, "I'm so glad you're going to eat something. I know you say you're feeling fine, and you look marvelous, but you do need to eat."

"You'll fatten me up yet, won't you."

"That will be the day," he said.

The weather, even in early March, was perfect for lunching on the patio. The temperature was in the mid-seventies, and a soft breeze from the ocean was nudging cotton-ball clouds across the sky. Elliot Kruger and Leanne sat in white metal chairs at the round table while Rosalia served them.

The soufflé was a feathery-light concoction of eggs, cream, and fresh bay shrimp delicately flavored with herbs from the garden. Kruger began to eat heartily, but his gusto waned when he saw that Leanne merely moved the food around on her plate, taking only a few tiny bites.

Feeling his eyes on her, Leanne looked up and smiled. "It's really delicious," she said. "I must remember to tell Wendell myself."

Kruger tried to keep his tone casual as he answered. "You know, I've been thinking. It wouldn't hurt for you to have a checkup. No big thing, just a general once-over."

"But I feel marvelous," she said.

"I know, darling, and you look even better," said Kruger. "All the same, you have been through a unique experience, and we have no way of knowing what the effects might be."

Leanne looked away. "I've never liked doctors much."

"I can't blame you for that," he said, "but it would make me feel easier."

"Not Dr. Auerbach," she said.

"Don't worry. Auerbach's through as far as I'm concerned."

"I'm glad. I heard him say some things the other night that were really cruel," Leanne said. "Called me 'unnatural.'"

"He's an old fool. No, I'd like Dr. Maylon to do the exam. Is he all right with you?"

"The cute one with a round face who smokes the pipe?"

"I don't know as I'd call him 'cute.' He's the young man who came Friday night after I ran Auerbach off."

"I guess he'll do," Leanne said, "if we have to have a doctor."

"He's young, but he comes well recommended," Kruger said. "And I liked the way he handled himself the other night. Did what he was supposed to and asked no questions."

"All right, darling, if it's really important to you."

Kruger watched her push the food around on her plate some more and fake a bite. He said, "It would make me happy."

Leanne leaned toward him across the table, and Kruger kissed her on the mouth. She tasted of minty mouthwash and only faintly of shrimp.

A sudden sharp barking came to them from somewhere beyond a laurel hedge that enclosed the patio. Rosalia, who had been hovering within call of her mistress, started at the sound. Kruger shot her a stern look.

"What's that?" Leanne said.

Kruger answered awkwardly. "We, uh, felt that until things were more stable around here and we all got used to one another again, it might be better to keep Pepe away from the house. So I, uh, had a pen built for him over by the tennis court."

"Oh." Leanne sipped at her wine and gave him a distracted smile. She looked down at the plate on which the food was barely touched. "I've made a pig of myself. I'd better stop before I burst."

Kruger studied his wife curiously. The little poodle had been her one indulgence. She treated it like a child. Since the unfortunate bedside scene with the dog Friday night, Leanne had not mentioned it. Kruger had expected an unpleasant scene when she learned that the little dog had been banished from the house. Her apparent indifference puzzled him. Did it mean, he wondered, that she had her emotions under control, or was it something else?

"It's getting a little cold out here," she said. "Shall we go in?"

"Yes, of course." Kruger rose quickly and offered his hand.

Leanne shook her head. "Please, dear, stop treating me like a sick person. I can get out of a chair without help."

He moved back then and waited for her to join him.

"See?" she said, and linked her arm through his. They walked together into the house.

Richard was waiting for them inside, holding a briefcase stuffed with papers. He gave Leanne a chilly look and spoke to his father.

"Will you be able to get to some of these documents today? Contracts, proposals, urgent reports. They've been piling up."

"Can't you handle them?" Kruger said, massaging his wife's arm.

"There are things that need your signature. And some questions that only you can answer."

Leanne patted his hand. "Darling, go do your work. I'll be all right left alone for a few hours. Really, I'm not going to disappear."

Kruger hesitated, then said, "I'll make it as quick as I can. If you need me for anything, we'll be in the upstairs office."

"Fine. And stop worrying."

"I'm going to call Dr. Maylon. Get him over here today."

"Whatever you say."

Kruger turned to his son. "Just give me a minute on the phone and I'll meet you upstairs."

He kissed Leanne lightly on the cheek and left them alone. As Richard turned and started toward the stairs, Leanne touched his arm. He turned and looked at her curiously.

"How's your wife, Richard. Sara, isn't it?"

"Sara's . . . fine," he said hesitantly.

"She doesn't come around."

"Well, she's busy with her own things. Charities, volunteer work at Mt. Sinai."

"I thought maybe it was that she didn't like me. You don't like me, do you, Richard?"

"I try not to make judgments."

"I wish we could be better friends," she said, her voice growing husky.

"You do?"

"Why not? We have to spend a good deal of time in the same house, and I just think it would be so much nicer if you liked me a little bit."

Richard swallowed, making the tight little knot of his necktie bob. "I don't dislike you, Leanne."

"But you don't approve of me."

He started to speak, and she placed a fingertip on his lips, silencing him.

"If we got to know each other better, I think you might learn to like me. Maybe a lot."

Richard's eyes narrowed behind the lenses of his unfashionable plastic glasses. Leanne traced the line of his mouth with her fingertip, then trailed it down his chin and over the soft flesh at his jawline.

"Tell Sara hello for me."

While Richard stared, she turned and walked unhurriedly away.

Dr. Peter Maylon arrived at the Holmby Hills estate promptly at five o'clock. He was an earnest man in his early thirties who had been taken in by a prestigious Beverly Hills medical group. A combination of boyish bedside manner and scalpel-sharp medical knowledge had made him immediately popular with the upscale clientele. He had arrived recently enough from Eugene, Oregon, to retain a sort of humorous country-boy charm and to still be impressed by the immense wealth of some of his patients.

As Rosalia led the doctor to the big second-floor bedroom, Elliot Kruger stepped out of his office and called him aside.

"You do understand that this is to be completely confidential," he said.

"Naturally. That's the way it works in any doctor-patient relationship."

"I know, but I'm asking for even more than your usual discretion in this case," Kruger said. "As you can imagine, if the details of my wife's . . . illness and recovery got out, this place would be crawling with the morbidly curious. I've already had some disturbing calls and been forced to increase security here."

"You don't have to worry about me, Mr. Kruger. I'm good at keeping my mouth shut."

"I'm glad to hear it. You did come highly recommended."

"Thank you. Now, is there anything in particular you wanted me to check Mrs. Kruger for?"

"Nothing really unusual. She looks wonderful, and she says she feels fine. Her appetite hasn't been what it should be."

"Mm-hmm. Anything else?"

"It's probably nothing, but she seems to have a cleanliness mania. She takes half a dozen showers a day and must brush her teeth every hour."

"Have you asked her about that?"

"I mentioned it, but she laughs it off. Says she wants to feel fresh."

"That's not unusual for people who have recovered from a long illness. Of course, your wife's case is different, but I doubt that it's anything to worry about."

"Still, I'd like you to look her over, without alarming her."

"I'll do what I can. You do understand I could be more thorough if I had her at the office."

"No," Kruger said immediately. "I don't want her to leave the grounds. Not until I'm convinced she's . . . herself again."

"So be it," said Dr. Maylon. They walked up the stairs together.

When at last he cleared the bedroom of everyone except the patient, Dr. Maylon took a seat at the side of the huge bed. Leanne Kruger reclined there with a mound of pillows at her back. She wore high-necked black lounging pajamas and a loose robe of Japanese silk.

"Well," he said, giving her his professional smile, "you don't look very sick to me."

"That's what I keep telling people," she said.

"Got any complaints? Aches and pains? Dizzy spells?"

"I'm afraid not. This is probably a wasted trip for you. I feel just fine."

"And you look fine," he said. "All the same, we—"

"Why, thank you, doctor," she interrupted. "Do you mean I look fine from a medical standpoint or"—she let the robe gap just a bit and smoothed the pajamas over her flanks—"just in general?"

"Both," he said briskly. "Your husband tells me you haven't been eating well."

"Elliot's like a Jewish mother. Always 'Eat, eat.' Do you think I look underfed?"

"No way."

"Are you married, doctor?"

He looked surprised. "Yes, I am."

"Children?"

"I have a little girl."

"That's nice." She reached down to straighten the robe, and her hand brushed against his thigh.

"What's her name?

"Kelly." He checked his watch. "Shall we get started?" he said.

"I'm ready. Do you want me to take off my clothes?"

"That won't be necessary." He plugged the tips of a stethoscope into his ears and became professional. "Suppose you just loosen your pajama tops a little."

Slowly, keeping her eyes on his, Leanne began opening the buttons from the throat. She had freed the third and had her hand on the fourth when Dr. Maylon spoke up.

"That's fine." He placed the diaphragm against the soft flesh high on her breast.

Leanne continued to open the buttons. "How do I sound?"

"Mmm." He moved the diaphragm lower. "Healthy. Lungs clear, heart strong."

She freed the last button, and the pajama coat slipped away. Her breasts rose and fell with each breath. A musky odor, tinged with soap, rose from her flesh.

Dr. Maylon started to take away the chest piece of the stethoscope. Leanne caught his hand and guided it back. She brushed his fingers across her nipple. It stiffened under his touch.

"Aren't you going to do me here?" she said, peering at him through lowered lashes.

"Do you?" He cleared his throat.

"Listen to me here."

Dr. Maylon pulled away hastily. "That won't be necessary." He slipped the stethoscope back into a pocket.

"I think you'd better have your husband bring you in to my office. I have a nurse there. And special equipment."

Leanne's eyes ranged down his body. "You didn't bring the equipment you need?"

"Mrs. Kruger," he said carefully, "I don't do this sort of thing."

She snaked a hand behind his head and with surprising strength pulled him down. She kissed him, openmouthed. He tasted mint . . . and something else. While part of his mind cried out at this terrible breach of ethics, he did not resist as Leanne guided his head down over the yielding flesh of her breasts until he took her nipple eagerly in his mouth.

Chapter 11

BILLIONAIRE'S WIFE, DEAD SIX MONTHS, RETURNS

Mac Fain stood in the Safeway checkout line on Wednesday, muttering to himself as he scanned the story on page three of the L.A. *Insider*. Didn't even make page one, for Christ's sake. That seemed to be reserved for the female stars of a prime-time soap, whose alternating love affairs and ailments were considered endlessly fascinating by the editors.

Furthermore, he had to read down to the third paragraph of Ivy Hurlbut's bylined story to find his own name. Okay, so maybe Elliot Kruger had more news value than McAllister Fain; they might still have mentioned him in the lead.

And where were all the pictures? Zeno must have shot a roll of film up at his place, but the only photo accompanying the story was one of Kruger that must have been some twenty years old.

At least his name was spelled correctly. Other inaccuracies, like the six months mentioned in the headline, peppered the story. Mac wondered about the "billionaire" business. If Kruger was close to that, he should have asked for more money. A lot more. At the time, thirty thousand had seemed like the jackpot. Now it was peanuts.

"Will that be all?"

Fain looked up from the paper to see he had reached the cash register.

He paid for the tabloid, carried it out of the market, and sat on the low wall bordering the parking lot to read the story again.

There were, of course, no quotes from Elliot Kruger or Leanne, although the story was written to imply that the *Insider* had had reporters right on the scene. By reading between the lines, Fain figured that the source for the story was Rosalia, the maid. He wondered if they had paid her for the tip.

The thought of payment brought him back to his own fee, which was looking smaller by the minute. With accountants and bankers and lawyers involved, especially that asshole Richard Kruger, Fain would be lucky to see any of the money he had coming before the end of the year. He was glad he had cashed the check for the retainer before somebody had put a hold on that.

He walked the two blocks back to his apartment, opened a Heineken, and settled into his recliner to read the *Insider* story one more time.

BILLIONAIRE'S WIFE, DEAD SIX MONTHS, RETURNS
BY IVY HURLBUT

A woman pronounced dead last year was returned to life over the weekend in a luxurious mansion in Beverly Hills. Before the unbelieving eyes of startled witnesses . . . [Enough of that, let's get down to paragraph three and the good stuff.]

McAllister Fain, 36, a well-known psychic and occult practitioner ["Well-known" is stretching it a little, but what the hell], operates out of a funky apartment in the picturesque Echo Park district of Los Angeles. [Funky? Picturesque? Nice way of saying seedy and run-down.] Fain, a personable young man with an engaging smile [Why, thank you, Ivy], declined to reveal to the *Insider* the methods he used in the astounding resurrection of Mrs. Kruger. [And with good reason. The well-known occult practitioner had not a clue as to what he had done last Friday night to make a dead woman live again.] Fain said only that a metaphysical strain running through many generations of his family gave him the power to perform feats outside the range of scientific knowledge. [Had he really said that? What utter bullshit.] He stressed that bringing back the dead was not his usual line of work. [They got that right, for sure.]

He read the story a last time and put the tabloid aside. It would make a nice entry for his scrapbook. If he had a scrapbook.

He called Jillian, got the answering machine, and made an indecent suggestion. Then he got out his address book and started a new list of his regular clients whom he had neglected during his brief adventure in the land of the millionaires. At least until he collected the rest of his fee from Elliot Kruger, he had better get back to work. Break out the trusty tarot deck. His ladies would be getting antsy waiting for word of the imminent ocean voyage and the mysterious, handsome stranger.

The next day Mac got two telephone calls from people who had read the *Insider* story. The first was from a pool-shooting, beer-drinking acquaintance who thought the whole thing was a rare joke. Fain let the guy have his laugh and hung up. The second was from an oily-voiced young man who identified himself as Dean Gooch, a columnist for the *Los Angeles Times*.

"You may be familiar with my work," he said.

"No."

"Oh. Well, I just read that *Insider* story about you and the Kruger woman." he said. "It gave all of us here at the *Times* a good chuckle."

"Glad to hear it," Fain said, working up a dislike for the guy.

"Not that I take it seriously for a minute, but I thought you might have something to say about it that I could use in my column. I do humorous stuff, you know."

"I'll bet you do," Fain said.

"I don't mean at your expense," Gooch said. "What I had in mind was taking a couple of shots at those supermarket tabloids and the lip-readers who buy the things."

"As opposed to the mental giants who read the *Times*?"

"What's that?"

"Forget it. What do you need me for, Dean?"

"Just a quote on how ridiculous the whole story is. I mean, bringing back the dead . . . after all."

"Why don't you just quote yourself like the rest of the *Times* gang? You know: 'Informed observers say . . .' That kind of thing."

"Wait a minute; you're not trying to tell me this story is true."

"You're a reporter. Find out for yourself."

He hung up feeling a little contrite about mouthing off at Gooch, but only a little. He was in a rotten mood, anyway, and the guy's smug attitude had been asking for a smack across the chops.

Mac goofed away the rest of the day, got no more calls, and went to bed feeling cheated out of even the fifteen minutes of fame Andy Warhol had once predicted for everybody.

On Friday the telephone woke him at seven-fifteen. He fumbled the receiver off the cradle and up to his ear and managed a hoarse "Hello?"

"Antichrist!" shrieked a woman's voice.

"What?" Fain held the receiver away from his ear.

"Devil worshiper!"

"What number are you calling?"

"Fascist! Blasphemer!"

"Wait a minute, lady—"

"Defiler of the grave!"

His brain began to function. The shrieking woman had read the story and looked up his phone number. Unfortunately, he was listed in the book.

The shrill voice continued. "Only the blessed Christ Jesus can make the dead to live again. You are an accursed spawn of Satan."

"Get stuffed," Mac told her, and cradled the phone.

Ten minutes later it rang again. Another woman's voice. This one teary and beseeching.

"Please, oh, please, sir, you must help me. You're the only one who can help me."

"Help you do what?"

"My darling Joseph, my husband of forty years, was taken from me before his time. I'm all alone in the world. If only you will bring him back to me, I'll be forever grateful."

In spite of himself, Mac felt a surge of compassion. As gently as he could, he said, "Ma'am, after forty years, maybe it *was* his time."

"I beg of you, don't refuse me. If I can't have my Joseph back, there is nothing for me to live for. These five years he's been in the ground have been misery for me."

Five years in the ground? "Lady, I'm sorry, really, but I can't do anything for you."

After a second's pause the woman went on in a hardened tone. "You did it for those rich people; why can't you do it for me? You only help millionaires—is that how it works? Ordinary people aren't good enough?"

"Lady, that is not the way it is."

"I know how it is, Mr. Big Shot. You're just like the doctors. You fall all over yourself when the rich guys want something, but for the poor people you're out to lunch. I know where you live, too. Think about that."

Fain hung up and thought about that. What was going on? How come the delayed reaction? he wondered. Did everybody go to the supermarket on Friday?

The next call was from a weak-voiced old man who was willing to pay every cent he had for the return of his dear dead wife. The one after that was from a little kid who missed his turtle, flattened by a UPS truck. Fain was shakily pouring his first cup of coffee when the fifth call of the morning came. It was Jillian Pappas.

"You're famous," she said.

"Tell me about it. The phone hasn't stopped ringing. I don't know what happened; the *Insider* ran the story two days ago."

"Fuzz the *Insider*. Haven't you seen this morning's *Times*?"

"The *Times*? Jesus Christ."

"I think he made it, too, but back in the Religion section. You're on page one of Metro."

"Balls. Hey, I've been trying to call you."

"Was that you talking dirty to my answering machine?"

"Never mind. When can I see you?"

"I've been real busy. Gotta run now; I've got a look-see for a McDonald's commercial."

"How about dinner?"

"Okay. Talk to you later. B'bye."

"Good-bye," he said to the dead phone. "Nice talking to you." He hung it up, and it began to ring immediately. He let it go this time and walked to the front door to retrieve the *Times*.

There it was, as advertised, under Dean Gooch's byline on page one of the Metro section:

Do Dead Return?
One Did, Says Tabloid

Tucked away among the stories of UFO's and miracle diets and singing fetuses in the pages of a supermarket tabloid this week was the news of a woman dead—not for minutes but for months—who was miraculously restored to life.

The alleged returnee to the land of the living is Leanne Kruger, 23, wife of wealthy industrialist Elliot Kruger of Holmby Hills. The engineer of this remarkable feat is said to be one McAllister Fain of Los Angeles, who bills himself, perhaps too modestly, as a "Master of the Occult."

A check of the records tells us that Mrs. Kruger was indeed reported dead last November 1. There were rumors at the time that her body was cryogenically preserved and maintained at the Kruger home, but this was denied by the family. According to an impressionable member of the Krugers' household staff, Fain conducted a bedside ceremony lasting several hours, after which Mrs. Kruger awoke and spoke to the people around her, seemingly restored to life.

Neither of the Krugers was available for comment. Richard Kruger, a son by a previous marriage, declined to be quoted but implied that the whole thing was a hoax. Dr. David Auerbach, the family physician said to be present at the time, was vacationing in Hawaii.

Fain, who works out of his apartment in Echo Park, refused to talk to reporters. We wonder if this means he is abandoning the resurrection game. That would be a pity, considering the wondrous things he might accomplish by bringing back, say, Abraham Lincoln or Galileo or Freud. Or how about W. C. Fields or Marilyn Monroe? The possibilities boggle the mind.

Fain sailed the Metro section across the room, watching the pages separate in midair and flutter to the carpet.

"Thanks a lot, Gooch," he said between clenched teeth. "Nice piece of writing. Asshole."

The telephone rang.

A woman claimed to have returned from the dead on her own and wanted to meet him and share experiences.

An agitated man talked nonstop in some language Fain did not recognize.

Another man wanted to know how he could arrange to be brought back when he had passed to the great beyond.

A young woman with a Middle Eastern accent proposed marriage.

Say what you will about Gooch, Fain thought, the man had his readers.

The telephone rang. This time it was Ivy Hurlbut.

"Did you read what that prick did to you?"

"Our friend Dean Gooch? Oh, yes."

"I take it you didn't talk to him."

"No."

"Or any other reporters?"

"Nobody's asked."

"They will, but hold out. You're hot now, honey."

"Hooray for me."

"The *Insider* wants me to do another piece on you. Front page this time, and definitely with pictures."

"No, thanks, Ivy. I'm through being the hero of the supermarket set."

"I don't blame you, honey. I put them on hold while I talked to *Los Angeles* magazine and *People*."

"*People?*"

"Sure. I've got contacts, honey. I don't just write schlock, you know.

"*People* magazine?"

"That's not all. I'm thinking book."

"Book?"

"Sure. An as-told-to autobio. I've got a friend who knows an editor at Bantam. They can crank these things out in less than six weeks."

"A book," Fain said again.

"When can we get together, honey? I can come over there."

"Let me get back to you. I've got a lot going on here at the moment."

"Don't wait too long, honey. Now's the time we want to jump in with both feet."

"Yeah, feet. I'll talk to you."

Mac hung up the phone and took two aspirin. His mind felt jumbled with all that was going on, like a file drawer dumped out and restuffed with no attempt to get things back right.

The telephone continued to ring.

There was a call from a woman who said that if he liked to do it with corpses, she could lie real still.

An older woman scolded him for contributing to overpopulation.

A thundering voice announced itself as God. Fain hung up on that one with his shoulders hunched reflexively against a thunderbolt.

The next call was from Barry Lendl.

"Barry who?"

"Lendl. Barry Lendl and Associates, Inc. Artistic and personal representation."

"You'll have to excuse me; I'm on my way out."

"Getting a lot of calls, are you?"

"Too many."

"Then I'm the man who can help you."

"Help me how?"

"Can you be at Nate and Al's by one o'clock?"

"What for?"

"For your future, my friend, your future. You need somebody representing you, and you need him now."

Short pause.

"You haven't got anybody else, have you?"

"No, but—"

"Good, then you might as well start with the best. Nate and Al's one o'clock. Or do you want to fight your own way through the yahoos who are calling you?"

"Nate and Al's," Fain said. "One o'clock."

Chapter 12

Richard Kruger stood uncomfortably at the side entrance to the Holmby Hills house, leaning as though anxious to continue through the open door to his Buick parked outside. He was held where he stood by the force of his father's tirade. Elliot Kruger held a rolled-up copy of the *Times* Metro section that he slapped into his other hand to emphasize his points.

"I want you to get on Bedlow right away and see what kind of a case we've got against these bastards."

"Sue the *Los Angeles Times*?"

"Hell, yes. Why not?"

"What about that rag the *Insider*?"

"I don't give a damn about them. It's this *Times* thing that's causing all the trouble. My friends read the *Times*."

"I don't know," Richard said doubtfully. "The way the story is worded, I don't see that we can claim libel."

"I don't care what the claim is, but I want to land on them with something. Have Bedlow figure it out; that's what I pay him for."

"I'll talk to him." Richard started to edge through the door.

"And I don't want you giving statements to any more reporters about anything."

"I told that Gooch person not to quote me," Richard protested.

"He didn't have to. Did you or did you not tell him there was a hoax involved?"

"I may have implied that I'm not totally satisfied that this Fain is all he says he is."

"Fain did what he said he would," Kruger snapped, "and that's all I care about. From now on there will be no interviews. Do I have to send you to the islands, too?"

"No interviews," Richard said, and was permitted at last to go out to his car.

Elliot Kruger stood for a minute in the doorway as his anger drained away. Then he went back inside and eased wearily into a chair. What had begun just a week ago as a blessed miracle was tarnished now by the intrusion of the press and the public.

A headache was beginning just behind his eyes. Kruger massaged them with thumb and forefinger. He had not been so foolish as to think Leanne's return would go unnoticed, but neither had he anticipated the sordid curiosity generated by one small item in the *Times*.

He did not worry about the L.A. *Insider* and the more sensational story they carried two days ago. The tabloid did not have anything like the clout of the *Times*. Then, too, it was through an ad in the *Insider* that he had found McAllister Fain.

The trouble had started this morning with a barrage of telephone calls from newspapers, wire services, and all three television networks. He also heard from respected members of the medical and religious establishments, educators, and uncounted cranks. Kruger had called in two women from his Wilshire Boulevard office and assigned them to do nothing but take the calls and dismiss the callers in whatever way they could.

Then a problem had developed at the gate. A crowd of morbid sightseers had gathered outside, and two teenage girls had somehow slipped in. They had been collared and hustled off, and now Kruger had extra security men patrolling the grounds.

But Kruger's greatest concern was the effect he feared this would have on Leanne. She had seemed to come through the months-long ordeal miraculously well. Early this morning she had slipped out of bed, saying she felt so well she wanted to go for a walk. When Kruger offered to join her, she had kissed him and said she'd like this little time alone. He could not refuse her that. She did agree to stay within the grounds.

Then she came back, looking flushed and upset. The damned gawkers outside the gate had caught sight of her. They shouted and whistled at her as though she were some kind of a freak. Kruger had immediately put his wife to bed and summoned Dr. Maylon. He was upstairs with her now.

Kruger turned at a small, persistent sound from the doorway behind him. Rosalia stood there, her brown hands nervously tugging at the sides of her dress.

"What is it?" Kruger said.

"I jus' want to say I'm sorry for all this trouble. I shouldn't have tol' nobody."

"It's done now, Rosalia. I know you meant no harm."

"Oh, no. I would never harm Mrs. Kruger. I am jus' so happy she is back that I want everybody to know and be happy with me. I didn't think people would be so bad."

"I know," he said gently. "It's not your fault. I hope you have learned, though, not to talk to anyone else about what happens here."

"No, sir. They can torture me but I never say one more word."

"I doubt they'll resort to torture, Rosalia, but I appreciate your sentiment. Is the doctor still in with Mrs. Kruger?"

"Yes, sir."

"As soon as he comes out, tell him to see me."

Rosalia bobbed her head and scurried off. Kruger sank back into the chair, feeling his age.

One of the security men came in carrying something wrapped in a towel.

"Excuse me, sir."

Kruger looked up wearily. "Yes, what is it?"

"I found this in the swimming pool." The security man raised one end of the towel. Under it was a small matted bundle of white fur.

"Oh, no, that's my wife's little dog. He was supposed to be penned up."

"Found him floating in the pool," the security man repeated. "Beats me why he couldn't have climbed out of there. Dogs are good swimmers, and the pool rim is low enough so even a tiny thing like this could have made it."

"Put it in the garage for now," Kruger said. "And please don't mention this to anyone. My wife was quite fond of the dog, and I'd rather she didn't hear about it just now."

He watched the man leave, feeling more tired all the time. Although Leanne had not been terribly upset about having Pepe kept away from her, something like this could be very painful to her, especially with all the other problems they had today.

Kruger lifted his eyes toward the ceiling. He wondered how the doctor was doing with his wife.

Dr. Peter Maylon lay on his back on the big bed in the master bedroom. His jacket and tie were hung carelessly over the back of a chair. His shirt was hiked up, and his pants were unbelted and pulled down around his knees. Leanne Kruger, naked, sat astride him. She rode him up and down, her buttocks smacking wetly against his upper thighs.

Maylon's face was turned away from her, his eyes squeezed shut. He moaned in tiny puffs of breath with each smack of buttock on thigh. Suddenly his body spasmed, and he reached down to clutch the smooth white flesh of the woman and hold her to him.

Leanne gazed down at him, her small white teeth glistening in a smile. She stayed atop the young doctor until his passion was spent; then she disengaged.

"Did you like that, Peter?" she said.

Still he did not look at her. "God, what are we doing?"

"I don't have to tell you, do I. You're a doctor."

He slid away from her and began pulling his clothes together. "That's the trouble. I'm a doctor. This is wrong. Wrong."

"My, how moral the doctor is now that he's all finished."

"Please, Leanne, I feel badly enough."

"Worried about your wife finding out?"

He fumbled his glasses from the night table and put them on. "This has to be the last time. I'm going to tell your husband I can't treat you anymore."

"What reason are you going to give him?"

"It doesn't matter."

"Oh, but it does, Peter darling. If Elliot had even the slightest notion what you were doing to me, he would destroy you. Maybe you think he couldn't do it."

"I'm sure he could." Maylon pulled his necktie into place and looked at her. "Why me, Leanne? What is it you want from me?"

She reached out to stroke his cheek. "Just exactly what I'm getting, darling. You're not going to take that away from me, are you?"

He pulled away from her, stood up, and finished dressing. When he spoke again, he tried to get some of the calm authority of the physician back into his voice. "It smells stale in here. Why don't you open the windows?"

"The windows are open."

"Well . . . The air isn't good."

Leanne got off the bed on the opposite side. She snatched a robe from the back of a chair, covered herself, and headed for the bathroom. "I'll see you tomorrow," she said without looking back. "Make it early."

The bathroom door closed behind her.

The young doctor stared after Leanne for a moment, then turned to check himself a last time in the mirror. He picked a loose black hair from his lapel and willed his facial muscles to relax. Then he went downstairs to face her husband.

Nate and Al's delicatessen on Hollywood Boulevard was one of the last reminders of Hollywood in the golden era. Long gone was Romanoff's, the Garden of Allah, Ciro's, the Trocadero. Grauman's Chinese was not Grauman's anymore, and the Brown Derby had closed for good. Among the gay bars and the porno flicks and the grease-smelling hamburger joints, Nate and Al's hung on, a reasonable facsimile of the deli where screenwriters used to gather and reminisce about New York and curse the studios. Back when there were *real* studios.

People from the industry still went to Nate and Al's, but now they were more likely to be front-office types than writers. They all read the trades, and they talked in loud voices so everybody should know it.

Mac Fain was halfway through a beer when Barry Lendl arrived ten minutes late. Lendl was a balding little man with two-tone smoked glasses and a ruddy complexion. He danced his way through the crowded room, scattering greetings like rose petals. "How you doing, Billy? How's the kid? . . . Lookin' good, Sammy. . . . Caught you on *A.M. America,* Blake. . . . Nice jacket, Sid. I wanta know where you got it. . . . Hey, Marv, let's do lunch soon." He pirouetted to a stop at Mac's table. "You must be McAllister Fain."

With a glance Fain took in the fitted designer jeans, the ultrasuede shirt, the Gucci loafers, the heavy gold neck chain. The man was a walking caricature of the Hollywood agent. He nodded and gestured to the open chair.

"Terrific. I'm Barry Lendl. What are you having? The pastrami's the best; take it from me." He beckoned a waiter over. "Maurie, how goes it? I'll have a pastrami on rye, heavy on the mustard, kosher pickle, and a diet Seven-Up."

Fain ordered pastrami on white and potato salad. He said, "What, exactly, was it you wanted to talk to me about?"

"Right to business, hey? Good, I like that. No bullshitting around. You may not know it, Mac, but today you're a hot property. I mean, did you or did you not bring a woman back from the dead?"

"That's what I read in the papers," Fain said.

"That's good enough. Tomorrow you could cool off, but we won't worry about that. The important thing is to make as much money as you can while you're still hot. Am I right?" He went on without waiting for an answer. "I'm here to help you do that."

"I'm not sure I understand."

"Maybe if I name some of my clients, it'll clear up the picture for you. Remember Louis Freitas?"

"I don't think so."

"He started out to paddle a kayak across the Pacific. Got eight miles off shore before he foundered. *Eyewitness News* did a little piece on him leaving, and the guy became a folk hero."

"I never heard of him," Fain said.

"In a small way, of course. When they pulled him out of the drink, I looked him up and got his story in the local dailies and put him on a radio talk show. With the publicity behind us, I booked him into survival schools, environmental meetings, yacht clubs, like that. Got him a tie-in with one of the builders at the boat show. He had a profitable three months just for paddling a stupid boat into the ocean."

"I must have been out of town," Fain said.

"How about Barbara Jean Mayer? You gotta remember her."

"It rings a bell. Faintly."

"U.S. women's gymnastic team. Cute blonde. Pigtails. Mary Lou Retton got most of the goodies, but we did all right with what was left over. I got her a couple of local endorsements, and she cut a record."

"A record of what, her falling off the balance beam?"

"Ha-ha, that's good. No, she could sing a little. Not much, as it turned out, but we did okay for a few weeks."

"I don't sing," Fain said.

"What I got in mind for you is to get as much local exposure as we can; then we go for club lectures, maybe some colleges. I know I can place some articles, and a book would sell right now."

"Somebody else mentioned a book."

Lendl leaned forward. "Not another agent?"

"No, a writer I know."

"Oh, well; they're easy to find. I got a ghost client who could crank it out in a week."

"I'd like to stay with mine. She seems to know what she's doing."

"A woman, hey. Well, put her in touch with me and maybe we can work something out." He leaned forward, getting serious. "You want to tell me how you did it? Made it look like the dead broad came back to life?"

Fain tossed a spoon into the air, caught it, tossed again, and the spoon vanished. "Magic," he said.

"Hey, that's not bad," Lendl said. "We can work it into the lectures. Seriously, you don't have to tell me if you don't want to."

"Seriously, I haven't got any more idea how I did it than you have."

"Fair enough. So how about it, Mac? Have we got a deal?" Lendl stuck out his hand.

Fain hesitated. "What's in this for you, Barry?"

"The usual—ten percent and expenses."

"Expenses?"

"Hey, only what's legitimate. I'm not one of these Hollywood hotshots who'll try to screw you."

After a moment Mac took his hand. "What the hell, we got a deal."

"Beautiful." Lendl checked his watch. "Look, if you'll excuse me, I want to get right on this while you're still news." He signaled for the waiter. "Hey, Maurie, check over here."

The waiter brought the check, which Lendl snatched up with a flourish. He grabbed at his hip, then grinned sheepishly.

"Can you believe it? I left my wallet outside in the Mercedes. Let me run out and get it."

"Never mind," Mac said, taking the check away from him. "I'll get this."

"Thanks, Mac. The next one is definitely on me. You'll hear from me in a day or so."

The little man made his exit. "Sheila, you're too lovely. . . . Nice job on the Switt pilot, Jack. . . . Christine, saw your work on *Dynasty*. Marvelous . . . Call me for lunch."

Les Freres Taix was a French farmhouse-style restaurant on the Echo Park stretch of Sunset Boulevard. It was located improbably among Mexican and Cuban food stands and clothing stores that specialized in bright polyester. Inside, the restaurant was dark and cool, with red candle lamps on the tables. The food and the decor were reasonably authentic French. The busboys were the traditional illegal aliens.

Jillian Pappas barely sipped on her chablis as Fain got into his second Jose Cuervo.

"You are not exactly bubbling tonight," he said.

"Sorry."

"How did the McDonald's thing go?"

"I won't know for a couple of days. I don't think I got it."

"Not enough bajoomies?"

"Too old."

"You're kidding."

"I don't kid about my work. Take a look at the women working in soft-drink and fast-food commercials. Even the atmosphere people you barely see in the background. None of them are old enough to vote."

They were silent for a minute. Fain looked at the menu; Jillian chewed at a hangnail.

"There's something else bothering you," he said.

"No, really."

He pulled a red napkin through his fist, and it came out white. "You can't fool the all-seeing eye."

His sleight of hand could usually cheer her up, but not this time. She said, "It's what you're doing, if you want to know."

"What I'm doing?"

"I mean all this mystical stuff. And now you tell me you've got an agent."

"So what? You've got an agent."

"That's different. I'm an actress. You're a . . . a . . . flipping grave robber."

"That's not fair."

"Maybe not, but it's close to the truth. And who's this bimbo who's going to write a book for you?"

"Oho."

"Don't give me 'oho.' I'm not jealous; I just don't feel like what you're doing is clean. I haven't liked it from the start."

"Jillian, I've already made more money that I ever have in my life. I didn't kill anybody for it." He smiled. *"Au contraire."*

"I hate it when you get smug. You were a much nicer person before you had money and your name in the paper. And now you're going ahead and exploit this necro . . . necro . . . whatever the word is."

"The word is necromancy, and I'm getting a little tired of all this uninvited criticism."

She stood up and slapped the napkin down on the red tablecloth. "Too bad about you. Well, I don't want to spend any more of my time with somebody who makes his living off walking corpses."

Jillian delivered the line with good projection right from the diaphragm and stalked out. The room fell suddenly silent, and Mac felt the eyes of the other diners on him. He swiveled around, giving them a ghastly smile. When they all had returned hastily to their meals, he swallowed the rest of his tequila and left.

Chapter 13

On Saturday, Mac Fain got three phone calls inspired by the article in the *Times*.

A television evangelist from Glendale offered to debate him on the air. Mac referred him to Barry Lendl, and the evangelist lost interest.

A woman called to ask if he was the McAllister Fain from Michigan. When he said yes, she hung up.

The third call was a juvenile voice shouting, "Boooo!" then hanging up in a storm of giggles.

On Saturday night he went up to Sixth Street Billiards and lost twelve dollars shooting pool. He was home and in bed with a slight beer headache by two A.M.

On Sunday, he woke up earlier than usual and dragged in the bulky *Los Angeles Times*. There was no mention anywhere of him or the Krugers. He read the sports page and the comics and the Calendar section, then tossed the paper aside.

He boiled a hotdog for lunch, checked the TV Guide, did part of the *Times* crossword puzzle, and finally it was two o'clock. Jillian Pappas never rose before two, and conversation with her any earlier was futile. He dialed her number.

"Hi. Still mad?" he said when she came on the line.

"Mad? What makes you think I was mad?"

"Oh, I don't know; maybe the way you called me a corpse lover and stormed out of Taix the other night."

"I was just upset about this magical mystery tour of yours."

"So I gathered."

"Mac, I worry about you. You seem . . . different."

"It's been a traumatic week for me. Why don't you come over and we can make up tonight."

"Hey, I would, but I've got this really important photo session."

"On Sunday night?"

"The photographer will do it for special friends."

"Uh-huh."

"Don't say uh-huh like that. He's gay, if it makes you feel any better."

"It does. Well, how about letting me take you to dinner tomorrow, then. Anyplace you name."

"Anyplace?"

"Name it."

"L'Hermitage."

Fain's throat tightened at the mention of the expensive French restaurant; then he remembered that he had banked twenty thousand of Elliot Kruger's dollars, with another ten thousand coming whenever Richard got through screwing around with the paperwork.

"You got it," he said expansively.

He felt a little better after talking to Jillian, but the feeling soon ebbed. Two days ago the phone would not stop ringing. Now the apartment seemed unnaturally silent.

"Fame to obscurity in three days," he grumbled. "I wonder what the world's record is."

By four o'clock Fain had sunk into a depression. Collapsed in his recliner, he stared glumly at a terrible old Elvis Presley movie on television.

A knock on the door jogged him out of his stupor. He got up and yanked open the door to find Barry Lendl standing outside. The little agent was looking nervously back down the steps to where a metallic-gray Mercedes 380SL roadster was parked at the curb.

"Am I safe down there?" he said.

"As long as it's daylight," Fain told him.

Looking doubtful, Lendl came inside. "Nice place," he said without looking around.

"It's home." Fain thumbed off the television set.

"You got anything on tomorrow night?"

"Well, a date."

"Cancel it. I got you a spot as featured speaker at the Eastside Social Club banquet."

"What is that?"

"These are some important people in the Latino community. For us it means a cool three hundred dollars."

"Wow."

"Hey, we got to start somewhere. You telling me you can't use three hundred dollars."

"I can use it," Fain said, "but I'm curious why these guys would want to hear me."

"You got a soda? Perrier? Anything like that?"

"Ginger ale."

"Sugar-free?"

"No."

"Oh, well, I'll take it. You ought to keep sugar-free."

Fain went to the kitchen and uncorked a bottle of Canada Dry. He poured it into a glass over ice and brought it out to Lendl, who perched on the vinyl seat of the recliner.

"Now what about these merchants?" Fain said.

"The truth is you aren't exactly their first choice. I had Carmela Lopez booked for the banquet, but she came down with dysentery."

"Who is Carmela Lopez?" Fain asked.

"She's very big on Channel Thirty-four. They call her Thunder Thighs."

"And you expect me to go on for Thunder Thighs?"

"You got something better to do?"

"Not really, but—"

"They were gonna go fifteen hundred for her. Naturally I couldn't get that for you, but I managed to talk them up from two to three."

"Barry," Fain said carefully, "I don't even speak Spanish."

"Not to worry, *amigo*. Most of these dudes talk English."

"What am I supposed to say to them?"

"Just general bullshit about life after death, that kind of thing. Throw in a trick like that spoon business you did for me. They'll love it."

"You think so? Barry, I haven't even started to put together any kind of a lecture."

"No sweat, *compadre*. Wing it. Give 'em five minutes of generalities, then call for questions. They'll carry it for you from there."

"Are you sure?"

"Mac, do you trust me?"

"I can't think of any reason why I should."

"I'll let that slide. I know the money is not huge, but this could lead somewhere. I happen to know TV is covering the banquet."

"Channel Thirty-four."

"Hey, it's better than nothing."

"Tell me something, Barry. Do these people know Thunder Thighs won't be there?"

"Their program chairman knows, guy named Silvera, but I didn't exactly broadcast the news."

"Oh, great. Well, I suppose I have to eat somewhere."

Lendl smoothed his thin hair across the speckled scalp. "Actually, the speaker's fee doesn't include dinner. I thought you'd rather have the money than heartburn."

"You're asking me to speak to a bunch of strange Mexicans on an empty stomach?"

"Mac, do you and me have a deal? Did we shake hands?"

Fain nodded reluctantly.

"Then do this thing for me. Don't worry; I'll be there to pull you out of any rough spots."

"Rough spots? What rough spots?"

"That's what I'm saying; I'll be there to make sure there aren't any. Trust me, baby."

"I don't know why," Fain said, "but I'll do it."

"Terrific. I'll go start the ball rolling. Say, Mac, I'd rather not drive the 'cedes in that part of town. Can you pick me up?"

"What about my Camaro?"

"How old is it?"

"Seventy-nine."

"They won't touch it. Six o'clock okay?"

"I guess so."

Lendl wrote down an address in Beverly Hills—the wrong side of Sunset. "See you then, *amigo*."

"*Arrivederci*."

Fain stood in the doorway and watched Lendl hurry down to the street, where he walked slowly around the Mercedes, counting the hub caps before he got in and drove away.

Jillian Pappas was not happy to hear about the change in plans.

"What you're telling me is no L'Hermitage," she said.

Fain smiled disarmingly at the telephone. "There'll be other times, honey. This is the first thing Lendl has set up for me, and I couldn't very well turn it down."

"No, heck no."

"So listen, why don't you come along?"

"To this Mexican banquet?"

"Eastside Social Club."

"What time is dinner?"

"Uh, we won't exactly be eating there."

"Oh?"

"You wouldn't want to sit there through four courses of tamales and enchiladas?"

"I don't want to sit there at all."

"Hey, it might be fun."

"Listening to you talk about raising corpses?"

"You don't have to make it sound so ugly."

"Tell me how to make it sound pretty."

"Jillian, don't fight me."

"Who's fighting? I just don't want to go and listen to you tell a lot of Mexicans how you bring people back from the dead, okay?"

"Well, how about Tuesday? You busy then?"

"I think so. Mac, I gotta go." *Click. Buzz.*

"Same to you, fella," Mac said to the dead phone, and dropped it into the cradle.

Ten minutes later when the phone rang, he let it go five rings before picking it up. No use letting Jill think he was poised there waiting for her to call back and apologize.

"Hi, Mac, you busy?" The voice was Ivy Hurlbut's, not Jillian's.

"Hello, Ivy." He tried to keep the disappointment out of his tone.

"Hey, if you're not tied up tonight, I thought we might get going on the book."

"You heard from Bantam?"

"Well, no, but a local outfit called Astro is interested."

"I don't think I know them."

"They're not one of the bigs, but as they say, better than nothing."

"Yeah." Nothing seemed to be going the way it was supposed to. Fain had a momentary impulse to get out the tarot deck and ask it what was happening.

"Well? How about it? Want to do some work?"

"Sure. Come on over."

Ivy showed up an hour later, wearing a Coors T-shirt and a pair of jeans tight enough to squeak. She brought a portable tape recorder and a bag of cassettes.

"I talked to Lendl. He says you're giving a lecture tomorrow night."

"So I hear."

"Can I come?"

"Sure, if you want to."

"It might be something I can use. I'll see if I can get Olney Zeno to come and take pictures."

"How about a drink?" he said. "Do you like margaritas?"

"Love 'em."

Fain went out to the kitchen and mixed a blenderful of margaritas—the real kind, with fresh lime juice, triple sec and tequila. None of that slushy foam the bars were serving.

They sat side by side on the sofa and sipped the drinks. Ivy fiddled with the tape recorder.

"This is the first time I've used one of these," she said. "I don't know what to ask first."

"How about do I sleep in the nude?"

"I already know the answer to that one."

"Oh, right."

She pressed the RECORD key and started the machine.

"Why don't you just give me your life story in your own words."

"Okay, but I warn you, it's not very exciting. I was born and grew up in Muskegon, Michigan. Straight-arrow, Norman Rockwell family. Not rich, not poor. Comfortable. Average student. Went to college at Western Michigan in Kalamazoo."

"Is that really a town?"

"So help me. I took psychology, graduated with a useless B.A. degree. Went to Chicago with a vague notion of getting into advertising. Struck out. Went to New York, got mugged twice, ran out of money. Hitchhiked to California ten years ago. Figured if I was going to starve, I might as well be warm while I did it. Started the occult dodge and found out I was good enough to make a living of sorts at it. And here I am."

"I have a feeling you're leaving something out," Ivy said.

"Probably, but you go ahead and fill it in with some of those spicy facts you people specialize in."

"I'll ignore that," she said. "Any brothers or sisters?"

"Nope, I was the only one. Dad was over forty when I was born. My mother was about the same age. I guess they'd about given up."

"Are your parents still alive?" Ivy asked.

"My mother died when I was seven. Dad's retired now and living in Fort Lauderdale. I haven't seen him in a couple of years, but we write."

Ivy squirmed uncomfortably on the sofa.

"I warned you my life hasn't been all that fascinating."

"It's not your life," she said. "It's these jeans. They're not letting me breathe."

"You know what I'd suggest?"

"Take 'em off?"

"Right."

"Good idea."

After considerable tugging and grunting, she managed to pull off the jeans. Fain was not greatly surprised to see that she wore no underwear.

"Okay, where were we?"

Fain gulped his margarita and refilled the glasses. "Do

you expect to get a coherent interview out of me with you sitting there bareass?"

"It was your idea."

"So it was. Want to hear another idea?"

"Try me."

He tapped the recorder. "Is this thing still running?"

She punched the OFF key. "Not anymore."

"Let's move the show into the bedroom."

"Don't you ever do it on the couch?"

"Only if I'm in a terrible hurry."

"You're pretty conventional under the funky facade, aren't you?"

"It's the Midwest upbringing."

He stood up, slipped one arm behind her back, the other under her bare bottom, and carried her into the bedroom.

"What about my tape recorder?"

"You can take notes," he said.

There were not a lot of preliminaries. Mac was not in the mood, and Ivy did not seem to require it. They came together forcefully and with a mutual hunger. It was over in less than twenty minutes.

They lay naked side by side for a while; then Ivy said, "Tell me about your other hobbies."

Chapter 14

Mac Fain locked up the Camaro and gave it a friendly pat, hoping he would see it again. Then he joined Lendl and Ivy Hurlbut on the sidewalk.

He looked up and down the block on Whittier Boulevard without enthusiasm. The stores were dark and locked, with folding steel grates pulled across the fronts. The only sign of life was the Sonora Café, which occupied the ground floor of the building where they had parked. A red neon sign in the window advertised Carta Blanca. Recorded salsa music could be heard faintly from inside.

Near the café entrance lounged several dark young men in muscle T-shirts and tight-fitting jeans. They wore colored shoelaces that identified their gang. The young men watched the three Anglos impassively, letting their eyes linger on Ivy Hurlbut.

Lendl led the way past the café and up a narrow flight of stairs to Chavez Hall, where members of the Eastside Social Club were holding their banquet. The spicy aroma of chilis was enough to bring tears to the eyes.

At the top of the stairs they were stopped by a scowling Mexican woman seated at a desk. Lendl identified himself and party. The woman checked them against a list and let them pass, not looking happy about it.

Inside, a trio of guitar, bass guitar, and mandolin provided non-stop music to which nobody seemed to be listening. Busboys hustled around clearing dishes off three long tables. At one end of the large room a smaller table stood on a riser at a right angle to the others. The men seated there wore suits and neckties, while the diners down below were more informal. A gray-haired man at the speakers' table said something in Spanish into a microphone. The diners laughed and applauded, and the man sat down, looking pleased with himself.

The laughter died gradually, and the eyes of the diners turned toward the newcomers. The crowd was not what Fain had expected. He was looking for something like a Mexican Rotary dinner, but this was more like a Gonzales family picnic. Whole families sat together, from elderly grandparents to lively dark-eyed children who raced among the tables, paying little attention to their parents' orders to sit down and shut up.

"Looks like a fun crowd," Fain muttered to Barry Lendl.

When they had stood uncomfortably in the doorway for a minute, a chesty, pockmarked man got up from the speakers' table and came over.

"You looking for somebody?"

"I'm Barry Lendl," said the agent. "I talked to a Mr. Silvera on the phone."

"That's me. Frank Silvera, program chairman." He looked Fain over with cold eyes. "This your man?"

"McAllister Fain," said Lendl. "The man you've been reading about."

"I don't read that much." Silvera nodded toward Ivy. "Who's this?"

"Miss Hurlbut," said Lendl. "She's writing a book about Mr. Fain."

"You didn't say she was coming."

"No extra charge," Lendl said with a twinkle.

Silvera looked at him coolly. "We better get up by the microphone. The kids are getting restless."

He turned and headed back toward the speakers' table. Ivy and Fain exchanged a look.

Lendl nudged them along after Silvera. "It's going to be terrific," he said. "You'll see."

Behind the speakers' table a young woman in pancake makeup and two men stood by a cluster of television equipment bearing the Channel 34 logo. One of the men balanced a Minicam on his shoulder. The woman talked briefly to Silvera, glanced over at Fain and his party, and signaled for the two men to start packing up.

"There goes TV coverage," Fain said. "I guess I'm just no Thunder Thighs Lopez."

At the speakers' table an extra chair had to be brought for Ivy and squeezed in beside Fain. Frank Silvera stood up and clanked a spoon against a glass for attention. The crowd settled slowly. Silvera blew into the microphone, bringing a *whoosh* of static from the cheap suitcase speaker.

"Unfortunately," Silvera said, "as you know, we couldn't get Carmela Lopez at the last minute."

Fain groaned softly. The crowd grumbled.

"But I was lucky in being able to get Mr."—he checked his notes—"McAllister Fain."

No response.

"He is the man who was in the paper for bringing a dead woman back to life."

Small rustle of interest.

"Mr. Fain kindly agreed to come here to tell us how he did it." Silvera shoved the small table microphone over in front of Fain.

Mac stood up and cleared his throat. Before he could speak, a piercing squeal cut through the room. Silvera rose and glowered toward the wall where the speaker was plugged in.

"Hey, you kids get away from there. *Pronto!*"

The children backed off a little, and the feedback squeal stopped. Fain looked around at the fifty or so people watching him and wished mightily that he was somewhere else.

"*Buenos noches,*" he said, using up all the Spanish he had prepared for the evening. The reaction was nil. "I know you were expecting Carmela Lopez tonight, and I hope you're not too disappointed. Well . . . anyway, I'll tell you a little bit about who I am and what I do, and then you can ask questions. Maybe we'll all learn something.''

Fain looked around and saw not one smile on all those dark faces. Quit being clubby and get to the serious stuff, he told himself. He grabbed a water glass from the table and drained it, wishing it were something a lot stronger. Stealing a nervous glance at his watch, he began to speak, improvising as he went along.

"Life and death. That's really what it's all about, right? Where does one stop and the other begin? A question that has cudgeled the minds of men from the beginning of time. Down through the ages, that last dark curtain at the end of a man's life has been the single greatest mystery. What lies beyond?''

He babbled on in this vein, growing increasingly nervous as he sensed he was losing the crowd. He should never have agreed to this. If it were possible, he would personally hand their money back on the spot and make a dash for the street. Maybe the gang out in front had not had time yet to strip his Camaro.

While Fain droned on about life and death without saying anything of substance, he saw Olney Zeno ease through the door, bedecked with his camera equipment. The lanky photographer raised two fingers in a small salute, and Fain could have kissed him. It was the friendliest gesture he had seen all night.

"There are stories," he went on, "told by people who claim to have crossed over into the realm of death and returned. I guess we've all heard or read about them.''

Not a flicker of agreement from the increasingly restless crowd.

"Well, anyway, there are such stories. Books have been written on the subject. But do we believe them? How can we ever be sure?''

He gazed around and caught the glint of light off a number of crucifixes resting on brown bosoms. Better touch on religion, he thought. Might make them less inclined to rip my arms off.

"And what does the Bible have to tell us about this matter of life and death?''

A loud *blap* from the speaker, a shower of sparks, and

122

the room went dark. For a terrible broken moment Fain thought God had spoken.

Silence for a slow beat of five, then a babble of voices. Chairs scraped back. Dishes clattered, feet thudded on the floor, bodies collided. Excited voices rattled a mixture of English and Spanish.

Fain stood where he was without moving, wondering if he was going to be blamed for this. He tried to remember where the exit was. Ivy Hurlbut grasped his hand.

Then the lights blinked once and came on. Everyone looked around a little guiltily. Several started to laugh. Then a woman screamed.

"Miguel!" she cried. "Miguelito! *Ai, Madre de Dios!* My little boy!"

There was a surge of people toward one corner of the room. For an instant, when no one blocked his view, Fain saw the prostrate body of a boy lying next to the overturned speaker. The boy's eyes and his mouth were open. He did not move. A man ran up and yanked the speaker's crackling electric cord from the wall plug. The crowd closed in around the fallen boy.

For the next few minutes the room was a confusion of babbling voices as the diners milled about. Women cried; men swore. Olney Zeno was standing on a chair, shooting over their heads.

The crew from Channel 34 hastily unpacked their equipment. The young woman fluffed her hair, and the man with the Minicam pushed his way toward the boy.

"Maybe we ought to get out of here," Lendl said.

"No, wait," Fain told him. "We can't just walk away."

"Why not?"

Frank Silvera whistled through his fingers for attention. "Okay, everybody, stay calm. The paramedics are called. They're on the way. Stand back and give little Miguel some air."

From the looks of the small, pale figure with the empty eyes, Fain did not think air was going to help.

A siren wailed outside, and footsteps pounded up the stairs. Two young paramedics rushed in with oxygen and first-aid equipment. They immediately started to work on the boy with mouth-to-mouth resuscitation and CPR techniques. A stout woman, apparently the boy's mother, stood by, wailing while friends comforted her and held her back.

The woman from Channel 34 was interviewing anybody who would talk, positioning herself so the Minicam could keep her in the frame with the rescue attempt.

"Let's go," Lendl said again.

"No."

Lendl and Ivy turned to stare at Fain. He was surprised himself at the firmness of his answer. He had no logical reason, but something he could not explain held him there. More quietly, he said, "It would look bad if we ran out now."

"I guess you're right," Lendl said grudgingly. He shot a cuff and checked his imitation Rolex. "I only hope this doesn't keep us here all night."

Some minutes later, one of the paramedics took Silvera aside. Fain heard him say, "There's nothing more we can do. There was a drink spilled there on the floor. The boy was standing in it when he grabbed the bare wire. It was a massive electrical shock. There's no respiration, no pulse."

"You giving up?"

The paramedic chewed his lip. "We'll keep working on him until the coroner's man gets here, but I'm afraid the boy's gone."

Silvera expelled a long breath and nodded. He walked over to the boy's mother and put an arm around her shoulders. He spoke to her softly in Spanish. The woman gave a keening wail and ran back toward her son. Several of her friends stopped her and held her before she could reach the boy.

"I don't like this," Ivy said. "Can't we go now?"

"Okay, I guess we might as well," Fain said.

"Well, thank God," said Lendl. "Let me just talk to Silvera about our check."

While Fain and Ivy waited for the agent to push through the crowd to Silvera, the mother of the little boy loomed suddenly in front of them.

"You!" she said, leveling a forefinger at Fain. "Why don't you help?"

"Me?"

"You made that woman come alive again after she

124

was dead. They said so in the newspaper. Do it for my boy now. Bring back my Miguelito.''

Fain held up his hands as though to fend her off. "I'm sorry, ma'am. You've got the wrong idea.''

By this time a dozen other people stood around the mother. Their eyes were on Fain.

"Believe me," he said, striving for the right note of sincerity, "if there was anything I could do to help . . .''

A bright light hit him in the face, and the man with the Minicam pushed into the growing circle of people. The young woman thrust a ball-head microphone under Fain's nose.

"Are you McAllister Fain?'' She had a pleasant, soft Spanish accent.

He nodded, looking around for help from Lendl.

"You are the man who claims to have brought a dead woman back to life last week?''

"Well, there was this story in the *Times*. . . .''

"And now this mother wants you to work on her son. The little boy the paramedics say they can't save.''

"Help me, *por favor*!'' cried the stout woman, moving into the bright light. She clutched at Fain's hand. "Save my little boy.''

"There's nothing I can do," Fain said, sensing a growing hostility in the people watching. "The paramedics are doing everything they can.''

"They can't help my Miguel. They say he is dead.''

"I'm sorry," Fain said. "I'm really sorry.''

A thin man with dangerous black eyes stepped forward.

"How sorry are you, man? As sorry as me? I'm Alberto Ledo. The boy is my son.''

Fain looked around for some sign of support. He found none. "Mr. Ledo—'' he began.

"What is the trouble, man? You don't like Mexicans? You only do your thing for rich Anglo ladies?''

Several voices seconded the accusation. Fain looked toward the exit and saw that his path was blocked.

"It's not like that at all," he said, fighting to keep his voice calm.

"Then why don't you help me and my wife? You're so good, let's see you bring Miguel back to life like you did the rich Anglo lady.''

The man's voice broke on the last word, and he looked angrily around at his friends, who voiced their agreement.

Barry Lendl squirmed past the Channel 34 crew to Fain's side. "Come on, you people," he said. "If there was anything Mr. Fain could do, he would. Make way now."

The crowd moved closer. Somebody shoved Lendl out of the way. Ivy clung to Fain's arm.

"He's not going to do nothing," somebody said.

"He wants to go home to his nice clean Anglo house."

"Let's teach him Mexicans are people, too. Teach all three of them."

"All right . . . *enough!*"

Fain's voice rang above the din in the room. The angry crowd fell silent. He looked slowly around at the ring of faces, giving them the gray-eyed stare. The Minicam moved closer. Alberto Ledo and his wife watched him expectantly.

"Take me to the boy," Fain said.

Lendl grabbed his arm and muttered, "What the hell are you doing?"

Fain gently removed the agent's hand from his arm and walked through a path made for him by the crowd. Close behind him came the Channel 34 crew.

One of the paramedics was still trying to force breath into the dead boy. He looked up as Fain approached.

"It's too late, mister. He's gone."

"Just give me a minute," Fain said.

The paramedic frowned, but he rose and stepped back from the boy's body. Fain spread his arms, turned his face toward the ceiling, and closed his eyes.

What the hell was he going to do now? These people actually expected him to bring the dead kid to life. From the tone of the crowd it was a good bet there would be some kind of violence if he did not look as if he were making an effort.

But he had no props. No candles, no colored powders, no assistant. He didn't remember any of the chants he had used or the symbols he had drawn on the floor. He vowed that if he got out of this in one piece, he would retire forever from the Lazarus game and go happily back to reading fortunes.

126

"Ralé Méné Vini." It was the only thing from the whole rigmarole that he could remember. *Call. Bring. Come.*

"Ralé. Méné. Vini."

Fain stood for a painfully long minute with his arms spread, eyes closed, head tilted back. The unnatural silence in the room pressed down on him. He felt the sweat run from his armpits down his sides.

Someone screamed.

"Él es vivo!"

"The boy is alive!"

Slowly, Fain opened his eyes and looked down. Mrs. Ledo was on her knees beside the boy, palms pressed to her plump cheeks. Her husband stood behind her, frozen in position. Miguel was sitting up, looking around. The boy began to cry.

Fain heard Lendl mutter, "Holy shit!" somewhere behind him.

The Channel 34 Minicam pointed at him, but the young woman was transfixed by the revived boy. Zeno moved through the crowd, shooting in all directions.

As Fain watched, Miguel's mother disengaged herself from the crying boy and came over to him. Before he could speak, she seized his hand and kissed it. She pressed the hand to her big soft breast and looked into his eyes.

"Gracias, sēnor, mil gracias," she said, then added fervently, *"Tu eres mi santo."*

McAllister Fain swept his gray eyes over the hushed crowd and gave them a gentle saintly smile.

Chapter 15

Nine-year-old Miguel Ledo rode to County General in an ambulance with his mother and father. The ride itself was exciting enough, but Miguel did not like the idea of going to the hospital. That was where they took people and never brought them back. And they had doctors there who were always poking at you where you didn't like it and jabbing needles into you. Miguel insisted that he felt fine, except for the burns on his hands, and wanted to go home to his own bed, but as usual none of the grownups paid any attention.

Miguel's mother, her tears still flowing, and his father, trying hard to appear macho, were occupied with their feelings of relief. Their little boy, whom they had seen with their own eyes lying dead, was given back to them. How it happened and why could be talked about later. This was a time for giving thanks.

They arrived at County General only a few minutes ahead of the reporters and the cameras. An ambitious employee at Channel 34 had passed along the story to the news director of Channel 5. He gave it to their radio station, and within an hour every news department in town was hot after the boy who came back from the dead.

The parking lot and the streets bordering the hospital

were soon jammed with cars, camera vans, reporters, and curious pedestrians. It was a slow news week, and Miguel Ledo's resurrection was a big story.

Inside the hospital, Alberto and Maria Ledo listened as a heavyset doctor with a tiny brush mustache told them about their son.

"He is a very, very lucky boy. From the looks of the burns on his hands and the soles of his feet, enough electricity went through him to kill a mule. But aside from those burns, which should heal in a couple of days, he seems to be all right."

"Seems to be?" said Alberto.

"His vital signs all register positive." The doctor's eyes flicked away for a moment.

"There is something else?" the father asked.

"Only a slightly delayed response in some of the neural reflexes."

"Is that bad?" asked Maria.

"I don't think so, but I'd like to make some more tests. If he could stay overnight—"

"Is he sick?" Alberto demanded.

"I wouldn't call him sick," the doctor said, "but there are questions—"

"The hospital is for sick people," Alberto said flatly. "My boy is going home with us."

"Well, of course it's up to you."

"That's right. Thank you, doctor. Can we take him now?"

The doctor started to say something more but decided against it. "I'll have him brought down."

The crowd waiting outside, which had heard a half dozen versions of what happened, none of them accurate, burst into applause when Miguel and his parents came through the door. Lights blazed; reporters and cameramen moved in. Police from the Hollenbeck Division cleared a path for the family to their car, which a friend had driven from the banquet.

"How does it feel to have your boy back?" was the question asked over and over as the Ledos pushed through the clusters of reporters.

Patiently, the parents answered as they made their

was through the crush. "Fine. It feels good. Real good." What else could they say?

A woman from Channel 7 with stiff blond hair thrust a microphone at them. "There are stories that a man who was at the banquet tonight brought your son back to life. Would you comment on that?"

"Our boy is alive," Alberto said. "A man helped, yes."

"Was the man McAllister Fain?"

"I think that is his name."

"What exactly did he do to revive Miguel?"

"I don't know, and I don't care. My boy is back with us. That's all that matters."

"That man worked a miracle," said the mother. "A miracle."

A policeman moved in front of the Ledos and spoke to the crowd. "Come on, folks, make way. These people have had a rough night, and they're tired. We're all tired. Let's go home."

Reluctantly, the reporters fell back, and Miguel and his parents were deposited in their car. A police car led them to the neat stucco bungalo in Alhambra where they lived. The officers discouraged the media people from hanging around, and the family was at last able to relax and feel what had happened to them. Several times during the night one or the other of the parents tiptoed into Miguel's bedroom for reassurance that the boy slept peacefully.

In the morning they awoke to learn just how much their lives were changed. Alberto's employer, who owned the Apex Furniture Mart in San Gabriel, insisted he take the day off with pay. Alberto was uncomfortable staying home on a workday, but his boss meant well, and he could hardly turn the offer down.

The reporters returned with the first light and wanted to know everything about the family. They took pictures of all of them inside and ouside the house. They interviewed the neighbors and the people in the little market at the corner. When they ran out of family and neighbors, they interviewed one another.

As soon as they had a chance, Alberto and Maria put

on their good clothes, dressed Miguel up, and drove across town to Holy Name. The reporters piled into cars and turned the trip into a motorcade. When they arrived at the church, Miguel, who until then had been enjoying the attention, did not want to get out of the car.

"Come along," said his father. "I don't want to stand out here all day."

His mother examined the boy's bandages. "Do your hands hurt, Miguelito?"

"No."

"What is the matter, then?"

"I don't want to go in there."

"It is our church. You have been there many times. Today is a special day for us. It is a day to give thanks."

"I don't want to go in."

Alberto's patience began to fray. "We will talk about what you want later. Now we are all going in."

Maria gave her husband a disapproving look, but the tone of his voice made its point with young Miguel. The boy climbed reluctantly out of the car, making more now of his injuries than he had before.

The cameramen and reporters gathered around for the surefire scene of the grateful family going into their church. Some of them went along inside and filmed Maria placing flowers at the foot of the Virgin and lighting a candle for her personal saint, McAllister Fain.

While his parents prayed, Miguel remained silent, almost sullen, avoiding the statue of the Virgin and the tragic eyes of the crucified Jesus. His father glanced at the boy with a worried look, but Maria nudged her husband back to their prayer.

As they left the church, Miguel seemed to regain his usual good spirits. He laughed and talked eagerly to the reporters, proudly displaying his bandaged hands. He posed happily for pictures while Maria looked on smiling and Alberto consulted his watch.

Back at their house, it was more of the same, with friends, relatives, neighbors, reporters, and strangers filling the little bungalow to a point where Alberto found it hard to breathe. While Maria prepared nachos in the kitchen, a gray-haired man in a powder-blue blazer motioned Alberto aside and handed him a business card.

"Mr. Ledo, my name is Hollingsworth. I'm with the Prime-Vita Company. You've heard of us?"

"No."

"Too bad. We're in the health-products field—nutritional aids, vitamins, dietary supplements."

"Good for you." Alberto was looking past the man at the crowd filling up his house and eating his nachos.

"I have for you a proposition that could mean several thousand dollars, with options for more if things work out."

"What proposition?"

"I'd like to use your boy in our newspaper ads and in a television spot."

"You want Miguel to say he eats your stuff, that's why he's alive today?"

Mr. Hollingsworth chuckled. "Actually, he wouldn't have to say anything. We'd just use his picture, and the copy would say a little about him and about Prime-Vita products. If the people want to make a connection, that's all right with us."

"It's not all right with me."

"What's that?"

"I don't want my boy in no commercials for phony vitamins an' your other junk."

"Now just a minute, Mr. Ledo—"

"I ain't got a minute. I think you better get out of here." He turned to the crowded room and raised his voice. "The rest of you, too. My family and me want some time alone. Please go."

After considerable milling around, the crowd thinned, and at last they had all gone. Alberto went into the kitchen and took a cold Coroma from the refrigerator. He popped the top and drank down a third of the bottle. Maria came in, and they sat down together at the kitchen table.

"You were not very nice to the people," Maria said in Spanish.

"They were making me tired. Do you know what one of them wanted? He wanted to use Miguel to sell his vitamins. That's when I told everybody to get out."

Maria touched her husband's hand. "It is all right. I am glad we are alone."

132

"Yes. I will be happy when they find some new miracle."

"This *is* a miracle, Berto," Maria said in a hushed voice.

"Maybe."

"No, really. We have seen a true miracle from God."

"That is not for us to say. It all happened so quickly. That man, that McAllister Fain—we don't know who he is."

"He is a saint."

"I don't understand what happened . . . what he did."

"Maybe we are not meant to understand it. We have our little boy back."

"Yes. Yes, we do."

"Be happy with me, Berto."

"I am. I am happy, only . . . "

"Only what?"

"I don't know. This thing troubles me."

A crash out in the living room brought them to their feet. Alberto was the first to reach the room, with his wife right behind.

A table lamp had fallen to the floor, knocked over by Miguel. The boy seemed not to notice as he drew feverish patterns on the painted wall with a Magic Marker. The designs were strange, angular forms in a pattern that looked like writing but was not.

"Miguel!" cried his father. "What are you doing?"

The boy whirled toward them, and for an instant his face was the face of a stranger. Then his eyes cleared, and he looked from one of his parents to the other. His lips quivered, and he began to cry.

Alberto stared at the scribblings on the living-room wall. "What is this? You scrawl graffiti like some *cholo*? And on your own wall? Have you gone crazy?"

Miguel began to cry louder, and Maria swept the boy into her arms. "Ai, Miguelito, it's all right. Tell him it's all right, Berto. He has had a difficult time."

Alberto stood frowning for another minute at the strange marks on the wall. "Sure, okay, it's all right. Now let's clean it up."

* * *

While the Ledo family scrubbed at their living-room wall, Mac Fain sat with Jillian Pappas in a dark back booth of the Jalisco Tavern on Alvarado Street. Barry Lendl stood talking into a wall-mounted pay phone with his hand cupped over the mouthpiece as though worried that someone might listen in. The only other customers were two Mexicans in their early twenties playing a listless game of pool and a weathered old man sitting at the bar.

"This place smells like a toilet," Jillian said.

"We had to come somewhere to talk," Fain told her. "You saw what it was like at my apartment—the phone, the people hammering at the door."

"You're famous," Jillian said. "You'll have to get used to it."

Lendl came back to the booth and sat down, looking pleased. He ignored the glass of beer in front of him, as did Jillian. Only Fain was drinking.

"I called my office," the agent said. "We're on our way. You saw the noon news on Channel Thirty-four?"

"I saw it," Fain said. "And the article in the *Times*. I made page one of Metro again. No pictures, though."

"It was too late for the deadline," Lendl said. "But wait till you see the *Herald*."

"Famous," Jillian said softly. She picked up her beer glass, tasted it, and set it down.

"Besides the *Times*," Lendl continued, "we're in the *Daily News* and the Orange County *Register*. They want you for talk shows on KABC and KIEV. Channel Seven's interested for an *Eye on L.A.* segment."

"Things sure happen fast once they start happening," Fain said.

"That's the way it is in this town," Lendl said. "What we want to do now is move fast but make sure we pick the right offers. I don't want you doing any shit. Excuse me, Jillian."

She waved him off without comment.

"What I mean," Lendl continued, "is you're on fire now and we got to take advantage. God, I can't hardly believe our luck."

Fain peered at him. "Luck?"

"That kid last night coming to right when he did. If it

happens while the paramedic's working on him, we're nothing. If he doesn't come out of it at all, we're in trouble with that crowd. Like they say, timing is everything."

"Were you worried?"

"Hell, yes, I was worried. Those people carry knives. But we can forget that now. First thing is we got to get you out of that shit-box apartment. I'll book you into a hotel we can use for a headquarters while we sift through the offers."

Fain turned to Jillian. "How about that, honey? I'm sifting offers."

"I'm thrilled," she said, not sounding thrilled.

They heard the bartender say, "Back there," and turned to see Ivy Hurlbut come toward them.

Ivy wore a "No Nukes" T-shirt and a pair of her squeaky-tight jeans. She carried a copy of the *Herald* like a banner.

"Take a look at this. You're gonna love it."

She moved the beer glasses aside and spread the paper out on the table. Three of Olney Zeno's photos were printed across the page above the story of what happened at the Eastside Social Club banquet. The first photo showed the prostrate Miguel beside the overturned speaker, looking very dead. Maria Ledo stood over him, hands clenched, her face a mask of grief. The second shot caught Fain standing over the boy, arms outstretched, head tilted toward the ceiling. In the third picture Mrs. Ledo knelt beside her revived son, her face radiant with love and relief. Behind mother and son stood McAllister Fain, his hand raised as in benediction.

"Beautiful," said Lendl. "Just beautiful. That boy Zeno does good work. You don't even have to read the story."

"I really like this one," Ivy said, pointing to the third of the photos. "If you had a beard, you'd look like Jesus Christ. Maybe you ought to grow one."

"That's not a bad idea," Lendl said.

"I hate it." When everyone looked at Jillian, she said, "I haven't met your friend, Mac."

Fain eyed her cautiously. "I'm sorry. Jillian Pappas,

this is Ivy Hurlbut, the writer I told you about. Ivy, Jillian.''

The two women looked each other over without visible warmth.

"I read your story in the *Insider*," Jillian said. "Cute piece of work.''

"Thanks," Ivy said. "What is it you do?''

"I'm an actress.''

"Isn't that interesting." She returned her attention to Fain. "I talked to Bantam this morning, read 'em the *Times* story. They're gung ho for the project now. Ready to talk about a real advance.''

"Sounds good," Fain said.

"That's not all. The *Insider* is all over me. They're ready to pay their top dollar for a page-one feature. The *National Enquirer* will double that.''

Barry Lendl held up a hand to quiet her. "I don't think we want to do the tabloids right now. They got no dignity. Besides, we don't need them. You weren't here, Ivy, but I got an office full of people looking to buy a piece of McAllister Fain. We can pick and choose. One thing sure, there'll be no more speeches for three hundred dollars.''

"Hey, you're going to be rich," Ivy said.

"Rich and famous," Jillian put in. "Just like a fairy tale.''

Fain looked at her. "Is something bugging you?''

"Who, me? Heck no, I'm just going with the flow. Waiting my turn for an autograph.''

"Sarcasm doesn't become you," he said.

"I just don't like this whole business.''

Barry Lendl jumped in. "What's not to like? By some fantastic coincidence, Mr. Fain gets lucky two times, and people come to life when he tells them to. The families are happy. The press is happy. We're happy. And the people who were supposed to be dead got to be happier than any of us. Everybody wins, nobody gets hurt. So what's not to like.''

"It sounds like you're turning him into some kind of franchise Messiah. Try our drive-through resurrection window. And you, Mac—I get the feeling you're start-

136

ing to believe it. I liked you better when you were doing card tricks and telling fortunes for lonely ladies.''

Ivy gave her a smirk. "This couldn't be a little jealousy, could it? Boyfriend getting more famous than you are?"

Jillian turned on her. "I don't need analysis from some scandal-sheet hack."

"Cut it out, you two," Lendl said. "We got to make some plans."

Ivy looked at the newspaper photos again, shaking her head. "This really is wild. We couldn't have staged it better if we tried. What do you suppose really brought the kid around? That CPR business the paramedics were doing?"

"Who knows?" Lendl said. "Kids bounce back from things would kill a grown-up person."

"Wait a minute," Fain said. "Just wait a minute, all of you."

They looked at him, silenced by the commanding tone of his voice. He locked stares briefly with each of them, his pale gray eyes luminous in the gloom of the tavern.

"What is all this talk about luck and coincidence and paramedics and kids bouncing back?"

After a moment, Lendl said, "I don't follow you."

"Why is everybody so damned sure I didn't really do it?"

"Do it?" Ivy said, blinking.

"Bring that woman and that little boy back to life. Why couldn't I be the real thing?"

Chapter 16

The Beverly Towers Hotel made it into Beverly Hills just barely, being on La Cienega and Wilshire, far from the glitter of Sunset. As for towers, that was open to doubt in the high-rise 1980s, when twelve stories was not in the towering class.

Nevertheless, the two-room suite rented by Barry Lendl looked good to Mac Fain when he moved in. There was an oversized sitting room with comfortable chairs, two sofas, impressionist prints on the walls, and a wet bar. The bedroom had a king-size bed with soft indirect lighting and a television set built into the wall. A considerable step upward from the Echo Park apartment.

"How much is this costing me, Barry?" he asked when Barry Lendl moved him in on Tuesday.

"Not to worry," Lendl said airily. "I've got a deal with the management, so they'll wait till we start cashing in on you."

"Let's hope they don't have to wait too long."

"Let me do the worrying," Lendl said. "You relax tonight, and tomorrow we go to work."

That night Fain slept alone, and he slept badly. Jillian was again tied up, she said, with an acting-class project that would last quite late and leave her too tired for anything but sleep. He next called Ivy, but she was anxious to finish an outline for Bantam Books so they could start negotiations on the advance. As he lay wakeful in the big bed, Fain had time to wonder if loneliness was part of the success package.

The next day he forgot all about being lonely. Barry Lendl was there early, closely followed by reporters, cameramen, hustlers, con men, crackpots, and a lot of people with no apparent reason for being there except curiosity. While Fain watched Lendl trying to restore some semblance of order, a smooth young man in a cashmere jacket maneuvered him to one side of the room.

"I'm Warner Echols," the young man said. "Federated Artists. You *have* heard of us?"

"I think so," Fain said.

"Most people have, even people not in the business. We're easily the strongest, most respected talent agency in town. I could reel off a roster of our clients for you, but why take up our time with bragging, right?"

"Right," said Fain on cue.

"To get right to it, Mac, we want to represent you. I don't have to tell you that F-A can do things for you that no other agency can touch."

"You want to represent me in what?"

"In all areas, Mac. F-A will take over every detail of your career, steering you steadily up the mountain, while you concentrate on . . . doing what you do."

"The thing is," Fain said, "I have kind of an understanding on that with somebody else."

Echols smiled indulgently. "Yes, I know. Barry Lendl, isn't it?"

"That's right."

Echols looked over to where Lendl was trying to keep out a large woman at the door waving an Instamatic. "I saw him when I came in. I admire your loyalty, Mac, but I've got to be frank. Lendl's clients are losers and second-raters. You don't belong with him. You want to travel first-class, and that's Federated Artists. Your whole future depends on making the right moves now. You're not under contract, are you?"

"No, but Barry has spent some money. He's into the hotel for this suite."

"You don't have to worry about that. F-A will reimburse him for anything he's put out and add a little besides, even though we're under no obligation."

"It's not only the money . . ." Fain began.

Echols leaned closer. Fain could smell the wintergreen breath sweetener. "Mac, sometimes in this business you have to be tough. Everybody in town knows Barry Lendl, and everybody likes him. Hell, I like him. He's a sweet guy and a beautiful human being, but face it, he'll put your career right in the toilet. You'll wind up as one of his flash-in-the-pan celebrities and make a thousand bucks lecturing at Kiwanis meetings, then disappear forever. Is that what you want?"

"No, but . . ."

"Then be tough, Mac. Move ahead now with F-A. Trust me, Mac. Barry Lendl wouldn't know how to handle you even if he had the resources, which he doesn't."

"And you people do?"

"Hey, I'm here to tell you F-A is the big leagues. When we put you into a book, it's hardcover with a window display in Brentano's. When we book a client on a talk show, it's not some Mickey Mouse local guy on Channel Twelve in Seattle. We're talking Carson, okay?"

"Sounds good," Fain said.

"Then we've got a deal?"

"I think you've made me an offer I can't refuse."

"Fantastic. On the chance that you'd make that decision, I've got Nolan Dix—he's our top attorney—on the way over with the papers to make it official. But there's no reason we have to sit on our hands until everything is signed and sealed. That's not the F-A way."

"I'm ready when you are," Fain said.

"That's what I like to hear. What do you say we step into the other room so Jesse can have a look at you?"

"Jesse?"

"Jesse Cadoret, our image specialist. The very best in the business, I don't mind telling you. He'll want an in-depth session with you later, but there's a lot he can do off a first impression."

140

"This may sound dumb," Fain said, "but what is an image specialist?"

Echols laughed shortly, showing a beautifully capped set of teeth. "I'll let Jesse explain it to you, Mac. It's strictly state of the art."

Fain looked around the room, and his eyes met those of Barry Lendl. He also saw Jillian Pappas, who must have come in while he was talking to Echols. She was puffing inexpertly on a cigarette.

"Give me a minute, will you?" he said.

Echols followed his glance and nodded. "Sure, but don't take too long. The sooner we rev the motors, the sooner we get off the ground."

Fain walked over to Lendl, who did not move to meet him.

"Barry, I've been talking to Federated Artists."

"So I see."

"I wish you and I had more time to talk."

Lendl shrugged. "What for? How much time do you need to tell a man he's out?"

"That's not the way it is," Fain said.

"Oh, no? You didn't just make a deal with that shark Warner Echols?"

"I need somebody now who has the clout to help me make the right moves, that's all."

"I was already started," Lendl said. "I've got feelers out. I had ideas."

"I'm sorry, Barry, but your ideas weren't big enough. Where you were talking East Side Social Club, F-A talks the *Tonight* show."

"Already you're sounding like one of them."

"Anyway, they're going to take care of you. You won't lose anything."

"Hey, that's nice of them. All heart, those people."

"Okay, if you want to take it that way, there's nothing I can do about it. I'll see you."

"Sure, we'll do lunch sometime."

"What about me?" Jillian said, smashing the unaccustomed cigarette into an ashtray. "Are your new friends going to take care of me, too?"

"Damn it, Jill, this is business. What do you want to give me a hard time for?"

"I just want to know where I stand."

From across the room Echols called, "Mac, can we move it along? Jesse's ready for you."

Fain gave him a wave and turned back to Jillian. "Look, I've got a hundred things going at once here. Why don't I give you a call later."

Jillian stood up and faced him levelly. She said, "Fuck you, Mac."

Fain stared as she walked out with Barry Lendl. It was the first time in their three-year relationship that he had heard Jillian actually use the F word. The door closed behind her with a solid chunk.

"Mac, are you coming?" Echols called across the room. "Jesse's got another appointment at two."

"Yeah," Fain said, still looking at the door where Jillian had gone out. "Yeah, I'm coming."

Jesse Cadoret was a lean young man with seriously receding hair that he wore cropped and brushed forward. He positioned Fain in the center of the room, then stood back and studied him with one hand cupping an elbow and the fingers of the other playing with his mustache.

"Wardrobe," he said, and made a tsk-tsk sound with his tongue. "Those clothes will simply have to go."

Fain looked down at his hopsack jacket, open-collar shirt and gray Sansabelt slacks. "What's the problem?"

"Too laid-back. Too California. People aren't going to take you seriously if you come on looking like a dressed-up beach bum."

"What do you suggest?"

"Earth tones. Dark colors. Plain shirts and tasteful neckties."

"I never wear neckties."

"You can learn. And for heaven's sake get rid of those awful Hushpuppies and put on some nice sincere wing tips."

"Wing tips," Fain repeated doubtfully.

"Don't worry; you won't have to shop for them yourself. I'll give Warren Echols a list, and he'll have somebody pick out everthing for you."

"Gee, thanks."

142

"Now, about that haircut."

Fain ran a hand over his shaggy hair. "A little long, I guess."

"A little? It's strictly 1970s. The neat look is in, if you haven't heard."

"I feel so out of it."

"Yes. You don't wear glasses, do you?"

"No."

"Good. They would definitely not suit what we want you to be."

Fain rubbed his jaw. "Somebody suggested a beard."

Jesse pinched his eyes together as in pain. "Oh, Lord, a beard, he says. I'll just bet a woman suggested that."

"As a matter of fact it was."

"I knew it. For your face, never. With your long, narrow jaw, you would look like Mephistopheles. Hardly the look we're shooting for."

"A mustache, maybe?"

"Sleazy riverboat gambler."

"Another wrong look."

"You're catching on."

Jesse Cadoret examined his thin gold wristwatch. "This will have to do for a starter. I'm due at CBS to try to make a soap-opera star into a macho adventure hero. A Herculean task, I'll tell you. See you again. Ta-ta."

"Ta-ta," Fain said to the man's retreating back.

As the image specialist went out, Warner Echols came in, accompanied by a hard-breathing fat man with an attaché case.

"Mac, this is Nolan Dix. He has the papers for you to sign that will make you officially a Federated Artists client."

Fain shook the attorney's plump hand and looked over the thick contract without really absorbing it. "I'd like a little time to study this."

"Time is money, Mac," Echols said. "I don't want to rush you, but F-A has already started the moves on your behalf. It would be a shame to shut down now. This is our standard client's contract. All it does is legalize a working agreement between us for one year with options for another five. We guarantee you our full services for twenty percent of what you earn through our joint efforts.''

"Twenty percent? What ever happened to ten?"

Echols smiled indulgently. "Mac, Mac, ten percent went out with the dollar martini. Remember, we aren't merely providing you representation; we are taking charge of your future. Federated Artists has faith in you. We believe you are going to be a huge success with the proper guidance, and F-A can provide that guidance. We'll manage your whole career—take the difficult decisions off your back, warn you about the pitfalls, pull you out of jams.''

"And choose my clothes."

Echols smiled. "Sure. Find you a girl if you want us to. Or whatever your taste.''

"Quite a service."

"That's what I'm telling you. So if you just want to sign the papers now . . .''

Fain accepted a platinum Cross pen and signed his name repeatedly as Nolan Dix wheezed and flipped the pages for him.

When he had finished, the attorney stuffed the contract back into his attaché case. "A pleasure to have you with us, Fain," he said. "Wish I had time to stay and talk, but you know how it is—rush, rush, rush. Let's do lunch sometime.''

Warner Echols clapped an arm around Fain's shoulder for a manly hug. "Way to go, Mac. Glad to have you on board. Now that you're officially under the F-A wing, the first thing we'll do is get you out of this hotel.''

"What's the matter with it?"

"It's *out,* Mac. That's what's the matter with it. You said Barry Lendl booked you in here?"

"That's right."

"It figures. Nobody stays at the Beverly Towers anymore, Mac, except washed-up stars trying to get a *Love Boat* walk-on and out-of-town book writers begging for a screenplay. It's Loser's City. A dump.''

"You should see my apartment."

"We won't even talk about that. No, what I have in mind for you is something special. It's a house in the Santa Monica Mountains above Mulholland.''

"A house?"

"It's owned by F-A. Do you know the name Walter Belmont?"

"No."

"Not many people do today. He was a star in the early twenties, up there with Jack Gilbert and Wally Reid. He made a bundle and spent it, a lot of it building this house in the hills he called Eagle's Roost. When the talkies came in, Belmont was finished. He had a voice like Bugs Bunny. He hit the needle, and the house went to pay debts to Arthur Garshied, who started Federated Artists in the thirties. It's been with the agency ever since. We use it when it's appropriate. For you the place is perfect. Great atmosphere. Completely furnished. You won't have to bring a thing."

"Eagle's Roost," Fain said, testing the sound of it.

"Corny but descriptive. You'll look down on the whole city. There's only one private road leading up there, so we can control the traffic. That's where we'll do interviews and picture layouts. And you can see your prospective clients.

"Clients?"

"People who want you to bring somebody back to life. We've already got a stack of letters at the office. We'll help you go through them and pick some of the likelier candidates to come up—with media coverage, of course. Then you tell them for this or that reason you can't help them, and we send them back down the mountain."

"Why can't I help them?"

"Hell, Mac, you don't want to be put into a spot where you're actually supposed to be raising the dead."

"Why not? I've been there before."

"Yes, but that was . . . I mean . . . we both know . . ."

"I thought that was what all this was about—bringing dead people back to life."

"Well, on the surface, yes, but what it's really about, Mac, is money. You don't have any objection to money, do you?"

"No," Fain admitted.

"Well, then, it's the peripherals we're talking about here. Books, movies, personal appearances. One of our people has even come up with an idea for a music video. Don't laugh; it could be a big money item."

"I'm not laughing," Fain said.

"Fine. Come on, I want you to meet Victoria Clifford. She'll be your secretary, assistant, gofer, and anything else you want while we're getting you under way. She's good."

Echols led the way back to the crowded living room and tugged Fain along to where a tall woman with sleek brown hair and bright green eyes stood frowning at one of the prints hanging on the wall.

"Victoria, this is McAllister Fain."

She extended a slim hand and said in a soft, husky voice, "It's a pleasure, Mr. Fain."

"Me, too," he said. "And you might as well call me Mac."

"Whatever you say . . . Mac."

Echols clapped his hands and rubbed them together enthusiastically. "Well, then, why don't the three of us bail out of here and run up to Eagle's Roost."

"Should I pack my things?" Fain said.

"We'll have somebody take care of that for you," Echols told him. "You're with F-A now, Mac, and you don't have to concern yourself with bothersome details. Shall we go?"

Victoria linked her arm through his, and they started out. At the door they were met by Ivy Hurlbut, carrying a manila folder and looking puzzled.

"What's going on, Mac?" she said. "I just saw Barry downstairs.

"There's been a change in plans," Fain said.

Ivy held up the folder. "I was hoping we could go over my outline for the Bantam thing."

"Well . . ."

Echols spoke up. "Look, Mac, F-A has writers already working on a book. It'll be hardcover and under your name. There's a movie deal in the works, so I think we'd better not screw it up."

Fain spread his hands. "I'm sorry, Ivy."

She stared at him for a moment. "That's it? You're sorry?"

"Mac, there's a car waiting."

Victoria squeezed his arm and let her sleek hip brush against him.

"I've got to go," he said, and left Ivy looking after him, the folder forgotten in her hand.

Chapter 17

"I've got to go," said Peter Maylon.

"No" she complained.

"Really." He struggled to pull free of Leanne Kruger's surprisingly strong grasp.

"Why do you have to go so soon? You've only just come."

"Please."

"That's a play on words, doctor." She was taunting him now. "Don't you think it's funny?"

"I don't think any of this is funny. Please let go of me."

"Maybe I won't. Maybe I'll just squeeze and squeeze until I pull it off." She tightened her grip around his limp organ. "I could keep it with me to fill me up while you're not here. What about that, doctor?"

"I don't like it when you talk that way."

"Oh? Do I bruise your little sensibilities? All right, then, darling, I won't talk naughty anymore if you don't want me to. Okay?"

She held on a moment longer, then released him. He climbed hurriedly out of the bed, reaching for his scattered clothes. The cloying smell of her perfume was heavy in the still air.

Leanne lay with the sheet over her lower body, watching him. Her pale skin was luminous in the dim light of the bedroom.

"You don't seem as . . . enthusiastic as you were at first," she said. "I'm beginning to wonder if you really like me."

Maylon buckled his pants and sat on a chair to put on his shoes. He said, "I'm trying to think of some way to say this that doesn't sound like a cliché, but there doesn't seem to be any. We've got to stop doing this, Leanne. It's wrong."

"Oh? And I was so sure we were doing it right."

"Stop playing. You know what I mean."

"How very moral you've become, doctor," she said.

"I suppose that's the way it sounds, but this has bothered me from the beginning. It goes against everything I believe in—my oath as a doctor, my religion, my marriage vows. I know how it sounds, bringing all that up right after we've . . . we've . . ."

"Fucked," she prompted.

"We should never have started, but I was weak. Now it's got to end. I love my wife, Leanne. I love my little girl. I can't look either of them in the eye."

"Your wife doesn't suspect, does she?"

"No, but she knows something is troubling me. God, she'd have to be blind not to know."

"Well, I wouldn't worry about it unless she finds out for sure. And there's no way she could do that, is there? Not unless somebody tells her."

Maylon stopped with his shirt buttoned up halfway. "You wouldn't do that, would you?"

"Me? Darling, why on earth would I do a thing like that? I mean, it would finish everthing you and I have together, wouldn't it. And I certainly don't intend to let that happen."

He made a little moaning sound deep in his throat. She reached out for him, but he moved out of her grasp.

"Poor Peter," she said with exaggerated sympathy.

"That's not all that worries me," he said.

"Tell me about it, darling."

"There's something wrong with you, Leanne."

She snapped to a sitting position in the bed. Her eyes flashed. "That's not true! I'm all right!"

"You're not all right," he said, his voice calmer now. "At first I wasn't sure, but it becomes more evident every day. It's in your eyes, your skin texture." He reached over and snapped on a lamp on the bedside table. "Look at you."

"Turn that off!" she snapped, and lashed out with her hand, knocking the lamp to the floor.

The light from the naked bulb, shining up at them, gave their faces a satanic cast. Maylon reached down and picked up the lamp, snapping it off as he replaced it on the table.

"You see," he said.

"The light startled me, that's all," she said, but her voice still held the edge of hysteria.

"No," he said. "You're not a well woman. I think it's connected with the time you were . . ."

"Dead? Is that what you're trying to say? Well, I wasn't dead. I was in a state of cryogenic suspension. There was no tissue damage afterward. No internal problems. You should know; you examined me yourself."

"You seemed all right at the time," he said, "but I wasn't allowed to do all the tests I wanted to. There has been a deterioration in your condition. I think it's accelerating."

"I don't want to hear any more about it."

"I'll have to tell your husband."

"You'll tell him nothing," she snapped. "There is nothing wrong with me."

"Leanne, it's no good denying it. All you have to do is turn on the lights and take a good look at yourself in the mirror."

She got out of bed and stood naked in front of him. Her body was smooth and pale in the dusk. The triangle of black pubic hair glistened with the juices of their coupling.

"Look at me," she said. "Just look and tell me if you see anything wrong."

He reached for the lamp.

"No!" She slapped his hand away. "You don't need that."

"You can't keep it a secret," he said.

"Peter, if you say anything to Elliot, I'll tell him you

have been forcing your way into my bed and into my body."

"But it was you who—"

"Do you think he'll believe that? I'll tell him you gave me some kind of pill and climbed on top of me while I was unable to resist. I can make him believe me, Peter; you know I can."

"Yes, I suppose you can," he said wearily.

"And do you know what Elliot Kruger would do to you then, Dr. Peter Maylon? He would make you suffer in ways you've never imagined. And believe me, he has the resources to do it."

Maylon turned away from her. He knotted his tie without worrying about making the ends even and shrugged into his coat.

Leanne came up behind him and ran a fingernail down the line of his backbone, making him shudder. "Same time tomorrow, doctor?" she said.

"I don't know. I'll have to see."

"You've already seen, Peter. You'll be here."

Maylon started out the door, then turned back. He said, "Why me, Leanne?"

She smiled, her teeth glistening in the dusk. "Because you're here, Peter, darling. Because you're here."

He left the bedroom, closing the door behind him. He could smell the woman on him. Moving swiftly, he descended the broad staircase and headed for the front door, hoping to be out and away without having to confront Elliot Kruger.

"Doctor."

Too late.

Maylon turned to face Elliot Kruger, who came toward him across the tile floor of the hallway. He needed a shave and seemed to walk more slowly than he had a week before.

"I was expecting a report from you," the old man said.

"Your wife seems . . . a little undernourished, maybe, but all in all she's doing well." The words were like bile in his mouth.

"I'm worried about her," Kruger said.

"Oh?" Maylon looked at his watch, edging toward the door.

"Why don't we go into my study."

Unable to think of a way out, Maylon nodded and followed Kruger into the book-lined room. He perched on the edge of a leather couch while Kruger took a chair facing him.

"She's been acting strange." When Maylon did not respond, he went on. "She stays in the bedroom most of the time with the blinds drawn and the lights dim. She isn't eating. She says things that aren't like her at all."

"Your wife has been through a unique experience," Maylon said.

"I know that," Kruger said impatiently. "But it doesn't account for everything. My wife has spoken harshly to her maid, Rosalia. That girl loves her, and Leanne never before raised her voice. Also, not once has she asked what happened to her dog. That isn't her. It simply is not like my wife."

"Mr. Kruger, we have to expect aftereffects. Unfortunately, there is no way of predicting what form they will take."

"But she seemed so . . . normal at first. But as the days pass, she seems to be getting worse."

Dr. Maylon took off his glasses and cleaned them. "In what way, specifically?"

"Well, our—" Kruger cleared his throat and started over. "Our sex life, for one thing. At first it was wonderful. Even better than before. But now it's erratic. Sometimes she seems insatiable. Other times she won't even let me in the bed."

Maylon felt his face burning. He thought surely Elliot Kruger must see his guilt, but the old man was focused within himself.

"And there's something else." Kruger hesitated. "I know it's old-fashioned of me, but I find it hard to talk about these personal details."

Maylon nodded, not trusting his voice.

"The thing is . . . Leanne has an odor about her."

"An odor?"

"Yes. An unpleasant smell. She bathes several times

a day and tries to cover it with perfume, but it's there, and it's getting worse."

Dr. Maylon leaned forward. "Mr. Kruger, at the time you called me in, I recommended that your wife check into the hospital for more extensive tests. I still think that's what you ought to do."

"No." Kruger shook his head vigorously. "I don't want a lot of people involved. The press would love to get at her. Ever since the business with McAllister Fain and that boy in East Los Angeles, they've been all over me. I will protect my wife's privacy at all costs."

"There is only so much I can do, Mr. Kruger. I want you to feel free to call in another doctor anytime."

"No, no, I don't mean to imply I'm not satisfied with you. Things are piling up on me, that's all. Not only do I have Leanne on my mind, but my son is behaving oddly, too."

"Your son?"

"Richard. He suddenly stopped coming around the house. And just when I thought he and Leanne were starting to like each other. But don't let me burden you with my personal problems, doctor. You'll see my wife tomorrow?"

"Yes," said Dr. Maylon. "Same time tomorrow." He rose and walked to the door like a man carrying a load too heavy for him.

On the other side of the city, Alberto Ledo came home from work to find his wife sitting in their living room crying.

"What is it, Maria?" he said, dropping his lunch pail on a table near the door.

"You're home early," she said.

"The planer jammed again; it will take the rest of the day to fix it. But what is wrong here?"

She got up and started for the kitchen. "Are you hungry? I will make you a sandwich."

"I still have the sandwich you made for my lunch." He took hold of her shoulder and turned her to face him. "Maria, I want you to tell me right now why you were crying."

She dropped her eyes away from his. "It's Miguel."

"What happened? He isn't painting the wall again?"

"No. He hurt little Juan Ramirez."

"His friend next door?"

"Yes."

Alberto gently squeezed his wife's plump shoulders. "That is not so serious. Little boys fight all the time. Then they make up."

"It was no fight," said Maria. "Miguel cut him."

Alberto's face darkened. "Cut him? With a knife?"

"Yes."

"Where did he get a knife?"

"From the kitchen. He took the butcher knife."

"*Dios!* Is the other boy badly hurt?"

"They took him to the doctor. He will be all right."

"Where is Miguel?"

"In his room. What are you going to do, Berto?"

"I am going to punish him; what do you think?"

"Berto, he is not the way he was. Not since he was . . . hurt and brought back."

"That is no excuse for using a knife on his friend."

"Please," she said.

"All right. But I will talk to him."

He walked past her to the small second bedroom at the rear of the house. The door was closed. Alberto opened it and walked in.

The room was unnaturally dim for the time of day. Alberto saw that a blanket had been hung crookedly over the window. He walked over and took hold of the blanket.

"What's this for?"

Miguel was sitting on the narrow bed, his head against the wall, his feet straight out in front of him. He said, "To make it dark."

"I can see that. What I'm asking you is why."

The boy shrugged and went on fiddling with a robot that could be folded into a star fighter.

Alberto ripped the blanket away from the window. The boy flinched from the light.

"When I talk to you, you answer me," Alberto said. "You understand?"

The boy nodded.

"I hear you been using a knife. I hear you cut the boy next door. Little Juan Ramirez. What do you say about that?"

"He wouldn't let me ride his bike."

Alberto stared at his son. "He wouldn't let you ride his bike, so you used a blade on him? Is that what you're telling me?"

"It was my turn. He said I could ride next, and then he didn't let me."

"You have your own bike."

"Juan's is better."

Alberto clenched his fists and breathed deeply. With an effort, he relaxed the taut muscles in his back and shoulders. He went over and sat on the bed with his son. "Miguelito, are you feeling all right?" He took the boy's hand and examined the healed burn mark across the palm. "Since you were hurt the other night, do you have any pain? Something you haven't told us?"

"No, I'm okay."

Alberto released the boy's hand and ruffled the thick black hair. "Miguel, using a knife on another person is a bad thing. They put people into prison for that, and they keep them there a long time. I know, because when I was a boy I came very close to going to prison myself. I want you to promise me that you will never take a knife from our kitchen again. And that you will never cut anybody."

Miguel looked away and did not speak.

Alberto felt the anger rising again. He took hold of the boy's chin and turned his head so that they were facing each other. "I want you to answer me."

"I won't do it anymore," the boy said. "I won't take the knife."

"And you won't cut anybody."

"An' I won't cut nobody."

A long moment went by as father and son faced each other. Then Alberto said, "Okay, then, it's finished. But if you do anything like this again, I'll whip you. Do you understand?"

A nod.

The father waited for the boy to say more. When he did not speak, Alberto finally stood up.

"This room stinks," he said. "Open your window."

He went out with a feeling in his gut that there was more wrong here than he could understand.

Chapter 18

His first look at Eagle's Roost came when the F-A limo rounded the last twist in the private road that led up off Mulholland Drive. McAllister Fain immediately hated the place.

The house was gray stone, three stories tall. It was a humorless house with towers and arches and parapets and dark, sullen windows. A perfect setting for a low-budget horror movie, thought Fain. In fact, the exterior had been used in several such productions. Warner Echols reeled off the titles of several screamers from the sixties and seventies. Fain was not impressed.

The interior of the house made him feel a little better. At least half of the forty or so rooms had been sensibly sealed off. Once you were past the vast entry hall, which was furnished in Frankenstein Gothic for atmosphere's sake, the rest of the house was done in a comfortable contemporary style. Fain decided he could live with that.

He perked up considerably when a van brought his recliner from the Echo Park apartment along with a few of his books and familiar things. He found a downstairs room into which they fit nicely, and it was there he spent most of his time.

As the days passed, Fain felt himself gradually growing into the house. Victoria Clifford was most helpful; she proved that her talents were not limited to secretarial tasks. With his upgraded wardrobe and a plentiful stock of good food and liquor, he began to feel like a true lord of the manor.

And he was kept busy. Warner Echols, using the resources of Federated Artists, had him on a full schedule of personal appearances, local talk shows, meetings with studio chiefs, and sessions with a team of writers who were preparing a biography. He was already booked for the *Today* show, and talks with Johnny Carson's people were under way.

At least three producers were bidding for an option on his life story. Robert De Niro was being mentioned for the lead. Fain saw himself as more the Clint Eastwood type, but De Niro was not chopped liver.

There was a steady stream of visitors to Eagle's Roost, all carefully screened by a private security force hired by Federated Artists. Armed guards prowled the grounds and manned the gate on the private road. Nobody who could not further McAllister Fain's career in some way was allowed in his presence. There were times, in spite of Echols's busy schedule and Victoria's recreational ideas, that he felt a little lonely.

One morning a week after they moved in, Warner Echols stomped into the house, brandishing a rolled-up newspaper like the Olympic torch.

"Damn it," he said, "this kind of thing isn't going to do us a bit of good. Did you know what she was up to?"

"Who? What?" Fain stuttered. It was the first time he had seen the unflappable Echols not in full control.

"This!" The agent thrust the paper on him.

Fain unrolled the tabloid to see the familiar masthead of the L.A. *Insider*. From page one his own face peered back at him. It was one of the photos Olney Zeno had taken in the first session at his Echo Park place. Not a bad shot, Fain thought.

He looked up at Echols. "Publicity?"

"Yes, but not ours. Read on."

The headline said, "Crystal Gazer to Christ Figure—the Miraculous Rise of McAllister Fain."

Christ figure?

The byline was Ivy Hurlbut's. A box indicated that this was the first of a two-part story. Fain scanned the article quickly. Although Ivy had exaggerated some events in his life and written the whole thing in the florid style of the tabloid, he found nothing libelous or patently untrue. If she made him sound a little freaky, he could not really blame Ivy. After all, he had not been completely fair with her.

"So what's the problem?" he asked.

"The problem," Warner Echols said patiently, "is that this rag is ripping us off. This . . . this"—he snatched back the tabloid—"this Ivy Hurlbut is using you without paying us a dime. You're a commodity, Mac. We don't give you away any more than Kellogg's gives away cornflakes."

"A flattering analogy," Fain said.

"You know what I mean. I've already got Nolan Dix on it. We'll come down on these pirates with more lawsuits than they can shake a stick at. We'll break this sheet and send Ivy Hurlbut back to writing copy for dildo catalogs."

"No lawsuit," Fain said.

"What do you mean?"

"Just that. I don't want any lawsuit."

"Hey, Mac, did you read that junk?"

"Ivy only used the stuff I gave her, with a little journalistic license. The pictures I posed for. They're kind of flattering, actually. No reason to sue anybody."

"An article in one of these rags isn't going to do the image any good."

"Let Jesse worry about my image. I can't see where this story can do me any damage."

"That's not the only problem. If we let this go by, next thing you know somebody will put you on a Mac Fain T-shirt, without any royalties to us."

"When the T-shirts hit the streets, you can sue," Fain said. "But I want you to leave Ivy Hurlbut alone."

Echols threw up his hands. "If you insist, but I think you're making a mistake."

"It won't be the first, and I've survived before."

"All right, Mac. I'll go call off Dix, and then I want to talk some business with you."

"Anytime," Fain said agreeably.

On his way out, Echols passed Victoria Clifford coming in. She wore a maroon velour top and tight silvery pants. Her rich brown hair was tossed into a carefully windblown arrangement. She gave Echols a look, then came on toward Fain.

"Something bugging Warner?" she asked.

"He wanted to sue somebody, and I didn't agree."

"Warner usually knows what he's doing."

"Good for him. I just thought it was time I made a decision about something. I don't even get to buy my own clothes anymore."

Victoria stepped close and kissed him on the lips. She tasted of cinnamon. "Macho man," she murmured against his mouth.

"Go ahead," he told her. "Make my day."

"Love to," she said, then took a half step back. "How about a little brunch? I make a sensational omelet."

"I'll bet you do," Fain told her, loosening up the Clint Eastwood squint, "but I'm not hungry."

"How about something to jog your appetite? I'm good at that, too."

"Yes, I know, but not right now." He showed her the copy of the *Insider*. "I want to read about myself."

"Maybe later, then," Victoria said. "You know where to find me."

"Sure."

Fain watched her walk away, the fine high buttocks rolling nicely under the silver stretch pants. He sighed and wandered into the stone-cold entrance hall, its vaulted ceiling lost in the shadows high above. Muddy oil paintings of people long dead hung on the walls. He avoided the tall straight-back chairs, which must have been built for some purpose other than sitting in.

"It reminds me of mine castle back in Transylvania," he said in a bad Bela Lugosi impression.

"Balls." He walked to one of the tall leaded windows and gazed out at the small clearing in front and the thick scrub pine that pushed up to the edge of the road.

Feeling depressed, he walked back into his personal room and sat in his recliner to read Ivy Hurlbut's story thoroughly. He also read about the feud between two female stars of the top nighttime soap. He read about a lamb born outside Butte, Montana, with a perfect image of the Christ child in its wool. He read about a woman in Hartford who cooked her husband's beagle and served it to his poker cronies. He read about the miracle diet that kept half of Hollywood's glamour queens looking good. He started to read about an African tribe that worshiped toads, but that was too much, and he tossed the paper aside.

"Balls."

McAllister Fain, sensation of the tabloids, sought after by talk shows, possible subject of a biography in Brentano's window, about to be portrayed on the screen by Robert De Niro, was bored and lonely. How would that look in one of the tabloids?

But it was true. Despite the comforting presence of Victoria, he missed Jillian Pappas and their little personal jokes, their small fights and large reconciliations. He had called her half a dozen times since moving into Eagle's Roost but had gotten only the recording. He had left messages, but there had been no return of his calls. Now that he was finally on the brink of making it, he didn't have anybody to share it with.

"Balls."

To hell with this line of maudlin self-pity, he decided. He levered himself out of the recliner and started for the grand marble stairway that led to the bedrooms and Victoria Clifford. He was halfway up when Warner Echols called to him from down in the entrance hall.

"Hey, Mac, are you ready to go to work?"

"What's up?"

Echols held up a handful of envelopes in assorted sizes and colors, most of them hand-addressed. "You had a lot of mail at the F-A office. I brought some of the more promising applications for your services. Thought we might go through them and select one or two lucky winners."

Echols led the way into a large sitting room with twelve-foot sofas and a deep spongy carpet. They sat side by side, and the agent spread the mail out on a massive coffee table.

The letters were addressed to Fain in care of local

radio and television stations where he had appeared. Some had been sent to his old address.

"There will probably be a bundle more mailed to *Insider*," Echols said, "but I don't suppose we'll get a look at those."

Fain chose several of the letters at random and scanned the contents. He looked up at Echols. "These are from people who want me to bring somebody back from the dead."

"Sure they are. That's your shtick, isn't it?"

"I thought you didn't want me doing it again."

"We don't. I mean, not the whole routine. But we need something right now to keep you from cooling off. If we announce you're going to animate another corpse, we get your name back in the papers, and your price goes up."

"What do you mean, 'announce'?"

"You're not actually going through with it, of course. But we pick some deserving person, get you together for the cameras; then you tell them you're sorry but for one reason or another you can't do it this time."

"I see. What reasons did you have in mind?"

"Hell, I don't know. Bad vibes. Planets in the wrong conjunction. The moon's out of phase. You're the master of the occult; you should be able to think of something."

Fain read through one of the letters. It was written in a shaky hand, the lines drooping toward the right side of the page. When he was finished, he looked up at Echols.

"Here's one with a damn good reason for not trying. The lady wants Henry, whoever he is, brought back to life. The trouble is, Henry died in 1935. He'd be nothing but a pile of bones, for Christ's sake."

"No, you're right about that," Echols said. "I should have screened that one out."

Fain picked up another. "And this one . . . the guy died only a couple of days ago, but he was ninety-one years old."

"So what?"

"Warner, that man was ready to die. I don't try to bring back anybody who belongs dead."

Echols looked at him oddly for a moment. "I see. Uh,

how do you decide, Mac, who should stay dead and who comes back?''

Fain studied the agent. "You don't think I can do it, do you, Warner?"

"Let's just say there are a lot of things I don't understand. Whether I believe or don't believe is not important. My job is to make you rich and famous."

Fain nodded slowly. "I really can, you know. Don't ask me how, or why it should be me and not somebody else, but I can do it. I can make dead people live again. This all started out as a scam, but I've tried it twice now, and twice it's worked. It's no scam."

"Of course not. Nobody said it was." Echols slapped his well-tailored thighs and stood up. "I have some details to talk over with Victoria. Why don't you look through the letters and pick one where we can put on a good show."

"Good show," Fain repeated.

"You know what I mean."

"Yeah, I know. I'll look them over."

With a smile that didn't quite make it, Echols walked out of the room. Fain riffled through the letters, giving only a few seconds to each.

A shop worker in Torrance had been caught in a conveyer belt and ripped in half before the machinery was stopped. His wife hoped Fain could restore her man to life. Maybe he could, Fain thought, but he doubted the woman would want the mangled remains shuffling around the house.

A twenty-three-year-old suicide victim in Burbank was a possibility, but he passed over the parents' plea. The decision to end your own life should be final.

A four-year-old girl was run over by her father's car. Fain winced at the man's pain, but the child had been buried for a year now. Too long.

And so it went. The victims were too old or too torn up or had been dead too long. Or maybe Fain just felt they were not right. How he felt this, he could not say, but he knew as surely as he knew his name that he must reject all of the applications before him.

In an effort to relax, he moved to the recliner, kicked back, and thumbed on the television set with the remote-control unit. A blow-dried newscaster he remembered from an earlier interview was winding up a cutesy feature on a baby parade in Norwalk. The camera moved in then, and the newsman shifted his handsome features into a solemn expression.

"Tragedy struck today in the gymnasium of North Compton High School."

A yearbook picture of a smiling black youth filled the screen.

"Kevin Jackson, honor student and member of the North Compton basketball team, collapsed during a pickup game with other students."

The newsman's face reappeared.

"When school officials and paramedics were unable to revive him at the scene, Kevin was taken to Martin Luther King Hospital, where he died less than an hour ago."

Fain levered the chair upright and leaned forward, staring at the television screen.

"Now here's Cindy with a report from Santa Monica where landlords and tenants clashed in a council meeting over changes in the rent-control ordinance. . . ."

Fain killed the television picture and jogged out of the room. He took the stairs two at a time and found Warner Echols and Victoria going over a computer readout in the second-floor room that served as an office.

"I've got him," Fain said, bursting in on them.

Echols looked up, startled. "What? Got who?"

"Our candidate. A high school basketball player collapsed on the gym floor. He just died at Martin Luther King Hospital. Let's get over there."

"That wasn't one of the letters."

"It was on TV just now," Fain said. "We've got to hurry."

"Basketball player," Echols said. "Is he black?"

"Yes, yes; now can we get going? The longer we delay, the harder it's going to be."

"Black is good," Echols said. "I'll need time to clear it with the office. Get the wheels turning, contact the media. Want to be sure we get the right kind of coverage."

"Come *on*!"

"What if the kid's parents don't want you to try anything?"

"Simple—then I don't do it."

Echols looked deep into Fain's pale gray eyes. What he saw there made him speak more softly than was his habit. He said, "Mac, are you sure you know what you're doing?"

"Hell no. It's a feeling, that's all."

"You're not going to rush into this and blow everything we're working for?"

Fain answered slowly and distinctly. "Warner, until now this has been your show. And you've run it well. Now it's my turn. You just leave this part of the action to me."

"Okay, Mac," Echols said softly. "Victoria, will you take care of the details?"

She nodded and was already on the phone as the two men headed down the stairs and out.

Chapter 19

News of their arrival had preceded them. When Echols and Fain pulled up to the entrance of Martin Luther King Hospital in the Federated Artists limousine, three television mobile units were already there with a dozen cameramen and a like number of technicians. There was a swarm of reporters from the print media and their more photogenic brethren from television, clutching their ubiquitous ice-cream-cone microphones. The husky limo driver and a pair of armed security men pushed an aisle through the clamoring news people to get Fain inside.

Although his concentration was elsewhere, Fain could not mistake the cynical mood of the press. He tried to ignore the muttered remarks about miracle workers and frauds and followed his escort up the steps past the rude shouted questions and background laughter.

They were hurried into an office where a thin, antiseptic man sat behind a desk. Perched uncomfortably on a vinyl couch was a weary-looking black woman with fine, handsome features. The man got up reluctantly when they entered.

"Mr. Fain? My name is Ivan Tibbs. I'm the chief administrator here. This is Mrs. Urbana Jackson. She's the mother of the boy who was injured."

"I'm awfully sorry about your son, Mrs. Jackson," Fain said.

She studied him with dark eyes clouded by grief. "He was a good boy. Never messed with gangs or dope or any of that truck. Why should he be dead when so many bad ones ain't?"

"I don't know," Fain said. "I don't think there's any answer to that question."

Ivan Tibbs cleared his throat carefully. "I think I should make it clear that neither I nor the medical staff of Martin Luther King played any part in bringing you here. That decision was Mrs. Jackson's alone."

The woman ignored him and spoke directly to Fain. "The people I talk to on the phone say you can bring my baby back to me. That true?"

"I can try, Mrs. Jackson, if you want me to."

"Doctors say they can't do nothing more. You might as well try."

"I'd like to have the father's permission, too."

"Ain't no father around. He long gone. I raise Kevin all alone. Done a pretty good job, too. You got my permission, Mr. Fain. If that's all you need, you go ahead, do what you can."

Warner Echols said, "Er, Mr. Tibbs, about the reporters outside . . ."

"What about them?" demanded the chief administrator.

"I think they deserve to have a representative present."

"Out of the question. I will not have a bunch of reporters and photographers shoving their way through my hospital."

"Naturally," Echols said quickly. "I would suggest they select a minimum group from their number to serve as a pool and share their coverage with the rest."

"I suppose," sniffed Tibbs, "if it can't be avoided."

Echols hurried from the office and was back in minutes. "It's all set. A three-man team from Channel Five will cover it. They've promised to stay out of the way."

"Then we might as well go up," Tibbs said, casting a doubtful glance at the TV crew as they left his office.

While they waited for the elevator, a thin-lipped man in a white lab coat joined them.

Ivan Tibbs gave curt introductions. "Dr. Quarles. He handled the Jackson boy's case."

Dr. Quarles looked Fain over as though he were a slice of diseased tissue and found nothing to say. He exchanged a long-suffering look with the chief administrator as the party entered the elevator.

The boy was in a private room on the hospital's third floor. He lay under snowy sheets in a tall bed in the intensive care section. The boy's eyes were closed, his complexion a muddy gray. His body was still attached to the various life-support machines. They hummed and beeped and muttered electronically, but none of the monitors showed any sign of activity in Kevin Jackson's heart, lungs, or brain.

Fain spoke to the disapproving doctor. "There are no vital signs?"

The doctor shook his head. "Nothing. He's been gone almost three hours."

"Then can we disconnect the machines?"

The doctor looked to the mother. "That decision belongs to Mrs. Jackson."

"Go ahead and unplug 'em," she said. "Ain't doing my boy no good, anyways."

"You do understand," said the doctor, "that the hospital accepts no responsibility once the life-support systems have been removed."

"I understand that," said Mrs. Jackson. "Now let this man get on with it."

While the tubes and wires were being removed from the boy's body, Warner Echols edged over next to Fain. Speaking in a low, confidential tone, he said, "Mac, are you sure about this? What you do here can affect your whole future."

"Just let me be," Fain said. "I can't stop now."

It was true. Some force outside himself seemed to be driving him on. A part of his mind carried the old what-am-I-doing-here feeling, but he knew there was no turning back.

He did not spend any time on the chanting rigmarole over Kevin Jackson. The experience with little Miguel Ledo had shown him he did not need it. He stood alone at the boy's bedside and stared down at him while his

168

mother, the doctor, the chief administrator, Warner Echols, and the Channel 5 camera team looked on. Fain could sense the varying emotions in the others—hope, doubt, anxiety, fear—but he forced all of it out of his mind and fixed his concentration on the still, silent body of the boy.

When his mind was clear of all distractions, Fain spread his arms, closed his eyes, and intoned, *"Ralé. Méné. Vini."*

The seconds crept by. Fain clamped his jaws together as the sweat broke out on his body. He could hear the tense breathing of the onlookers.

Again. *"Ralé. Méné. Vini."*

The Minicam purred softly.

A sheet of paper rattled.

Someone stifled a cough.

The dead boy moved.

A murmur from the watchers.

Kevin Jackson opened his eyes, looked around, and said, "Man, what's happening?"

Fain stepped back as the others in the room surged forward to surround the bed. Mrs. Jackson hugged and kissed her son while the doctor went for his pulse. The cameraman ground away. The reporter thrust his microphone at everyone.

Warner Echols stayed back. He looked at Fain with new eyes.

"My God, you did it."

Fain nodded. He was weary. Anxious to be away from here, somewhere he could rest.

"You really did it."

"Can we get out of here?"

But the reporter and cameraman were coming at him now.

"Give the people a short interview," Echols said, "and I'll take you anywhere you want to go."

The questions posed by the young man were polite and restrained. Once, when Fain held up a hand to ward off the too close approach of the cameraman, the reporter crisply ordered him back. When Fain indicated he was through talking, the reporter thanked him profusely and hurried out, taking the cameraman and technician with him.

"Are those the same people who were laughing at me out in front?" Fain said.

"Converts," said Echols. "I think you're going to see a big difference from now on in the way people react to you."

While Fain was thinking that over, Dr. Quarles approached him.

"Mr. Fain, I owe you an apology."

"Oh? I didn't think you said anything."

"The apology is for what I was thinking. I don't pretend to know what it was you did in there, but I saw the results. I know—I mean, I was certain that boy was dead. Somehow you restored him. I still can't say I approve of your methods, but your results are undeniable. My congratulations."

He put out a hand. Fain waited a moment, then took it. "Thank you," he said, and turned away, steering Echols toward the elevator.

"What did I tell you?" Echols said from the side of his mouth.

Back out in front of the building, the waiting media people surged toward him in a wave, brandishing microphones and cameras and shouting questions. This time they were eager, but there was no mockery. The security men moved in to hold back the crush, but one smallish reporter with thinning black hair and an overbite wriggled past them and planted himself in Fain's path.

"We heard what you did in there, Mr. Fain, and I want to say that like everybody else I'm impressed."

"Thank you," Fain said, and tried to get by.

"I wonder," the reporter persisted, "if you could spare just a couple of seconds to tell me your feelings about reviving the Jackson boy."

"You agreed on the reporting pool," Echols broke in. "They got it all on tape."

The reporter ignored him. "Just a brief comment for my column, Mr. Fain. I'm with the *Times*. You may know my work. Dean Gooch."

Echols motioned for one of the security men, but Fain

held up a hand. "We've talked before, haven't we, Mr. Gooch."

"Uh, yes, briefly. On the telephone."

"And you even wrote a column about me. In kind of a smartass vein, if I remember."

"Well, that was before I'd actually seen what you can do."

"But that didn't stop you from writing about me, did it."

The reporter gave him an oily smile. "We've all got to make a living, Mr. Fain."

The smile slid away as Gooch looked into the pale gray eyes. They seemed to glow with a light from somewhere inside the man's head.

"Tell you what, Mr. Gooch," Fain said. "You go make your living off somebody else. I've got no time for cheap little fucks like you."

Gooch staggered back as though he'd been slapped. Echols and Fain moved on behind the security men to the limo and got in as the car pulled away into the dusk.

"I'm not sure you should have talked to Dean Gooch like that," said Echols. "It's a bad idea to make enemies in the press."

"He's an asshole," Fain said. "And we don't need him anymore, do we?"

"You've got a point there," Echols said. He pulled out a small leather-bound notebook and began making swift notes as the limo pulled onto the Harbor Freeway. "This is going to change our whole campaign."

"You mean now that you know I can do it."

"I mean now that the whole country will be seeing you do it on the eleven o'clock news."

The agent paused in his jotting and looked at Fain. "Mac, if I had any doubts—and I admit I did—forgive me. I've been handling phonies and hustlers and liars and cheats for so long, I can't recognize the genuine article. You are something special, Mac, and I promise you it won't go unrecognized. Or unrewarded."

Fain said nothing. He eased back into the plush upholstery of the limo and let the tension drain away from his body. Echols was right. He *was* something special. From now on things were just going to get better and better.

They ran into a traffic jam at the foot of the road leading up to Eagle's Roost, caused by people who had already heard the news from Martin Luther King Hospital. It took the combined efforts of the F-A security force and the LAPD to clear a path for the limo to drive up to the house.

Once inside, Fain headed for the master bedroom to lie down. Victoria came in with a tall, cool drink for him, but he sent her away. For a little while he just wanted to be alone to empty his mind.

Downstairs in a conference room that evening were gathered the top executives of Federated Artists. Warner Echols, who heretofore had been given only the agency's second-string talent to handle, was elevated to new prominence by his association with the new star, McAllister Fain. Plans were made, schedules laid out, logistics studied as in a major military campaign. When the star came downstairs to join them after an hour of meditation, they received him with respectful deference.

Fain sat in the most comfortable chair, while the others arranged themselves around him. He listened calmly to their grandiose plans for him, commenting now and then, amused by the eagerness of these powerful men to agree to any small change he suggested.

It was past midnight when the agency executives began to gather their materials to leave. One of the uniformed security guards entered. He looked from Echols to Fain and back again, unsure of who was in charge now.

Fain resolved it for him.

"What is it?" he said.

"There's a, uh, woman outside who says she has to see you, Mr. Fain."

"Take care of her," Echols said testily. "That's your job."

"This one is very determined," the guard said.

"Everybody's determined. Get rid of her."

"Wait a minute," Fain said. "Did you get her name?"

"I was coming to that," the guard said. "The lady says she's your mother."

172

"That's impossible. My mother's dead. She died a long time ago."

"Yes, sir, I read that on your fact sheet. But this lady was really determined."

"She is not my mother," Fain said.

"Right." The guard touched his cap. "I'll send her on her way."

Half an hour later the F-A executives and Warner Echols had left. Fain sat alone in his favorite room, tipped back in his recliner. His hands were clasped across his chest. He watched shadows from the fireplace dance across the ceiling.

The woman was obviously a crank. He supposed he would have to get used to that now—people using all sorts of phony stories to get close to him. The price of fame. He could learn to deal with it.

Sure, that's all it was. A crank.

So why did he feel so cold inside?

Chapter 20

Riding in the back of his custom Rolls-Royce, Elliot Kruger adjusted the reading light to his newspaper. He read carefully the account of McAllister Fain's new triumph in restoring the life of the young black basketball player. The paper treated Fain very respectfully, in contrast to the stories that followed his work with Leanne, and even when he revived the Mexican boy.

Kruger expelled a long breath and ran a hand through his hair. It was falling out in clumps these days, leaving bare patches of scalp, but Kruger hardly cared. He raised his eyes from the paper to the square shoulders of Garner, the chauffeur, seeking something solid and familiar in a world that had been suddenly knocked askew.

Although the morning was warm and he wore a suit and vest, Elliot Kruger shivered. He adjusted the rear-seat heater control, but the warm air that flowed instantly from concealed vents could not ease the bone-deep chill.

Again this morning Leanne had refused to have breakfast with him. She no longer left the bedroom; nor would she allow him in. The only people she saw now were Rosalia and Dr. Peter Maylon.

How long had things been going badly? Kruger tried to calculate when was the last time he and his wife had been together, relaxed and happy. But his mind was blurred with worry and lack of sleep. He could not count up the days. Too damn long—he knew that much. And it started less than a week after McAllister Fain had restored Leanne to him. That was when she had begun to change.

He started trying to reach Fain when he read about the Mexican boy and had called repeatedly with no luck. There was no answer at the Echo Park apartment. This morning he got a phone-company recording telling him the number was no longer in service. There were ways a man with his resources could find the occultist, but Kruger was reluctant to involve other people.

He had also tried Fain's assistant, or girlfriend, or whatever she was—Jillian Pappas. She had been cordial enough but said she had not seen Fain for weeks and did not know where he could be reached. She gave him the number of a man named Lendl, who she said might help, but he, too, denied any recent knowledge of Fain.

Now, sick with worry about his wife, Kruger was going hat in hand to the old friend he had dismissed for speaking his mind about McAllister Fain and what he had done to Leanne.

Garner pulled to the curb before one of the tall, featureless buildings in Century City, and Kruger got out. He entered the lobby and walked across the terra-cotta floor to the bank of elevators. Inside the car he pushed the button for the thirtieth floor.

The Thousand and One Strings played "You Light Up My Life" as the car rose silently. The music was wasted on Elliot Kruger.

The carpeting in the hallway, a dark rust color, was deep enough to muffle his footsteps. Kruger found the office bearing the name of Dr. David Auerbach. He hesitated a moment, squared his shoulders, and walked in.

The receptionist gave him a professional smile. "Good morning, Mr. Kruger. You can go right in. Doctor is waiting for you."

At least Doctor did not make him sit in the chilly chrome-and-glass waiting room. Considering the way Kruger had treated him, Auerbach would have been justified. And Kruger would have sat there and waited as long as he had to.

He found David Auerbach sitting behind his neat, polished desk. The doctor did not offer to rise as Kruger entered. Behind him, the window overlooked broad Olympic Boulevard to the east. The morning was still overcast, and the view did nothing to lighten Kruger's mood.

"Hello, David," he said. "How have you been?"

"Well enough." The doctor motioned Kruger into a chair. Reflected light from the desk lamp glinted off the lenses of his tiny spectacles.

"I guess the best way to start is with an apology," Kruger said.

"Not necessary," Auerbach told him.

"Maybe not for you, but it is for me. I brushed aside a friendship of many years because I was so blindly happy at having my wife back. That was all I could think of. I would not, could not, listen to anybody who questioned my happiness. What it amounts to, David—I was a damn fool."

"You'll get no argument from me on that," Auerbach said.

"And about that ticket to Hawaii . . ."

"Ah, yes, the bribe."

"I have no defense for that, either."

"That was what really pissed me off," Auerbach said. "That you thought you would have to bribe me not to talk about what I saw at your house that night. And you thought I would take it. Elliot, you should have known me better."

"Yes, I should have. I was sure of it when you sent the ticket back by messenger. I tried to call you then, but all I ever got was your answering service."

"I know."

"And no call back."

"You were not a patient."

Kruger spread his hands beseechingly. "David, I've told you I'm sorry. I'm not much good at groveling. What more do I have to say?"

Dr. Auerbach leaned forward across the desk. "You're

not looking good, Elliot. Are you eating all right? Getting exercise? Enough sleep?"

"No to all three questions," Kruger said. "But it's not about me I came to see you."

"Oh?"

"It's Leanne. She isn't doing well, David."

Auerbach stroked his cropped beard and said nothing.

"She stays in the bedroom all day long with the curtains drawn. She won't come out and won't let me in. The maid takes her meals in and brings back the tray barely touched. I'm worried sick about her."

"What do you want me to do?"

"I want you to come and take a look at her. Find out what's wrong. Take her to the hospital if you have to."

"You took me off the case, remember?"

"I'm putting you back on. If it's a matter of money—"

He caught the sudden tightening of Auerbach's facial muscles.

"Sorry, David. Please come back."

"Isn't she still in the care of your new doctor?"

Kruger frowned. "Maylon. That was another mistake. He seemed competent enough at first, but lately I can't get anything out of him. He gives me a lot of medical double-talk and won't look me in the eye. He's coming over this morning. I plan to dismiss him. Then will you take over?"

"Once Leanne is no longer his patient, I'll be glad to see her."

Kruger dropped his head into his hands. When he looked up, his eyes were moist. "Oh, God, thank you, David. I can't tell you what this business has taken out of me."

"You don't have to," Auerbach said. He scribbled on a prescription pad, tore off the top sheet, and handed it to Kruger. "Have this filled and take one at mealtime and one before going to bed. You're a mess. You should have a complete physical."

"Later." Kruger took the prescription and stuffed it into a pocket without reading it. He pushed himself out of the chair. "I'll let you know as soon as I get rid of Dr. Maylon."

The doctor stood up and came around the desk. The

two men walked out together through the waiting room. Auerbach said, "Have you seen any more of that Fain fellow?"

"No, but I've been reading about him."

"So have I, and I don't like what I read."

"I should have listened to you, David. You were right about him from the start."

The doctor shook his head. "No, I don't think so. At the time, I thought he was a fraud and a con man. Now I'm afraid he may be something far more dangerous."

They shook hands at the door. Kruger strode back down in the elevator, left the building, and climbed into the waiting Rolls.

He had been home less than twenty minutes when Dr. Peter Maylon was admitted. The young doctor looked thinner. There were brownish shadows around his eyes, and he had missed a patch of his jaw in shaving that morning. It was as though everyone associated with Leanne shared her affliction.

Kruger moved into his path as Maylon headed for the stairs. "Doctor, I'd like to have a talk with you this morning when you've finished with my wife."

Maylon faced him with some strange emotion in his eyes. Then he looked quickly away. "Yes, sir. There's something I want to tell you, too."

"I'll be in my study."

The young doctor continued up the stairs. Kruger watched him out of sight, then walked to the sideboard and poured himself a highly uncustomary morning brandy.

Leanne Kruger's room was, as usual lately, in deep shadows. On her orders, Rosalia had removed all the bright light bulbs from the fixtures. Heavy draperies were pulled across the windows day and night. The only illumination came from a low-wattage pink bulb in one of the bedside lamps.

Dr. Maylon stood in the doorway for a minute to let his eyes adjust. The air in the room was heavy with Leanne's perfume and the floral incense she had taken to burning. Still, they could not mask the fetid smell that grew daily more offensive.

"Come in, Peter. Close the door." Leanne's voice had lost its musical quality. She spoke now in a shrill, whining tone. "Come over here, where I can see you."

He approached the bed. Even in the faint and flattering pink light he could see the signs of her deterioration. Although the makeup was heavy on her face, lines showed through. Her eyes had a feverish brightness. A royal-blue satin coverlet was pulled up to her chin. The fingers of one hand, which played with the coverlet, had thinned and bent into bony claws.

Leanne smiled at him. He winced at the effect, then removed his glasses and polished them to cover his embarrassment. Leanne's gums were shrunken and pale. Her teeth were stained. Switching on his professional manner, the young doctor strode to the bed and took her wrist for a pulse count. He could feel the bones just beneath the rubbery skin.

"Don't I get a hello kiss?" she said.

"How do you feel?"

"Same as yesterday, only a little worse." She seized his arm with her free hand. The strength in her skeletal fingers surprised him. "Come into bed and make me feel better."

He looked down into her face, clownlike with the heavy makeup. A trick of the shadows turned her eyes into empty sockets. And yet he felt the familiar surge of desire. He wanted this woman beyond reason. He would always want her.

With an effort, he pried her fingers from his arm. "No more, Leanne. I want to end this now."

"Stop teasing me."

"No, I mean it."

She pushed herself to a sitting position. Her hair still held its luster. "You *don't* mean it, Peter. You know you don't. You love me."

"No," he said. "It's not love. It was never love. I wanted you. I . . . lusted for you. And God help me, I still do. But it's finished. The only reason I came today was to tell you that."

Leanne pushed aside the covers and stood up. Her pale blue nightgown hung to the floor, touching the tips of her breasts and the soft roundness of her belly.

Even as the sight gave him the beginning of an erection, Maylon recoiled from the memory of the mushy, flaccid feel of her flesh. He backed away.

She followed him, her brightly painted mouth turned down in an exaggerated pout. "Have you forgotten the talks we've had?" she said in her new harsh voice. "Don't you remember what I told you Elliot would do if I told him about us?"

"I'm going to tell him myself," Maylon said. "There's nothing he can do to me that's worse than what I'm doing to myself."

She backed him up against one of the curtained windows. "And what about your loving, trusting wife, Peter? What was her name? Oh, yes, Ann; that was it. A simple name for a simple, trusting little wife. What do you think she will say when she finds out."

"She already knows," Maylon said.

"What?"

"I told her. Last night. These weeks have been hell for me. I couldn't keep it up any longer, so I told her. Do you want to know what she did? I'll tell you. She cried, and she called me a bastard and a few other names that I richly deserve. Then she held me and said she loved me, and we both cried. I love her, Leanne, more than I could possibly love anyone or anything. I am going to devote the rest of my life to making her happy."

"You're lying!" Leanne said.

"No. For the first time in a month I'm telling everybody the plain truth."

"You can't leave. You can't. You love me, not your mousy little Ann. You love *me*!"

The young doctor's composure slipped. He snatched the heavy drapery away from the window and let the cruel morning light stream in through the glass.

"Love you? You think I love you? Look at yourself! How could anybody love something that looks like that?"

She stood frozen for a moment, face caked with makeup, eyes deeply shadowed, hands bony and spotted. Then she screeched wordlessly at him and seized him by the front of his jacket.

Peter Maylon was jerked to one side as though he

were a rag doll. He felt himself pushed powerfully backward. He hit the window, and the glass shattered as he lost his balance and flipped backward over the thigh-high sill.

There was an instant of weightless terror as he saw the white face with its cavernous mouth growing smaller above him. The rushing air roared in his ears. His last thought was *My God, I'm going to hit head fir—*

Downstairs, Elliot Kruger heard the *blatt* out on the patio. He dropped his glass of brandy and ran to the French doors. Peter Maylon lay facedown on the flagstones, arms and legs spread in a skydiving position. His head was cracked open like a cantaloupe, a mess of blood and brains.

Kruger's stomach lurched. He spat out a mouthful of regurgitated brandy. A crow cawed raucously above him, snapping him out of a momentary shock. He whirled and ran inside. He took the stairs two at a time and burst into the dark bedroom. Leanne sat on the bed, her face buried in her hands. The curtains fluttered gently at one of the windows. Kruger ran to his wife and knelt before her.

"Leanne, what happened?"

"He—he started touching me. Pawing me."

"Maylon?"

"Yes. I told him to stop. He'd never done anything like that before. He was like a crazy man. He p-pulled up my nightgown. He was going to . . . going to . . ." She broke off into a fit of sobbing.

Kruger sat beside his wife on the bed. He put an arm around her shoulders. The flesh had an odd spongy feel through the silky fabric. There was a powerful mingling of odors in the room. Perfume, incense, and something very sick.

"Take your time, darling," he told her. "It will be all right."

Her sobs eased off. Still not looking at him, she said, "When he grabbed hold of me, I . . . I pushed him. He stumbled and fell backward. He . . . he went through the window."

"I know. Hush now, Leanne. I'll call Orrin Bedlow. He'll know how to handle this."

For the first time she let her hands fall away and looked up at him. At the same moment, a soft breeze moved the curtain just enough to let the morning light fall on her face.

Elliot Kruger choked off a groan.

Chapter 21

The death of Dr. Peter Maylon was little noticed outside his modest home on the unfashionable side of Sunset in Beverly Hills. The whole thing was handled with quiet efficiency by the legal firm of Orrin Bedlow & Associates, attorneys for Kruger Industries. Although no liability was admitted, a generous cash settlement was arranged for the widow and a trust fund established for the young daughter.

The media virtually ignored the story. It was covered sketchily by the *Times* in the page-two roundup of local news. The victim was identified as a "Beverly Hills physician who died of head injuries in a fall from a second-floor window." The names of Elliot and Leanne Kruger were not mentioned. Nor was that of McAllister Fain. The short paragraph was sandwiched between threats of a transit strike and the naming of a new president at Cal Poly.

McAllister Fain did not read the story. He had little time these days for reading anything other than news about himself. Of that there was an abundance. After Ivy Hurlbut's series in the L.A. *Insider*, both *Time* and *Newsweek* had done features on him. *Los Angeles* magazine was ready with a lead article. A couple of "unauthorized" paperback biographies were already on the stands, while the Federated Artists ghostwriters rushed the official version to completion. The clipping service they employed provided a fat daily envelope of news stories from all over the country.

Life at Eagle's Roost had changed dramatically since the widely reported resurrection of Kevin Jackson. The sealed-off rooms had been opened. A full staff of servants was now employed. Federated Artists had a virtual branch office located in the house, with switchboard, secretaries, a receptionist, files, and a Xerox machine.

Fain was on a balcony off his bedroom, eating a breakfast of poached eggs, ham, English muffins, and grapefruit, when Warner Echols found him. He looked up at the agent's entrance and waved a spoon.

"Warner, what do you say? Had breakfast?"

"Yes, thanks."

"Have some coffee, then." He touched the side of the silver carafe. "You'd better call downstairs for a fresh pot. This is cold."

Echols hesitated only a moment, then went into the bedroom and used the newly installed intercom to call Fain's order down to the kitchen. Then he rejoined Fain on the balcony.

"Some good news," he said. "We've got you all but signed on Carson for Wednesday."

"So soon?"

"A piece of luck there. The San Diego zoo lady had to cancel, and they need somebody hot to fill in."

Fain put down his spoon. "Wait a minute. Are you telling me I'm going on as a replacement for the zoo lady?"

"You're in the second spot, right after Don Rickles."

"Oh, great. People are tuning in to see this month's cuddly animal, and there I am sitting on the couch next to a put-down comic."

"Mac, the exposure is unbeatable. Johnny will mention the book, and that means another twenty-thousand in sales."

"I won't do it," Fain said.

"Mac, you don't say no to Johnny Carson."

"Then say I've got an attack of the gout. Say it's a religious holiday for me. I don't care. When I do his show, I want my own spot, not substitute for a koala bear."

Echols sighed. He took out his notebook and wrote something.

"Okay. So what do you think about doing Michael Jackson Friday?"

Frowning, Fain looked up from his eggs. "Radio?"

"It's nework, Mac. ABC, coast to coast."

"But radio? We don't need that, do we?"

"Henry Kissinger has done it. Gerald Ford. Leonard Nimoy."

"Politicians and actors," Mac said. "I'll bet each of them was plugging a book."

"Remember, you've got a book to plug, too."

Fain laid down his fork. "Warner, you know that book is going to sell. We don't need some radio talk guy with a fruity accent to hype it. TV, now, that's something else. You go back to Carson's people and tell them I can't make it on such short notice. I guarantee you they'll find a spot for me where I can be first string and where I don't have to worry about zingers from Don Rickles."

"I can try," Echols said.

"You can do better than that. David Letterman picked up five Nielsen points when I did his show last week. Merv Griffin's packager added half a dozen markets after I did him. Carson's people can read the numbers."

"So that's a no to Michael Jackson?"

"You got it."

"Okay." Echols jotted something else in the notebook. "Can we take a meeting here with Universal at one o'clock?"

"I thought we were dealing with M-G-M."

"We are, but Universal has a counteroffer that gives us more points."

"To hell with points, Warner. I'm not going to play games with studio accountants. Get it up front or forget it."

"We'll put it to them that way at the meeting, okay?"

"Make it two o'clock. I've got Jesse Cadoret and a barber coming in at one."

Echols gave him a long look. "Two o'clock, then."

Victoria Clifford came out onto the balcony, wearing one towel and drying her hair with another.

"The plumbing in this place is primitive," she said. "Fourteen bathrooms and not one shower works decently."

"Can you get somebody on that, Warner?" Fain said.

"I'll see about it." Echols turned and started away.

"Oh, and Warner, I'll want to look at some letters from the public this afternoon."

"You're not thinking of doing another, uh . . . ."

"Resurrection?" Fain supplied. "Not right away. They take a lot out of me. But eventually I'll want to get back at it, and I want to have a feel for my prospective clients. Pick out twenty or thirty of the best, will you?"

Echols made another note and left without further conversation.

Victoria stood behind Fain and massaged his neck as he ate. She said, "I wish this place had a pool. I'd really like a swim."

"Don't blame me," Fain said. "You're company picked it out."

"I don't know if I want to go on working for F-A. I mean, what if they assigned me to somebody else?"

"They're not going to do that."

"Maybe not, but they could. I don't have any feeling of security. How would it be if I came to work for you, Mac?"

He stopped eating long enough to turn and look at her. "Work for me? As what?"

"Secretary. Girl Friday. Whatever you want. I'd do the same as I'm doing now, only I wouldn't have to answer to anybody but you. Wouldn't you like that?"

"We'll talk about it later," he said.

A boy came in with a carafe of fresh coffee. Fain poured himself a cup and drank. He did not offer any to Victoria.

The rest of his morning had been set aside for interviews with people who felt they and McAllister Fain could be of mutual benefit. He received them in a small office with Warner Echols and one of Nolan Dix's young legal assistants present.

The first was a fast-talking promoter from San Francisco who somehow managed to slip by the F-A screeners. He wanted to market a McAllister Fain T-shirt with a Jesus Christ tie-in. Instant rejection.

A cable-TV representative pitched a live ninety-minute special during which Fain would bring some deserving souls back to life. The young attorney had doubts, but Fain told the man to get back to him with a detailed presentation. It would have to be in good taste, he said. No stand-up comics, no rock groups, a minimum of glitter.

A well-known personal manager wanted to handle endorsements for Fain. He claimed to have commitments from Dewar's, Brut, Botany 500, and a new line of Adidas.

"Running shoes?" said Fain. "I wouldn't run from here to the corner."

"Doesn't matter," said the personal manager. "It's the name that counts. Do you think Bill Cosby really eats Jell-O?"

Warner Echols cleared his throat. "Uh, Mac, I'm not sure endorsing products it the way to go at this stage. We've got to consider the dignity factor."

"I suppose you're right," Fain said reluctantly. "But I kind of like the sound of the Dewar's."

"I'll have a case brought in," Echols said quickly, and the personal manager was dismissed.

A representative from CBS was there to feel him out about doing a *60 Minutes* segment.

"Which one of the people would do it?" Fain asked.

"Mike Wallace."

"Not a chance. Morley Safer or Diane Whatsername, maybe. Mike Wallace, no way."

He agreed to lend his name to a campaign fighting multiple sclerosis.

He turned down an opportunity to join the fight against AIDS.

A popular national evangelist made an emotional appeal to Fain to appear with him in a giant revival meeting in the L.A. Coliseum. Fain politely declined, saying he did not want to endorse any religion.

At one o'clock he cut off the interviews and went

upstairs for image enhancement by the barber under the direction of Jesse Cadoret.

Victoria stood by, watching, much to the annoyance of Jesse. She said, "You're not going to cut it real short, are you? It would look nice blow-dried."

"We are not trying to create an anchorman here," Jesse said icily. "We want to present an image of dignity, credibility, and humility in the presence of grandeur."

"Jesus," Victoria said under her breath.

"Now you're getting the idea," said Jesse.

In the Alhambra home of the Ledo family another haircut was getting an inspection. Nine-year-old Miguel sat in the living room, staring sullenly past his father, who stood with his arms folded. So intense was the family meeting that the conversation was held in Spanish despite the resolve of the parents to speak only English when Miguel was present.

"I can't believe what you're telling me," Alberto said to his wife.

Maria Ledo stood behind her husband, chewing nervously on a thumbnail as the two of them faced their son.

"I would like to hear it from you," Alberto said to the boy. "Did you take the barber's scissors and try to cut him?"

Miguel shrugged and rubbed at the stain on his jeans.

"You answer me when I talk to you."

The boy looked off at a corner of the ceiling.

"I haven't used my belt on you in a long time," his father said, "but that doesn't mean I won't do it."

He started working at his buckle. Maria stepped forward and took his arm.

"Please, Berto."

"I won't have a son of mine behving like an animal."

"He said the barber hurt him first."

"Mr. Gomez has been cutting hair since I was a little boy and my parents took me to his shop. He does not hurt children."

"Maybe we should take Miguel to the doctor."

"I've had enough of doctors. They charge you a lot of money and do nothing."

Maria put a hand on her husband's wrist, staying him from pulling the belt free. "Please, Berto."

He relaxed slowly and rebuckled the belt. To the boy he said, "You go to your room. We will talk about this later."

Moving without haste, the boy rose and sauntered out of the room.

"And take a bath," the father said. "You smell like a stale burrito."

The parents stood where they were until they heard the sound of the boy's bedroom door closing.

"He isn't himself," Maria said. "He has been like a different person ever since last night."

"He is being spoiled," said Alberto. "Children take advantage whenever they can."

"We should take him to the doctor."

"For what? The last one could find nothing wrong with him. A good strapping is what he needs."

"No, Berto, he is acting strange. Not like our little boy. He gets into fights. The neighborhood children do not want to play with him. Not even Juan Ramirez. Not since the knife business."

"You can't blame Juan for that," said Alberto.

"And in school he is not doing his lessons. He makes trouble in the class. Now this business with Mr. Gomez."

Alberto dropped wearily into a chair. He ran a hand through his coarse black hair. "What should we do, Maria?"

"I think a doctor is best," she said. "Maybe not a medical doctor; maybe one for the mind."

"You think my son is crazy?"

"No, Berto, no. I think he needs help."

"You read too many magazines. We'll talk about it later."

On the asphalt surface of a playground in the Willowbrook district of Inglewood a spirited two-on-two basketball game was in progress. One of the players was Kevin Jackson.

The doctor had cautioned Kevin about strenuous activity until his physical condition was thoroughly checked, but he was not about to give up the game. Not even for a little while. Basketball had occupied most of his waking hours since he was old enough to hold the ball.

He fired a twelve-foot jumper, a shot he used to make with his eyes closed. *His* shot. It clanged off the back rim into the hands of Porky Edwards. Porky passed out to Nero Krutcher, who faked Kevin once and went in for the easy layup.

Elray Dickenson, who was teamed with Kevin, stood with hands on his skinny hips and stared at his partner.

"Sheeit, man, what the fuck's the matter with you? You can't hit shit."

"Don't fuck with me, man," Kevin said. "I'm a little off is all."

"Little off? Man, you playin' like a faggot."

"Shut your mouth, motherfucker. I'll rip your heart out."

The other three boys stared at him.

Porky Edwards finally said, "Man, we gonna play, we gonna jiveass around?"

"Fuck you, motherfuckers," Kevin said. "I don't need this shit." He dropkicked the ball against the chain-link fence and strode out and away down Manchester Boulevard.

The boys looked after him.

"What's his story, man?" Nero Krutcher said.

"He never pulled no shit like this before," Porky said.

Elray Dickenson looked thoughtfully after the departed Kevin. "Something ain't right with him. Something happen when he have that heart attack and that dude bring him back to life. He ain't s'posed to be here. He's s'posed to be dead."

"Weird," said Porky.

"Let's play horse," Nero said, retrieving the ball.

Chapter 22

The editor shook two antacid mints out of the bottle, tossed them into his mouth, and chewed solemnly. He was a dark-browed man with hollow cheeks and a sour outlook on life. The placard on his desk read: Phillip Yardeen, Managing Editor.

"No," he said.

Dean Gooch planted both hands on the desk and leaned over it toward the other man. "I want this one, Phil. Something's going on. I know it is. I can smell it."

"No."

"Damn it, are we running a newspaper here or what?"

"This is not *The Front Page,* so stop doing Hildy Johnson."

Gooch straightened up. "Listen to me, Phil, just listen. Okay?"

Yardeen leaned back with a long-suffering expression and folded his hands across his stomach.

"This McAllister Fain is becoming the biggest celebrity in the country since Elvis Presley. And why? Because he raises people from the dead. Just think about that a minute. Let it sink in." Gooch repeated it slowly, emphasizing each word. "He raises people from the dead. Now look me in the eye and tell me that is not a

191

load of bullshit. Tell me you really believe people can die and come back."

Yardeen belched into his fist. "Dean, what I believe or don't believe matters not a damn. A lot of people think he's on the level. We had Elliot Kruger's wife, which could have been a freak happening, but then there was the little Mexican kid, and it happened again. Now the whole country has seen the videotape of McAllister Fain reviving a boy who the doctors pronounced dead. Millions of people read an interview the man gave immediately afterward in the nation's newspapers. The *Times*, I am embarrassed to say, was not one of those newspapers."

"That's a dig at me, isn't it?"

"You were covering the story, I believe."

"Phil, the man's a fraud. He's a charlatan. I don't know how he's doing it, but he's faking. Have you seen what he's doing now? He's preparing a grand cross-country tour on which he will pause here and there long enough to make corpses walk. He's not only a fraud; he's dangerous."

"Just a minute. Weren't you telling me a minute ago how this was a load of bullshit? Now you're starting to sound like a believer."

The columnist's eyes flickered away for a moment. "To tell the truth, Phil, I'm not sure what to believe anymore. But I'm as certain as I'm standing here that somebody has to sit on this man or he'll do real damage."

"Are you sure your nose isn't out of joint because he refused to talk to you?"

"No, damn it. I've got enough other reasons to worry about the guy."

"Let's hear one."

"How about that Dr. Maylon who did the dry dive out of Leanne Kruger's bedroom window?"

"Accidental death," Yardeen said. "That's what the coroner found, and that's what we reported."

"I know," Gooch said, "and I know the pressures that were brought to bear on that case. All I want you to do is assign me to McAllister Fain. I was a damn good investigative reporter before I started doing the column. I still can be if you'll put me on this."

"Dean," the editor said with exaggerated patience, "you already did a column on Fain, remember?"

"That was just kidding around."

"Uh-huh. We're still getting flak on that. McAllister Fain is not a man we want to kid around about."

"Are you telling me he's now on the untouchable list?"

"There is no such list."

"Come off it, Phil. We all know who they are—people who can do no wrong in the public prints. Billy Graham, Coretta King, Robert Redford, Lech Walesa, John Paul the Second. Sammy Davis, Jr., used to be on it until he hugged Richard Nixon."

"I don't want to talk about it anymore," said Yardeen.

"I've got one more suggestion," said Gooch. "What if I take some of my vacation time and work the story on my own?"

"I couldn't stop you, but you've got no guarantee the *Times* will print anything you come back with."

"You'll print it, all right."

The editor belched again. "When do you want to start?"

"Right now."

"Okay, Dean, you're on vacation and on your own."

The columnist grinned at his editor and hurried out of the office.

The streets around Elliot Kruger's mansion were quiet again after the flurry of excitement over the thawing and revival of his wife. While their name still popped up in stories about McAllister Fain, the focus had shifted to the man himself.

Dean Gooch eased his Thunderbird slowly by the gated entrance and saw that a security man was still on the job there. It was not likely the guard would admit a reporter, so he would have to find another way in. The prospect started the adrenaline flowing for the columnist as it had not since his early days in the business.

He parked up the street in a spot where he could watch the entrance and put his mind to work on a plan to get him in. The problem was solved for him when a van with Bel Air Pharmacy tastefully lettered on the door pulled to the curb across the street.

A young man got out carrying a package. He checked the label and looked up at the Krugers' gate. When he started toward it, Gooch climbed out of his car and hurried across to intercept the boy.

"Just a minute," he said.

The delivery boy turned with a question in his eyes.

Gooch gestured at the package. "Are you taking that to the Kruger house?"

The boy looked down at the piece of paper. "Yeah. Delivery from Bel Air Pharmacy."

"I'll take it in for you."

The boy started to protest.

"It's all right." Gooch dug out his wallet and flapped it open to his honorary sheriff's badge that he carried next to his official-looking *Times* ID card. "FBI," he said.

The boy looked at the badge and card without reading them. Nobody ever read them. Gooch clapped the wallet shut.

"What's going on?" asked the boy.

"FBI security matter," Gooch said, unsmiling. "I'll take the delivery in for you."

"Somebody has to sign for it."

Gooch seized the boy's order pad and scribbled something indecipherable. "There you go."

The delivery boy still looked doubtful, but he let Gooch take the package from him.

"That's all," the reporter said. "You can go now."

The boy returned to his van. Gooch walked purposefully toward the entrance gate as the van drove past.

As soon as the van was out of sight, Gooch turned and went back to his car. There he examined the package. It was wrapped with green paper and string. Leanne Kruger's name was typed on the delivery label. He carefully opened it and checked the contents.

Skin creams, fungicides, pancake makeup, perfume, deodorant. Odd assortment, but so far it meant nothing. He rewrapped the package, left his jacket and necktie in the car, rolled up his sleeves, and went back across the street.

194

"Delivery from Bel Air Pharmacy," he told the guard at the gate. Gooch waited while the man phoned the house for confirmation.

"Okay," he said. "Take it around back."

All was quiet inside the grounds as Gooch walked up the curving drive to the house. In the rear he found what he took to be the service entrance and rang the bell.

A pretty, young Mexican woman opened the door.

"Bel Air Pharmacy," he said, holding up the package.

"Thank you. I will take it."

He pulled the package back. "I have to get Mrs. Kruger to sign for it."

"Mrs. Kruger don't see anybody," the maid said. "She is sick."

"She *is* here?"

The maid's eyes flickered up at the ceiling. "She's here, but she don't see anybody."

"Gee, I don't know. I'm supposed to get her to sign before I leave the stuff."

"I can ask Mr. Kruger if he come and sign it."

"That'd be okay," Gooch said. He peeled the label from the package and handed it to the maid. "Here, you can just get his signature on this so he doesn't have to come out."

As soon as the maid walked out through one swinging door, Gooch stepped swiftly through another. He found himself in a formal dining room that looked as though it had not been used recently. Moving quietly, he enjoyed the heart-pounding sensation of danger that he had not felt since his days on the police beat. He knew a kind of wild exultation that had been missing in his years as a feature-page columnist.

He made his way through the kitchen and found a back stairway. He climbed silently to the second floor. There all the doors except one were open onto the wide hallway. Gooch hurried toward the closed room, glancing into the empty bedrooms on either side as he passed them.

He tapped lightly on the door. There was a rustle of movement from inside, and a voice said something he could not make out.

Feeling like a burglar and loving it, Gooch tried the brass door handle. It moved. The door opened inward.

The room was dark. Heavy curtains across the windows blocked any light from outside. A single lamp glowed pale pink on a bedside table. Something moved on the bed.

"Peter?" The woman's voice had a shrill, grating quality. "Peter, is that you?"

"Mrs. Kruger?" Gooch advanced two steps toward the bed.

The woman sat up. Her face was shadowed, the eyes two darker holes in the darkness.

"Who are you?" she said.

The air was heavy with a cloying perfume. Under the heavy sweetness something smelled bad.

"My name is Gooch, Mrs. Kruger. I'm a reporter."

"You're not supposed to be here," said the woman.

A man's voice, angry but weak, said, "No, Mr. Gooch, you're not."

He whirled to see Elliot Kruger standing in the doorway, silhouetted in the light from the hall.

"Mr. Kruger, I—"

"Come out of my wife's room," the old man said.

With a last look at the woman on the bed, Gooch eased past Kruger into the hallway. Kruger pulled the door firmly closed.

"I would be within my rights to call the police."

But you're not going to call any police, are you? Gooch thought. Feeling himself out of danger, he took the offensive. "I understand your wife is ill, Mr. Kruger?"

"My wife's physical condition is none of your affair. Now I want you to go downstairs and leave the way you came in."

"Those ointments and skin treatments from the pharmacy—they have something to do with Mrs. Kruger's problem?"

Some of the old strength returned to Kruger's voice. "Damn you, if you don't get out of here, I'll have you thrown out."

It was time to retreat. Gooch headed down the stairs, with Kruger following. On his way to the door the reporter took one more shot. "Have you been in touch with McAllister Fain?"

"Out of here," Kruger said.

Gooch left through the kitchen where a frightened-looking maid stood, still holding the label he had torn off the package. Feeling jaunty, he gave her a wink and left through the service door, saluting the frowning security guard as he headed for the street.

Back in his car, Gooch jotted quick notes in his personal shorthand. Something was very wrong at the Kruger house. Leanne Kruger had been widely described a few weeks ago as vibrant and alive, looking none the worse for her year in deep freeze. The apparition on the bed was far from vibrant. Although he could make out no details in the dim light, Gooch could see that the woman was not healthy. The whole room had an aura of decay. *Decay!* There was his hook. Dean Gooch closed his notebook and, humming, drove east across the city.

He pulled the Thunderbird to the curb on the quiet street in Alhambra and double-checked the address of the Ledo family. This was it, all right. Neat little house, trimmed lawns, flowers. A new Chrysler was parked directly across from him. Not exactly ghetto. Too bad, in a way. A ghetto story would have been more dramatic.

He crossed the street and approached the Ledos' studio bungalo, walking up the short concrete path to the front door. The sound of voices shouting inside brought him to a stop. Gooch caught only a few of the Spanish words, but the angry tone was unmistakable.

The front door burst open, and a balding man in a dark suit rushed out. He held one hand wrapped in a white cloth on which a dark red stain was spreading. A woman Gooch recognized as Maria Ledo appeared in the doorway. She held out her hands as though to pull the man back.

"Doctor!" she cried. *"Por favor, no vaya!"*

Ignoring Gooch, the man turned and spoke to her in angry machine-gun Spanish. All Gooch could make out were the words for "son," "bite," and "lunatic." More than enough to convince the reporter he was on the right track.

He stepped into the path of the departing man. "Excuse me, sir. I'm with the *Los Angeles Times*. Can you tell me what's going on here?"

"No," the man said brusquely, and tried to step around the reporter.

"May I have your name?" Gooch persisted. "Are you a member of the Ledo family?"

"I am not. I am Dr. Horacio Vasquez. Please let me pass."

"Is Miguel sick, doctor? What happened to your hand?"

"I have nothing to say. Please move aside."

The doctor marched determinedly past Gooch and headed for the Chrysler.

As the woman started to close the door, Gooch hurried toward her. "Mrs. Ledo?"

She looked at him doubtfully. "Yes?"

"My name is Dean Gooch. May I talk to you for a moment?"

"I don't know you."

"I'm a reporter. The *Times*?"

"What do you want from me?"

"Just to talk. People are wondering how Miguel is getting along." He caught the flash of pain in her dark eyes. "Is anything wrong?"

"My boy is . . . not well."

Gooch used a portion of his tiny Spanish vocabulary. "*Lo siento, señora*. I'm so sorry. Is there anything I can do?"

"No. Nothing. Uh, thank you, Mr.—"

"Gooch. I wonder if I could see the boy."

Alberto Ledo came out of the house behind his wife. His face was dark with anger. "I told you the boy needed a strapping. Now look what he has done—bitten the doctor's hand to the bone."

"Miguel bit the doctor?" Gooch said.

Alberto whirled. "Who are you?"

"I'm a reporter. *Los Angeles Times*."

"Go away."

"Mr. Ledo, I'd like to help you."

"Nobody can help us. Something is wrong with our boy, and nobody can help. Not you, not the doctor, not God."

Maria's hand went to her mouth. "Berto, don't say that."

"I'll say what I please. The first thing we did was go to the church and give thanks to the Blessed Virgin. And look what we have—a boy I don't know. A boy who stinks of the slaughterhouse, who will not do his lessons, who hurts his little friends and fights the doctor like an animal. Don't tell me God is good."

Dean Gooch cursed himself for not bringing a tape recorder, but he tried to remember Alberto Ledo's words as closely as possible to help him build the growing story.

"Mr. Ledo," he said, "I wonder if I could just—"

Alberto jerked his head around in surprise, as though he had forgotten Gooch was there. "I got nothing to say to you. All you reporters with your cameras and your microphones—maybe it was you made my son crazy. You get out of here now while you still got your *cojones*."

Gooch did not need a translation of that. He nodded to both parents and retreated hastily across the street to his car. He drove out of sight before stopping to add new notes to what he had written after the visit to the Kruger mansion.

Willowbrook is an unincorporated area of Los Angeles County jammed in between Compton and the Harbor Freeway. It was not quite a slum, but still several steps down from the tidy little street in Alhambra. Here were liquor stores, their windows boarded over, the boards splattered with graffiti. It was a neighborhood of greasy hamburger joints, auto-body shops, dark taverns, and old houses chopped up into cramped rooms and tiny apartments.

Old men with hopeless eyes and bagged bottles wandered aimlessly. Scowling younger men strutted the streets, proudly wearing the colors of their gang—blue for the Crips, red for the Bloods. In alleys and doorways and parked cars dope was bought and sold with little attempt at concealment.

Dean Gooch rolled up his windows and locked the doors as he drove slowly along, watching the street numbers. He was relieved to see that the block on which the Jacksons lived was in a somewhat more civilized area. He parked and locked his car in front of a little grocery store and, painfully conscious of the eyes on him, walked to the square brick apartment building.

Mrs. Urbana Jackson was listed on the third floor. Gooch climbed through layers of cooking odors and loud, recorded rhythm and blues. On the third floor he found the right door and knocked. No answer. He knocked a second time and a third. Nothing.

Annoyed, he turned and started down the stairs. Then he froze.

Three black youths ranged themselves across his path halfway down. They were not smiling. The only good news for Gooch was that they were not wearing any gang colors.

"Hey, man, you lost?" said the biggest of the three. He wore a black muscle T-shirt that showed off his gleaming brown deltoids. One of his companions was tall and blade-thin, the other chunky and watchful. Dean Gooch had the feeling any one of the three would kill him if he twitched the wrong way.

"I was looking for Mrs. Jackson," he said carefully. "Guess she's not home."

"What you want with her?" said the one with the muscles.

"Actually, it's Kevin I wanted to see."

Three pairs of opaque eyes watched him without expression.

"I'm a reporter. Working on a story for my paper about Kevin?" Was he sounding too white? Gooch wondered. Hell, it was probably safer than trying to sound street hip and getting the idiom wrong.

"Ain't no story here," said the spokesman.

"Guess not," Gooch said, working his lips into a smile. "That's the way it goes some days."

The three black youths made no move to get out of his way. Gooch began to perspire.

"Well, see you," he said, and moved tentatively down the steps. When they still failed to move, Gooch swallowed hard and said, " 'Scuse me, men."

The tall, thin one spoke for the first time. "You got any money?"

Big trouble. "Well, uh, yeah, I've got a little."

"Just a little, huh?"

"Forty dollars. Fifty, maybe?"

The young men looked at each other. Gooch felt his scrotum tighten like a fist.

"Man, you shouldn't walk around here in them nice clothes with forty, fifty dollars on you. Sheeit, man, they's people rip your throat out for that little bit."

Gooch's windpipe closed up on him. Dear God, he thought, don't let me faint.

"I was you, man, I'd tuck that money away, get in my T-bird, and hustle on back to my own part of town. Hear?"

"I hear." Gooch scarcely recognized his own voice.

They moved just enough to allow Gooch to squeeze between the muscular one and the tall one. He walked swiftly down to the second-floor landing, then around and down again toward the street. From above him he heard the boys' rich laughter. In his relief, he could have joined them.

Back in the blessed sunshine, he hurried to his car.

"Hey, man."

Gooch had the car door open when the voice called him. He turned to see the chunky black youth come out of the building. Keeping one foot inside the car, Gooch waited as the boy approached.

"You want to hear about Kevin?"

"Do you know where he is?"

"Huh-uh. He don't hang out with us no more. He don't hang out with nobody. Keeps to himself all weird like."

"Tell me about it," Gooch said.

"What's it worth?"

"Twenty dollars."

"This for all three of us, man?"

"Thirty?"

"Fifty."

What the hell, he could write it off. "You got it."

Gooch popped the lock, and the chunky youth climbed in on the passenger side. "Nice car. Let's go for a ride.

Don't look good for me to be sittin' talkin' to a white dude.''

Gooch started the engine and pulled away from the curb.

''First time we seen Kevin goin' weird was one day he was shootin' some baskets. . . .''

Half an hour later, when Gooch dropped the boy back on Kevin Jackson's street, he parted happily with the fifty dollars, figuring it might have just brought him one hell of a story.

Chapter 23

McAllister Fain leaned back in the burgundy leather judge's chair behind the desk in his Eagle's Roost office. Warner Echols sat across from him. Fain idly made shiny red balls multiply and vanish between his fingers as Echols held up eight-by-ten glossy photographs for his inspection.

"I like that one," Fain said, pointing. "It gives me kind of a macho Clint Eastwood look."

"It's good," Echols agreed quickly, "but is macho really what we're looking for here? I mean, for your book jacket something a little more spiritual, I think." He held up another photo in which Fain appeared to be looking at something off in the misty distance. "This, for instance."

"I remember that one," Fain said. "Somebody walked in just as Zeno took the shot. I'm looking up to see who it is."

"That brings up another point," Echols said. "About Zeno . . . I know you like his work, but we have professionals at F-A who specialize in this kind of thing."

"Olney Zeno is my man," Fain said, putting an end to the discussion."

"Right, Mac. It was just an idle thought. Do you suppose we can choose one of these now? The publisher wants to move them into the stores by the end of next month. He's already got orders up to here."

"You don't like the Eastwood shot?" Fain said.

"I'm not saying I don't like it, just questioning whether it's right for this application."

Fain made four balls turn into one and then vanished the last ball. "Okay, I'll go along with the mystical look if you think it'll help sell books."

"It fits the image," Echols said.

"Yeah, the good ol' image." Fain was thoughtful for a moment; then he got businesslike. "Will the book be available when I start the tour? A lot of people will want to buy it while I'm in their city."

Echols carefully squared up the stack of glossies. "About the tour, Mac—I wonder if that's such a good idea right now."

"What are you talking about? I've been planning on it. We've got rooms full of mail. Those people want to see me in action."

"I know we've got mail, but they aren't all fan letters, you know. A considerable number are pretty vicious. Threatening, even."

"So what? Even the pope gets hate mail."

"And you remember what happened to the pope. The truth is I'm worried about your safety."

"My safety? Hell, the Russian ambassador goes wherever he wants to, and he's got to have more people out to hit him than I have."

"The Russian ambassador has the protection of the United States government. You are a private citizen. All security arrangements would have to be privately arranged. A national tour like you're talking about would just put too much strain on our resources."

"You're telling me I have to stay locked up here in this mausoleum when I'm probably one of the ten most popular men in the country?"

"No, no, nothing like that. You can move around the area all you want; we can have men assigned to you full-time here. It's just the cross-country thing we object to."

Fain moodily rolled a half-dollar across his knuckles.

"All right, I'll shelve the tour for now, but I do want to go back to work."

"Work?"

Fain spoke with exaggerated diction. "Yes, Warner, work. Doing what I do. I haven't been active since the Jackson kid. People are dying every day who wouldn't have to stay dead. Families are torn up with grief. Widows are left without funds. Little kids are orphaned. God knows there are enough tragic stories in one day's mail to supply a year of soap operas. I can fix some of those things, Warner."

Echols chewed on his upper lip while framing an answer. Finally, he said, "Mac, we're a little edgy about doing any more of those."

Fain snapped forward in the judge's chair. His pale gray eyes bored into Echols. "We? *We?* Who is this *we* you're talking about? I'm the one who does the business. I'm the one with the power. Me. McAllister Fain. So you want me to cancel the national tour? All right. I may not agree, but I'll go along. But what are you saying now? Are you saying I should not bring anyone else back to life? Because 'we' are a little edgy? What if it was your wife, Warner? Or your little boy died suddenly? Would you be edgy then, or would you want me to bring him back?"

Echols held up both hands in defense. "Mac, Mac, I'm only thinking about your career. Moral questions are not my department. The thing is, you've done enough now to assure you of a sizable income for years to come. Especially after the national coverage we got on Kevin Jackson. All it takes now is careful management of the spin-offs and you'll be a rich man for the rest of your life."

"I'm already rich," Fain said. "I've seen the bankbooks. How much more money can I use? I want to give something back. This power I have must not be hoarded. I can give the gift of rebirth. A second chance at life. What would people say about me if I had the gift and didn't use it?"

For several moments the room was deathly quiet. The only sound was a persistent mockingbird outside the window. Finally, Warner Echols said, "Mac, you're starting to sound like . . ."

"Like what?" Fain snapped when he hesitated.

"Never mind," Echols said quietly. "I'll start the wheels turning."

"Start them turning *now*, Warner. I want a list of potential returnees in my hands by this afternoon."

"Returnees," Echols repeated dryly.

"Call them whatever you want; just get me the list."

"This afternoon," Echols said, and rose to leave.

"Another thing," Fain said, stopping him. "Victoria Clifford. I want her out of here."

"Victoria? What's the trouble?"

"No trouble; she's getting on my nerves is all. Pull her out and get me somebody else."

"Whatever you say, Mac."

Warner Echols left the office without further comment.

Fain tossed the half-dollar into the air, caught it on the back of his other hand, flipped his hand, and the coin disappeared. He got up from the chair and walked over to the window. The mockingbird still sang its varied repertoire somewhere in the branches of the California live oak outside. Fain scanned the tangled branches but could not locate the bird.

He walked back to the desk, sat down, and drummed his fingers. It was a rare minute alone for him these days. In minutes, he knew, someone would come through the door with papers for him to sign, a question for him to answer, a decision to be made. But for this minute or two he could enjoy the solitude.

Or could he? Having people with him at least kept him from thinking, and lately he found unwanted thoughts creeping into his mind. As convinced as he was about the rightness of what he was doing, there were times when unasked questions nagged at him for an answer. Times when he was alone.

Maybe he had been hasty in getting rid of Victoria. She was, after all, available to him anytime he wanted her. No, he decided, Victoria was a purpose girl. She was looking out for Victoria, and the time she spent with him was strictly for her own benefit.

Without really thinking about it, he picked up the phone and punched the private-line button—the one that cut off the recorder. He keyed in a number and listened as the receiver buzzed in his ear. It rang four times on the other end. He was about to hang up, then:

"Hello?"

So surprised was Fain to hear Jillian's voice that at first he could not find his own. He had not even tried to call her in weeks, and before that he got only her answering machine.

"Hello?" she said again.

"Hi," he got out at last. "I caught you at home."

"Hello, Mac."

The familiar husky voice was like mulled wine.

"How've you been?" he asked.

"Fine. I've been reading about you."

"They keep me pretty busy."

"So it seems."

"What about you? Are you working?"

"I'm in *Three Candles;* it's a bedroom farce. Nothing heavy, but I've got a nice part."

"Sounds great. Where is it?"

"At the Northside Theatre, an equity-waiver house in the Valley."

"I'd like to come and see you."

"I wish you could, but we close tomorrow night, and we're sold out."

"Oh, well . . ." He cleared his throat. "Maybe we could get together?"

A long pause on Jillian's end.

"I don't know, Mac. I'm pretty busy. And I know you are, too."

"I'll make time. And you're closing tomorrow."

"I go right back into rehearsals."

The pause this time was on his end.

"I see. Well, glad to hear you're making it, kid."

"I don't know about making it, but it's good to be working."

"Yeah. Let's keep in touch, okay?"

"Sure, Mac."

"G'bye then."

He hung up the phone and for several minutes sat looking down at the dead instrument. Outside, the mockingbird had stopped singing.

The return of McAllister Fain to the resurrection business was given wide and favorable media coverage, thanks to the publicity department of Federated Artists. The first carefully chosen subject was a city fireman who died of smoke inhalation while rescuing several elderly patients from a nursing home. The fireman's family was tearfully grateful, but Fain waved away their thanks. The mayor and city council voted unanimously to give Fain a special commendation. His modest acceptance on national television would have done credit to the young Jimmy Stewart.

The next was a sixteen-year-old girl in the San Fernando Valley. Despondent over a failed love affair, she sealed up the garage, started the engine of the family Caprice, and sat behind the wheel, inhaling carbon monoxide. They found her the next morning. The pleas of the grief-stricken parents persuaded Fain to break one of his own rules and bring back a suicide.

A popular television-series star died under anesthesia during cosmetic surgery. Fain brought her back, to the joy of her international fan clubs. The media failed to report that the star was also a client of Federated Artists.

To prove that he served not only the rich and famous, Fain resurrected a transient who was asphyxiated while trying to sleep inside a barrel recently used to haul toxic chemicals. The man's gratitude at being restored to his meager life was limited.

Having broken one of his rules with the young suicide, Fain had less trouble breaking the one against working with trauma victims. Especially in a good cause. A policeman was shot to death by a doped-up armed-robbery suspect not far from Fain's old apartment in Echo Park. The officer was killed by a bullet that entered his cheek and traveled upward through the brain. After he was revived the wound refused to heal, but that was overlooked in the general celebration of the hero's return.

From the shooting victim it was a short step for Fain

to take a young working mother of three who had been struck down in a crosswalk by a hit-and-run driver. He performed the short ceremony, which now came as naturally to him as the Pledge of Allegiance, and the mangled body stirred to life. Doctors doubted that they could put her back together in a recognizable shape, but that was their problem. McAllister Fain had triumphed again.

It became inconvenient for Fain to travel to wherever the deceased happened to lie, so it was decided that a centralized location would be provided where the victims could be brought to him. The site selected was a theater on Vine Street that had begun life in the 1930s as a movie palace. In 1955 it had been refurbished as a television studio, and there originated many of the comedy-variety shows of the day. The present owner was losing money renting it out for rock videos, and he was happy to accept the inflated offer made by Federated Artists out of the ever-growing profits of McAllister Fain.

While one triumph followed another for Fain, he became ever further removed from the public that clamored for a glimpse of him. While his earliest performances had been under makeshift circumstances, sometimes surrounded by strangers, he now worked on a stage with the latest in professional lighting and sound. The live audience was carefully controlled.

He was surrounded at all times by F-A security personnel and by a growing entourage who leaped to grant his every whim and shielded him from any adverse comments. He was scheduled for meetings, luncheons, appearances, telecasts, and script conferences during every waking hour. Fain was kept so thoroughly focused on the progress of his own fortunes that he was unaware of events unfolding in other parts of the city.

Leanne Kruger sat hunched forward in her darkened room before her dressing-table mirror. She looked into the shadowed eyes of the dim image in the glass and shivered. The face, caked with makeup and puffed out of proportion, belonged to a stranger. Leanne crushed the bottle of cologne she was holding. The fingers of her hand were deeply lacerated. No blood flowed from the cuts. She never bled anymore. And she never healed.

It was not only her face but her mind that troubled Leanne. In moments of lucidity like this one, she felt despair at what was happening to her. At other times—and they were growing more frequent—she felt a wild, unfocused rage and a need for revenge against . . . against whom?

Lately, voices filled her head. Strange voices of people she had never known. They reached out to her, called to her. There had been only one at first—the voice of a young boy. She heard it faintly the first time a week or so after her return. A young boy, alone and frightened. Then there had been another. Not so young but still less than an adult. Each day the voices grew louder—the words more distinct but still garbled.

For a while there were just the two of them. They called to Leanne, cried out for help. She denied the voices at first. Fought against them. Tried to close them out. But as she began to see the changes in her body and feel her mind slipping loose, she began to listen.

Now there were more voices. Three, six, ten. All of them lost and in pain, feeling the things she felt. Leanne sent her own thoughts out to them and sensed that they received her.

It was time to act.

One thought burned clearly through the fog that had dimmed her mind. She had to leave this house. She had to go to the owners of the voices. She could not have named the people or the meeting place, but something like a physical force pulled her. She would find them.

She rose from the padded bench that faced the mirror and walked out of the bedroom. The light was brighter in the hall, and Leanne winced. She had lost count of the days since last she had left the bedroom.

At the foot of the stairs Elliot came to meet her. His expression told her more clearly than the mirror what her face had become. He tried not to show it, but it was there. The horror.

"Leanne! Are you all right?"

She walked past him, saying nothing.

"Where are you going?"

"Out." Like some disobedient child.

"Wait! You can't go out like that."

She wore green satin lounging pajamas, a short belted robe, and slippers. What was wrong with that? Leanne continued toward the door.

Elliot moved directly in front of her. Reflexively, he turned his head away, then forced himself to look. "I can't let you go outside."

"Get out of my way." Even to her own ears Leanne's voice sounded harsh and unfamiliar. She was unaccustomed to using it lately.

"No, stop." Elliot took hold of her by the shoulder.

With a sweep of her arm she sent him stumbling across the floor and into the wall. He went to his knees, stunned as much by Leanne's phenomenal strength as by the impact.

She opened the heavy front door and stepped out into the night, letting the darkness close around her like a warm bath. By the time Elliot Kruger came out and shouted for the security guard, Leanne was gone.

The day after Leanne Kruger disappeared in Bel Air, Alberto Ledo came home in Alhambra to find his wife looking even more distraught than usual for these trying days.

"Maria, what is it?" he asked, hurrying to the front door, where she stood, teary-eyed, biting hard on a knuckle.

"Miguelito is gone," she said.

"Gone? What do you mean gone?"

"He didn't come home from school today. I waited and I waited, and finally I called the school. He never even went there."

"But you sent him off this morning."

"Yes, but you know how he has been lately. He acted very strange, wouldn't even talk to me. I should never have let him go."

Alberto took her in his arms. "It is not your fault. You were right—Miguel should have seen a doctor. I should have listened to you."

"Berto, what will we do?"

"Find our boy. I'll get the men in the neighborhood to help me. If we can't find him, then we will call in the police."

At about the same time, a spirited basketball game stopped suddenly in Willowbrook as a woman walked out onto the asphalt playing surface. Sometimes girls would come and stand around, making suggestive remarks while the boys played and pretended to ignore them, but older women, mothers, never came to the playground.

"You boys," she said.

They watched her, silent, wary.

"You . . . Nero Krutcher, Elray Dickenson, you . . . Porky. Come over here."

Reluctantly, the three boys disengaged themselves from the others and slouched over to the woman. She looked at each of them in turn, her dark face creased with worry.

"Any you boys seen my Kevin?"

Three heads rolled solemnly from side to side.

"You his friends. He always with you when he ain't home."

Nero Krutcher, his bare muscular torso gleaming with sweat, spoke in a mumble. "He ain't been with us. We seen him, you know, on the street two three times, but he don't hang out with us no more."

"He didn't come home last night or the night before," Urbana Jackson said. "I'm worried he might be in trouble or hurt or somethin'."

The boys shrugged. The short, stocky one looked down at his new Nike court shoes.

"You know somethin' you not tellin' me, Porky?"

"Some white dude came around lookin' for him," Porky Edwards mumbled.

"Not the police?"

"No. Man said he was writin' a story."

"And you ain't seen Kevin?"

"Not since . . ." Porky looked at the others—"three days back? Yeah, three days. Just saw him for a minute across the street. Looked kinda sick."

"Well . . ." The woman seemed to want to ask more

questions but abruptly changed her mind. "All right. You see him, you tell him get hisself home, hear?"

"We'll do it," Porky said.

The three boys watched Urbana Jackson, suddenly grown older, walk out of the playground. Then they returned to the game.

The surface under his feet undulated like a poorly filled water bed. McAllister Fain fought to move, but he could make no headway. In the shadows around him were . . . things. They rustled and hissed at him. Obscene little sounds. They were coming for him, closing in.

He tried to run, but the billowing surface mocked him, blocked him from any escape. The things moved closer. They multiplied and pushed in on him. He fell, bouncing in slow motion as they covered him with their rotting, stinking bodies. He tried to claw his way out, but he came away with handfuls of loose dead flesh.

He screamed. His open mouth was filled with . . . pillow.

Fain sat up in bed, his eyes wide and staring at the jiggling shadow pattern made by the trees outside his window. His pajamas were soaked through with sweat.

Gradually, the horror of the dream dissipated, and his breathing returned to normal. There were maybe a dozen other people sleeping somewhere in the big stone house, but never in his life had he felt so alone. He lay back down but slept no more before the dawn.

Chapter 24

Warner Echols slid his Porsche 911 to a stop in the gravel driveway in front of Eagle's Roost and leaped from the cockpit before the engine had stopped turning over. He dashed up the steps to the entrance and banged on the carved oak door, ignoring the bell.

The maid who answered the door recognized Echols and admitted him at once, stepping back out of the way when she saw the look on his face.

"Where is he?" Echols demanded. He gripped the rolled copy of the *Los Angeles Times* in his fist like a weapon.

"Mr. Fain?" the maid said.

"Hell yes, Mr. Fain. Who do you think?"

"H-he's relaxing in the hot tub."

"Relaxing," Echols repeated through clenched teeth. He pounded through the great entrance hall and on out toward the terrace where Fain had directed them to put in a hot tub.

The maid watched the agent's retreating back with wide, frightened eyes.

The water bubbled and steamed and swirled about the interior of the six-foot redwood tub. The effect, according to the ads, was supposed to be soothing, but neither of the occupants looked particularly at ease.

"Damn it!" Mac Fain scowled at the soggy Marlboro that was falling apart between his fingers. "Why don't they make those things waterproof?" He wadded the debris into a small ball and dropped it over the edge of the tub. He took a long pull from the Bloody Mary that was balanced on the wooden ledge.

"You shouldn't smoke, anyway," the blonde said. "It's bad for you."

Fain stared into her empty blue eyes. Then he looked down at her fine plump breasts bobbing happily atop the bubbles. He had to think for a moment to remember her name. Debbie? Candy? Sandi? That was it. Sandi. And don't forget to spell it with an "i."

"Honey, do me a favor," he said, "stop with the medical advice."

She worked on him down under the water with a practiced hand. "I just want to keep you well and strong."

"Thanks, I'm touched."

"Everybody knows cigarettes cause lung cancer," she said.

"Will you quit?" he snapped.

The blonde withdrew her hand.

"Not that," he said, replacing her hand, "nagging me about cigarettes."

She was silent. Her wide blue eyes showed hurt.

"Anyway, nobody lives forever," he grumbled.

Actually, Fain had given up smoking eight years ago and only recently took it up again when his nerves began jumping. With a sigh he grabbed the rest of the pack from the tub ledge, crushed it in his fist, and tossed it into the trees.

"There, satisfied?" he asked.

"It's really better for you not to smoke," she said.

This from a girl he had watched snort about two-hundred dollars' worth of cocaine to get herself going that morning. Fain shook his head and reached for the Bloody Mary.

The French doors opened behind him, and Warner Echols came out onto the terrace. "I've got to talk to you, Mac."

"Does it have to be now? I'm getting a health lecture."

"Yes, it has to be now. It's important."

"So talk," Fain said, shifting his position gently so as not to dislodge the blonde's hand. "You know Debbie, don't you?"

"Sandi," said Sandi.

"Alone," said Echols.

Fain edged around to look at the agent. "Can't this wait?"

"No, goddammit."

Frowning, Fain pulled Sandi's hand free and gave her a squeeze. "Take a hike," he said.

"Are you going to want me later?"

"I don't know. Stick around in case I do."

Sandi climbed gracefully out of the tub, giving Echols an opportunity to behold her gleaming ass before wrapping herself in an oversize towel.

Echols paid no attention to the naked girl. He stood shifting his feet impatiently, glaring alternately at Fain and at the newspaper in his hand.

When Sandi had strolled on into the house, Fain said, "All right, what's the problem? Every time somebody comes at me with a newspaper in his hand, it's trouble."

"Have you read the *Times*?" Echols said.

"No."

"You'd better read it."

Fain hoisted himself up onto the tub seat so that the water level was at his waist. He reached out, and Echols handed him the paper.

" 'New Setback for Tax Program,' " he read. "So what?"

"Not that. The left-hand column on page one."

Fain held the paper carefully up out of the water and read:

BACK FROM THE DEAD
—BUT BACK TO WHAT?
By Dean Gooch
(FIRST OF A TIMES INVESTIGATIVE SERIES)

He read quickly through the story, which was continued twice on the inside pages, and looked up at Echols.

"What about it? This Gooch character has had a hard-on for me since day one."

"If I were you," Echols said, "I'd be a little more concerned."

"Why? I've had bad press before."

"I know, but this time it's not the L.A. *Insider*. This is the *Times*."

"The *Los Angeles Times* can be wrong, you know. It's not the Bible."

"I don't think they're wrong this time," Echols said. "I've had Gooch's story checked as far as I could. We sent private investigators to see all three of those people—Leanne Kruger, Miguel Ledo, and Kevin Jackson."

"And?"

"And they're all missing. The Mexican kid and the basketball player for sure, Leanne Kruger probably. Kruger wasn't talking, but our man sounded out her maid. All three people just walked away."

"So they're missing. That doesn't mean all this shit of Gooch's is fact."

"He says in there you were 'unavailable for comment.' What does that mean?"

"It means I gave orders that Dean Gooch was not to be allowed anyplace close to me. That SOB dumped on me when I was nobody. Now let him get his news by reading the *Herald*."

"That's not a good attitude, Mac. Gooch swings a lot of weight down at the *Times*. And his column is syndicated around the country."

"I will not kiss up to that asshole. So he writes one critical story. That's not going to kill me. Overall the media has been favorable."

"And it's important we keep it that way. If you don't think the media can turn on one of its darlings, think about what happened to Jesse Jackson."

"I'm not running for office," Fain said.

Echols drew in a breath and let it out slowly. "Damn it, Mac, don't you see what kind of effect this will have on our whole program? The book, the movie, the public appearances—everything depends on keeping a positive image in front of the public. A thing like this could blow us right out of the water. We've got to do something to counteract the bad effect this has already had, and we've got to do it fast.''

Fain hauled himself out of the hot tub and pulled on a thick terry-cloth robe. ''What do you expect me to do about it? Apologize for bringing people back to life? I've got a power; I use it. I can't be held responsible for what happens to these people once I've revived them.''

''Maybe you can,'' Echols said darkly.

''What's that supposed to mean?''

''I'm thinking of the Oriental custom where you save a man's life, you become responsible for him from then on. You went a lot farther than just saving these people's lives; you brought them back from the dead.''

''Do me a favor, Warner. Knock off the Oriental philosophy. If you think we're in trouble here, let's have some positive input.''

''I know we're in trouble,'' Echols said. ''We started getting calls at F-A early this morning. You must be the only person in town who didn't read Gooch's story.''

''I got up late.''

''What I thought we might do,'' Echols continued, ''is have you make public appearances with some of the other people you've brought back. The more recent ones. Sort of a reunion showing that you're okay and they're okay.''

''If you really think it's necessary,'' Fain said.

''I do.''

''Then go ahead and set it up.''

In the days that followed, Warner Echols became increasingly worried. The people he sent out to contact Fain's recent ''clients'' came back with troubling reports. So troubling that Echols went out to see for himself.

His first stop was at the home of Glenn Meiner, the heroic fireman killed in the nursing-home blaze. He was taken into the living room by Meiner's pregnant wife. The venetian blinds were tightly closed, locking out the sunlight. A moist, unhealthy smell permeated the room.

Meiner sat slumped in a frayed easy chair. He did not

look up when Echols came in. His wife hurried over to take a position behind him. The fireman responded to Echols's greeting and his questions in a voice that had been drained of life.

"I don't want to be on any TV show," the fireman said.

"You wouldn't have to go into a studio or anything," Echols said. "We could do the interview right here. As a matter of fact, it might be better that way."

"I don't want them coming here. Too much fuss, too many people, too many lights."

"We could make it as simple and quick as you like," Echols persisted. "Just a short conversation between you and McAllister Fain."

"I don't want to see him."

Echols leaned forward, trying in the dim living room to read the face of the man sitting across from him. "Mr. Meiner, I'm not asking a lot of you, and it could be very important to Mr. Fain."

"No."

"May I ask why?"

"I don't want to, that's all." He raised his head to face Echols for the first time. Something dangerous glimmered in the shadowed eyes. "Now get the fuck out of my house."

"He doesn't mean that," Meiner's wife said quickly.

"I mean it," the man said. "All I want is to be left alone."

Echols rose from the chair and walked stiffly out of the living room and through the front door into the sunshine. Mrs. Meiner followed him.

"I'm sorry about Glenn," she said. "That isn't like him at all. Not the way he used to be. He was always a kind, laughing man. We were always having people in and going places. Now all he does all day is sit there in the dark. He won't see anybody. He won't do anything. He won't go back to work; he doesn't hardly eat anything. We don't laugh anymore."

"Is it something physical?" Echols said. "An after-effect from the fire?"

"I don't think so. The doctor checked him over and

said he was fine right after. He was fit to go to work if he'd wanted to. But I don't know . . . he just keeps sitting there. He won't let the doctor near him now."

Sharon Isaacs, the would-be suicide in the Valley, was even less encouraging to Echols than the fireman. He learned from her parents that Sharon had been in a more or less constant state of hysteria since her revival. The psychiatrist that the Isaacses called in recommended putting the girl in an institution, but so far the parents had resisted. They kept her upstairs in her old room, hoping she would come around, but so far Sharon was in no condition to talk to Echols or anybody else.

Paula Foster, the actress who had died during what was supposed to be minor surgery, was welcomed back to *River Falls* by a cast party. Her return a mere three days after the ordeal was considered miraculous. The day after the party she returned to work. The reports of what happened then were sketchy and guarded, but Echols managed to piece together a rough scenario.

Paula, who was known as a delight to work with, had immediately picked a fight with her costar and refused to do a kissing scene. In rapid succession she argued with the director, the producer, the writers, the network, and anyone else who crossed her path. She walked off the set and was placed on an indefinite leave of absence while her part was "temporarily" written out. Now she was reported to be holed up in her Malibu beach house, seeing no one and refusing to answer the phone. Not even her longtime personal agent at Federated Artists could reach her.

Barney Quail, the homeless man who had inhaled the lethal chemical fumes, had simply dropped from sight. Since his release from the hospital, he had been absent from his old haunts. There were no known relatives, and no one much seemed to care, so the trail ended.

John Corely was the clean-cut, well-liked young policeman who had been shot through the head while thwarting a robbery. Echols discovered he was currently in custody in the hospital ward of L.A. County Jail. One week after McAllister Fain brought him back, Corely had emptied his .38 special into the body of his wife.

Ada Dempsey, the mangled hit-and-run victim, had stayed in the hospital after her vital signs were restored. Then one night she somehow pulled together the torn flesh and shattered bones and dragged herself out of the hospital. No one saw her go. No one had seen her since.

The next time Warner Echols met with McAllister Fain, there was no blonde, no hot tub, no Bloody Mary. The meeting took place in one of the rooms of Eagle's Roost appropriated as an office by Federated Artists. The secretary was dismissed, and the door was closed as the two men faced each other.

"What we have here, Mac, is a crisis situation," Echols said.

Fain lit a Marlboro with a shaking hand, took a puff, ground it out. "Don't you think you're exaggerating the problem?"

"Exaggerating? Hell, if anything, I'm underplaying it." He ticked off the points on his fingers. "First we have disappearances of the original three people—Leanne Kruger, the Mexican kid, and Kevin Jackson. No word, incidentally, on any of them."

"Are the police in on it?"

"Only with the Mexican kid, officially. Elliot Kruger has his own security people looking for his wife. Jackson's mother won't have anything to do with the cops. Something about a roust of her neighborhood a couple of years ago."

Fain slumped in his chair, looking glum.

"Now we've got a man who sits and mopes in a dark room, a girl who screams all night, an actress who's locked herself away from everybody, a missing bum, a cop with a hole in his head and a murdered wife, and a bag of bloody bones that once was a woman out on the streets somewhere. If all that doesn't add up to a major crisis, you'll have to show me what does."

Fain ran fingers through his thick black hair. "Okay,

Warner, we've got a problem. What do you suggest we do?''

Echols hitched his chair closer. "That's what I came to talk about."

Chapter 25

"What we want you to do," Warner Echols said, "is drop out of sight for a little while."

"Drop out of sight?" Fain repeated.

"Until this situation smooths itself out."

"How long a time are we talking about?"

"Say, a year."

"A year? Jesus, you're asking me to disappear for a whole year? I won't do it."

Echols tapped the desktop with a forefinger to emphasize his point. "Mac, I am not asking you to do anything. If you'll read your contract with Federated Artists, you'll see that the agency has final control over all decisions that affect your professional career. This decision has already been made, and what it is, is for you to vanish. Believe me, this has been kicked around at the highest level, and it's the best possible move for you, considering the situation."

"To run away," Fain said.

"If that's the way you want to look at it, yes. Any other course would be foolhardy."

"What about all our plans? My commitments?"

"Let's be honest here," Echols said. "Your career is dead in the water."

"But there's the book," Fain protested. "The movie."

"The book is on hold. Bookstores have canceled orders to the point where it wouldn't pay to set the thing in type. And frankly, the publisher is not anxious to be associated with your autobiography with all the bad publicity going down. As for the movie, M-G-M is out, and there isn't a producer in town who will touch you, the way things are."

"All of this because of what that sleazy SOB Dean Gooch wrote?"

"All he did was break the story. It would have come out anyway. Hell, Mac, you can't hide what's happening to the people you worked on. They're turning into zombies. Dead meat. Carrion."

Fain looked around as though for a jury to hear his side of the case. "It's not fair. All I ever did was try to help people."

"Life isn't fair," Echols said.

Fain jammed his hands into his pockets and strode back and forth in the office. Finally, he came to a stop in front of Echols. "I won't do it," he said. "I won't run away. There's got to be some way to fix things."

"Do I understand that you're refusing to abide by the agency's decision?"

"Bingo."

Echols withdrew a thick number-ten envelope from his breast pocket and laid it on the desk in front of Fain. "In that case, I have to tell you that Federated Artists is severing all professional connections with you as of this date. You'll find the legal papers to that effect in the envelope. You can sign them when you get around to it."

Fain's eyes narrowed to silvery pinpoints. "This is what you wanted me to do, isn't it. You came all prepared to dump me."

Echols put out a hand toward Fain's shoulder. Fain pulled away.

"Mac, I'm truly sorry about this. On a one-to-one basis, I like you, but you can understand that we have to leave personal feelings aside. We didn't have a long time together, but you weren't too hard to work with. At first. But over the weeks I've watched you turn into something else. And in my heart I started having doubts about the whole project."

"Just what the hell does that mean?" Fain said.

"Honest to God, I don't know what you did to those people, and I don't think I want to know. Maybe it's a trick; maybe it's some weird kind of folk medicine. Or maybe it's magic. Whatever it is my gut feeling is that you should never have started. I'm not a religious man, but I think you stepped across a line that men should stay well back of."

"I cannot believe I'm standing here listening to a sermon from the same guy who was so eager to jump on the bandwagon when it looked like I would make a bundle."

"I was hoping you wouldn't take it like this, Mac. I know there are no hard feelings on my part. Speaking for myself and for the agency, I only want to say good luck."

"Gee, thanks, Warner. That warms my heart." He picked up the envelope and turned to go.

Behind him, Echols said, "Uh, how soon do you think you can be out?"

"Out?"

"Out of Eagle's Roost. I mean, there's no need to keep the place open any longer, and the agency would like to button it up."

Fain stared at him. "Will this afternoon be soon enough?"

"That'll be fine. we'll have a truck here for your personal things. Agency expense."

"If you do me any more favors, I may cry."

"It's a tough business, Mac."

The staff of servants and the agency personnel cleared out of the huge old house so fast it seemed to Fain he was watching a time-lapse film. At noon, the Bekins truck came for the things that Fain had brought with him from Echo Park—a pitifully small grouping in the big van. When the driver asked him for a destination, Fain realized he had no idea where he was going.

"We gotta take it somewhere, buddy," the driver said, licking the point of his pencil.

"Can you put it in storage?"

"Sure. You gotta sign."

"I'll sign," Fain said.

Ten minutes later, he watched all his worldly goods except two suitcases of clothes and personal things roll away from Eagle's Roost and down the hill.

He felt he ought to say good-bye to somebody, but there was no one left on the grounds that he knew. Warner Echols had disappeared right after giving him the news. He never really knew any of the staff by name. Debbie or Sandi was gone. Only the cleanup crew sent by F-A was on the grounds, and they kept throwing sidelong glances at Fain as though they wished he'd leave.

Coming out of Eagle's Roost was more of a shock than Fain had anticipated. Up there he had been surrounded by people who flattered him, agreed with him, protected him. The gate was closed to anybody who might upset him. News from the outside world came to him filtered through the agency. When he left the old stone house and drove down the hill into Hollywood, it was like a bucket of ice water in his face.

Dean Gooch's series was continuing in the *Times*. He had covered the three original people Fain had brought back and was now into the bizarre stories of the later ones. Other newspapers had picked up the story and were playing it big, along with television and radio.

There was talk of an official investigation of his activities as soon as it was decided which governmental bureau had jurisdiction. The religious community, unusually silent during the weeks Fain was a hero, were now after him like a pack of hounds. Editorials from all points of the political compass were unanimous in condemning the man they hailed as a near Messiah a couple of weeks earlier.

Fain parked on Hollywood Boulevard and wandered the tacky street like a drugged alien. He bought a *Times*, a *Herald*, and a *USA Today* and read of the disintegration of his people and the calls for his own punishment. He began to feel as though he might be seized at any moment and dragged off to some dank dungeon.

He returned to his car and drove up near La Cienega to a small, expensive hotel where celebrities stayed who did not want their pictures taken. It was done in California mission style with a central patio containing outdoor tables and a small sparkling pool. Fain parked on the street out in front and went into the small, tasteful lobby to register.

The clerk read the card he filled out and looked up at him in surprise. "McAllister Fain?"

"Yes. You *do* have a room?"

Still staring, the clerk nodded and handed him a key. "It's number fourteen, through the patio and on the right. Do you have luggage, Mr. Fain?"

"I'll bring it in later. Right now I just want to relax." He took the key and headed for the glass doors leading out to the patio. He could feel the eyes of the hotel staff on him. He went outside and crossed the small patio to reenter the hotel on the far side. His room was the first one off the hallway on his right.

The furniture was in soft earth tones and of excellent quality. Restful framed prints hung on the walls. A sliding glass door gave out on the patio and pool area. This was now curtained by heavy drapery.

Fain double-locked the door, peeled off his jacket, and dropped into a chair. It was still early afternoon, but he was bone-weary. He leaned back, closed his eyes, and let his mind drift.

Some fifteen minutes later, he jolted out of a light doze to the sound of a disturbance in the courtyard. It was a subdued babble of voices and the rustle of people moving around. He got up to part the draperies and look outside.

He recoiled at the sudden sight of faces looking at him. A crowd of maybe twenty people had gathered outside his room on the patio. When Fain pulled back the curtain, they surged toward him, pointing and calling out to one another. Their words came clearly to him through the glass.

"There he is."

"Is that really him?"

"Sure, he looks just like his picture."

"What's he doing here?"

"Is somebody dead in there?"

"If he's staying here, I'm leaving."

For a frightening moment he thought they were coming right in through the glass after him. He whipped the drapery back across the window and backed away. The voices were louder outside now; there were shouts and heavy footsteps as more people came to see what the excitement was.

Fain snatched up his jacket and bolted from the room. He dashed up the hallway and sprinted across the courtyard to the hotel's lobby. He ignored the goggling clerk as shouts rose behind him, and he heard the sound of running feet. The sound of the crowd had changed from curiosity to anger. For the first time in years he knew cold physical fear.

Out in front of the hotel he leaped into his car, fired the engine, and peeled away as the crowd spilled out under the canvas marquee and pointed toward him. Not until he had made half a dozen fast turns and was sure no one followed did he slow down and relax.

He pulled into the lot of a Thrifty Drug Store on Western Avenue and sat in his car for several minutes while his heartbeat returned to normal. He pushed down the panic and began to make plans. With an idea at last of what he was going to do, he went into the store and bought a Dodger baseball cap and a pair of nearly opaque sunglasses. Outside he put them on and checked his reflection in the plate-glass show window. With the cap pulled low and the glasses concealing his eyes, he was not so recognizable.

He drove off again and this time chose a seedy motel near Western Avenue. He paid the bored clerk in advance for a room and was relieved when his Dodger cap and shades drew no more than a passing glance.

The bed was narrow, with a ragged brown spread over what appeared to be army blankets. The vinyl furniture was spotted with cigarette burns, and the whole place smelled of deodorizer. But at least for the moment he was secure.

He knew it would not last. Too many people in Los Angeles knew him on sight, and the cap and glasses would not hide him for long. The best move, he decided, would be to get out of town and let things cool down. For that he would need money, but that was something he had plenty of. It was time to collect some of his earnings. He used a pay telephone in the tiny lobby to call Federated Artists.

When he got past the switchboard, a familiar voice said, "Mr. Echols's office."

"Hi, Victoria," he said. "Put Warner on."

"May I say who's calling?"

"For Christ's sake, it's Mac Fain."

"One moment, Mr. Fain. I'll see if he's in."

Soft tinkly music came out of the telephone. Fain ground his teeth.

Victoria returned. "Mr. Echols is out of the office. May I take a message?"

"Oh, for— No, forget it."

He slammed the receiver back into the cradle. A week ago a call from the star client would have had the agency falling all over itself to accommodate him. So much for fame.

He returned to his seedy room, put on the cap and shades, and left for the Sunset and Cahuenga branch of the Bank of California, where the agency had opened an account for him. He took out the leather-covered virgin checkbook and wrote his first check. He made it out for a thousand dollars and took it to one of the tellers. She looked at the check, smiled at Fain, and excused herself. She went away with the check and returned a minute later with a smooth-faced Oriental man.

He showed no surprise at the baseball cap and dark glasses. This was, after all, Hollywood. "I'm Benson Kano, Mr. Fain, operations officer. May I help you?"

"Yes, you can cash my check."

The operations officer clicked a professional smile on and off. "I'll be glad to, Mr. Fain, as soon as you get the other signature."

"What other signature? It's my account. I've got more than a hundred thousand dollars in the account."

"Yes, sir, it's all in order, but the account was set up so that in addition to yours we require the signature of Mr. Nolan Dix of Federated Artists."

"I don't believe this," Fain said. "Is there someone else here I can talk to?"

"Of course, sir," Kano said politely. "I can take you in to see our manager, but I assure you—"

"Ah, never mind." Fain was already drawing curious looks from the bank employees. He did not have time to get into an argument with the manager. It would be easier to get the agency attorney to sign the required check, or several of them.

The offices of Federated Artists were housed in an English Tudor-style building along the most fashionable stretch of Sunset. Fain left his disguise in the car this time and entered the building.

He breezed past the Miss Universe receptionist and strode to Warner Echols's office. Victoria Clifford sat at a desk outside his door, talking on the telephone. She flicked her eyes up at Fain with no sign of recognition. He waited a full minute for her to hang up.

"Tell Warner I'm here," he said.

"Mr. Echols is still not in, Mr. Fain," she said with icy courtesy.

"When *will* he be in?"

"I really couldn't say. Probably not for the rest of the day."

"Yeah, I'll bet."

He stepped past Victoria's desk, ignoring her protests, and pushed open the door to Echols's office. It was empty.

"I told you," Victoria said, arching one of her perfectly shaped brows.

"So you did."

He left the plush suite of offices where the agents entertained clients and entered the more conservative legal department. Nolan Dix's secretary, unlike those in the rest of the suite, looked as though she could really type. She smiled at Fain, apparently not recognizing him.

"I'd like to see Mr. Dix," he said.

"May I say who's—" she began.

"Never mind," he cut her off. He understood by now that his name would not get him past any doors here. He walked unannounced into the attorney's office and found Dix at his desk, studying a boating magazine.

"Well, hello, Fain," he said, seeming not terribly surprised.

"I just came from the bank," Fain said.

"Yes?"

"I was told I need your signature on my checks to draw out any of my money."

"That's customary," Dix said smoothly. "It's done primarily for the protection of our clients."

"I fail to see how that protects me," Fain said, "but don't bother to explain." He lay the checkbook on the glass desktop in front of Dix. "Just sign half a dozen of those for me and I'll be on my way."

Nolan Dix ran his manicured fingertips across the leather checkbook as though savoring the texture. He said, "I'm afraid I can't do that."

Fain stifled an impulse to pound the desk and yell at the smug attorney. In a tightly controlled voice he said, "Why . . . not?"

Dix looked up at him. His small eyes were cold under the heavy lids. "There is litigation involved here."

"What's the bottom line, Nolan?"

"Just this—I have been informed this morning that you, and by implication Federated Artists, have been named in two lawsuits, with others imminent."

"Somebody is suing me? Who? Why?"

The attorney slid out a desk drawer and produced a folder. He opened it and read from the top sheet. "The family of Sharon Isaacs is charging misrepresentation, fraud, practicing medicine without a license, and causing great pain and suffering to their daughter."

"Pain and suffering? She was dead, for Christ's sake. A suicide. Those people begged me to do something for her."

Nolan Dix went on as though Fain had not spoken. "Mr. and Mrs. Alberto Ledo have contacted the Latino Legal Assistance League and filed essentially the same charges on behalf of their son, Miguel, now missing."

"That's ridiculous."

"So it may be, but I have advance information that

the families of Ada Dempsey, the hit-run victim, and Barney Quail are preparing similar suits.''

''Barney Quail was a goddamn transient,'' Fain said. ''A bum. He didn't have a family.''

''It seems one turned up,'' Dix said. ''And I very much doubt that these will be the last. ''So you see, it's really impossible to free up your funds at the present times, considering the upcoming legal problems.''

Fain started at him as the words sank in. ''Nolan, I have exactly''—he took out his wallet and counted the bills—''exactly a hundred and forty dollars. I can't show my face anywhere in town without inciting a lynch mob. I need money to get away.''

Nolan Dix spread his hands. ''I'd like to help you, but there's nothing I can do.''

The intercom unit on his desk beeped electronically. The attorney touched a key and said, ''Yes, Miriam?''

''There are reporters out here, Mr. Dix. And a television cameraman. They heard somewhere that Mr. Fain is with you.''

''Oh, shit,'' said Fain.

Dix pointed to a door at the rear of the office. ''There's a hallway out there that will lead you to the rear entrance,'' he said. ''I don't suppose you feel like dealing with the media just now.''

Fain gave him a long look but, with the rising clamor in the outer office, swallowed his anger and slipped out the back way.

Chapter 26

Fain lay on his back on the narrow motel bed and followed a crack in the ceiling with his eyes. It roughly outlined the shape of a scorpion, its stinging tail poised to strike at the light fixture.

He imagined the tail jabbing forward into the light bulb and through it into the socket. A shower of sparks sprayed out and drifted to the floor.

His fantasy was interrupted by sounds coming from the adjoining room. Through the wall he could hear a woman squeal in feigned ecstasy. A man laughed through phlegmy lungs. The Horizon Motel, he had discovered, was a favorite of the down-scale hookers of Western Avenue.

He closed his eyes and willed his other senses inward as he concentrated on his predicament. It all seemed so unfair. He had not set out to hurt anyone or to profit off the misery of others. All he wanted to do was help people, make them happy. If he could get rich doing that, why not?

Rich. Hah. What did all those contracts and TV shows and personal appearances add up to? One hundred and forty dollars and a bed in a hot-sheet motel. And that hundred and forty would shrink fast. He had better get his brain working.

A sound gradually intruded on his concentration. A staccato percussive sound. Someone was knocking at his door.

Fain rolled off the bed and moved cautiously over to stand next to the door. Another crowd of hostile curiosity seekers? Process server? Police?

Shit, he was getting paranoid.

"Who is it?"

"Let me in." The voice was female, low and vibrant. Something in the tone compelled him to obey.

He unbolted the door and opened it.

The woman who stood outside was nearly as tall as he. The skin was dark and smooth across wide cheekbones. Her mouth, full and firm, was not smiling. The thick hair that fell loose to her shoulders was midnight black with strands of silver, giving it a lively sheen. The woman looked at him with eyes of pale gray that were a startling contrast to the dark face.

"Hello, McAllister Fain." She stepped past him and seemed to flow into the room. She wore a long, colorful dress that moved with her body.

Fain stared at her. He knew at once who she was even though he had not seen her in almost thirty years. It took the logical portion of his brain several moments to catch up with the intuitive.

"Darcia?"

"Yes."

A hundred questions pushed forward in his mind. He asked one of them. "How did you find me?"

"That was not so hard. I have known where you were since I called you at your apartment many weeks ago."

Fain thought back to Echo Park and when all his troubles began. A telephone voice registered on his memory. He said, "A woman asked if I was the McAllister Fain from Michigan, then hung up."

"I was that woman. When I read in the paper what you had done, I knew it must be you and that you had discovered your power. But I had to be sure."

He shook his head as though to clear it. "Darcia, why are you here?"

"I have many things to tell you. May we sit down?"

234

"Yes. Sure." He pulled the room's one comfortable chair over for her, and he sat on the bed.

"What did you mean when you said I had discovered my power?"

"The power to make the dead walk."

"That was as big a surprise to me as to anybody."

Darcia shook her head. "You always had it locked deep within you, but you needed the key. You must have found someone to give you the key."

Fain could not take his eyes off the woman. Her gaze held him like a physical bond. He said, "I went to an old shaman called Le Docteur. He told me what to do. I thought I was just fooling around. Later, I found it was all for real, and I didn't even need most of the rigmarole he gave me."

"Ah, yes. All you needed was the key. It would have been so much better if you had never learned what you could do. No matter what happens now, you must never, never use this terrible power again."

"I already decided that," Fain said. "I've got nothing but trouble now because of it."

"That is always the way, but it was inevitable that one day you would learn about yourself and would have to try."

"How do you know all this?" Fain said. "What is this power, and where does it come from? Why me?"

"I will come to that," said the woman. "Listen to me carefully now as I tell you of the danger you are in and what you must do."

"What danger?" he said.

"Desperate danger of life and death. Those you brought back understand by now what has been done to them. They have one common goal, and that is to destroy you."

"Are you kidding?" He looked into the luminous gray eyes. "No, you're not kidding."

Darcia continued. "They will come at night, and they will come very soon."

"But why should they want to hurt me?" Fain said.

"Revenge," said the woman.

"For what? I only wanted to help them and those who loved them."

"That is not important. The souls of those people no longer inhabit the bodies. The things that now walk the earth—the things you brought back—are soulless, mindless creatures that know only that you are the one responsible for their agony. As their physical bodies continue to decay, they have only one mission—to destroy you."

The woman was silent for a moment. Fain was not sure how seriously to take all this. She might be completely wacko. But in his heart he knew better. This woman spoke the truth. Finally, he said, "Suppose I just took off? How could they find me?"

"I found you," she said. "You can run; you can keep running. You may stay ahead of them for a day or a month or a year. But you cannot run forever, and when you stop, they will find you. You are tied to them forever, and as long as they exist and you exist, you will not escape."

"Sounds pretty grim," he said.

"There is more," said Darcia. "The danger is not only to you. Your friends will suffer, too."

"I have no friends," he said. "Not anymore."

"Yes, you have. There are those who care for you, those who have helped you, wittingly or not. The living dead ones will strike at you through them if they must. It is up to you to warn them."

Fain leaned forward, bringing his face closer to the woman's. "Who . . . are . . . you?" he said.

"You know," she said. "Look at my eyes."

He did. The woman's eyes were the same shade of pale gray, silver-flecked, as his. Deep within those eyes he sensed a reflection of the same fire that smoldered in his own.

"I am your mother," she said.

For a moment he could not speak. He knew instinctively that what the woman said was true. Finally, he managed, "And my father?"

"He is the man you have always believed him to be."

"You and he . . ."

"Yes."

236

"And my . . . my father's wife— What about her?"

"She was a very kind woman. Because of my illness I was unable to raise a child. She adopted you and brought you up as her own."

"Did she know about you and my father?"

"She never spoke of it. None of us did. But she was a perceptive woman. I think in her heart she knew."

"And you stayed with us."

"I did. Until your father was widowed. Then it was time for me to go. I promised myself I would never interfere in your life. Not unless it was necessary. Now it is. I tried to see you when you were in the big house in the hills, but I was turned away."

"You told them you were my mother."

"Yes."

Fain closed his eyes and massaged them. "God, this is all happening so fast." He looked at the woman again. "This . . . power—where does it come from?"

"From my family, my blood. There is a Shawnee word for it, but it would mean nothing to you. We all have a little of it. Some of us can read thoughts; others foresee the future or find lost objects. But the power to make the dead walk is given blessedly to only a few. One male child in every other generation. My father had the power. His grandfather. Now you, my son. I pray that you will be the last."

"Darcia, what can I do?"

"You must protect your friends. Through no fault of their own, they are menaced by your acts."

"I'll do what I can. But isn't there some way to end this horror?"

"You must send them back. All those you called from beyond the shadows, you must return there."

"But how? How can I do that?"

"I cannot tell you, my son. The man who gave you the terrible key to your power must show you how to reverse it. There is no other way."

The tall Indian woman rose from the chair. "I must go now."

He stood up and faced her. "When will I see you again?"

"You will not. There is no time left for me."

"But—"

She reached out and gently placed two fingers on his lips, silencing him.

"Good-bye, my son."

She turned from him and floated out the door, closing it soundlessly behind her. Fain stared after her but made no move to follow. He knew she would be gone.

As he stood there, trying to assimilate the things Darcia had told him, he became slowly aware that it was growing dark in the room.

They will come at night and they will come soon.

Well, if his walking corpses were coming after him, he was sure as hell not going to make it easy for them. He shrugged into his jacket and left the room, heading for the lobby.

The clerk sat behind his Plexiglas shield, reading the *Herald* sports page. A heavily made-up woman in a miniskirt and white vinyl boots was on the telephone, arguing with somebody. Fain waited impatiently for her to finish.

Finally, he tapped her on the shoulder. "I have to make a very important call. Would you mind . . . ?"

"Fuck you," she said, withering him with a look.

He seethed impotently while she talked for another two minutes. Just as he was ready to bolt out and find another phone, she hung up and sashayed past him with a sneer.

Fain dug out a fistful of silver and dropped coins into the machine. He dialed Jillian's number, the black receiver slippery in his sweating palm.

"Hi. This is Jillian Pappas. I'm sorry I can't take your call personally right now . . ."

"Shit!" The clerk did not bother to look up from his sports page at Fain's expletive.

Friends. Was there another friend besides Jillian? No one he had met during the past couple of months, for sure. And before that? It was scary to realize how few real friends he had ever had.

He dug through his wallet, looking for another number, and found it scribbled on the back of some forgotten realtor's business card. He fed more coins into the pay phone and dialed again.

The receiver buzzed ten times in his ear. Fain ground his teeth and tried to will an answer on the other end.

"So hello." Ivy Hurlbut's voice was tight with irritation, but Fain sagged with relief at hearing her.

"Ivy, it's Mac."

"Wow, the modern Messiah calling poor plain little me. I'm thrilled beyond words."

He ignored the sarcasm. "Listen, this is important. I've got to see you right away."

"Are you drunk?"

"Stone sober."

"Then what the hell is the idea? You dropped me like a hot potato when you went big time with your Hollywood agency and six-figure-a-year writers. Now you call out of the blue and want to see me. Right away, no less. Well, I'm working, hotshot. I've got a deadline day after tomorrow, and I've got five thousand words to go on a ten-thousand-word story. I should have left the phone off the hook."

"Wait a minute, Ivy," he shouted into the mouthpiece. "Don't hang up. You can call me all the names you want to later. I deserve it. But I have to see you tonight."

"You don't sound so good," she said.

"I'm not. Tell me the quickest way to get to your place and I'll be right there."

"Where are you?"

"Sunset and Western."

"You're calling me from a massage parlor?"

"I'll explain later. Just give me your address."

"Come all the way out the Santa Monica Freeway, hang a left on Main. Drive a couple of miles, past the Auditorium, then hang another left on Violet. It's a little-bitty street right where Santa Monica turns into Venice. I'm half a block up on the right. You can't miss it, I'm the only house on the street."

"Stay put," Fain said. "I'll be there as fast as I can."

"Mac?" All the anger was gone from her voice.

"Yeah?"

"What's going on?"

"I'll explain as best I can when I get there," he said. "It would sound too crazy over the phone."

He hung up the receiver gently.

Ivy Hurlbut sat for a minute with the phone in her hand after Mac had broken the connection. She had been prepared to really chew him out, dumping her the way he did, then calling when she was trying like hell to squeeze words out of an idea that wasn't working. But the tone of his voice had drained her indignation. Chilled her.

She replaced the instrument and shivered. She was not close enough to the ocean to hear the surf, but the nightly mist curled in around her little house shortly after dusk. She crossed the living room to close the front window and went back to the desk she had set up in a corner of the bedroom.

The frame cottage where Ivy lived was the last survivor on a street where similar little houses had lined both sides. A shopping center was going in there—as if the city needed another one—and her cottage was the last survivor. It was scheduled for bulldozing next month.

She tried to concentrate on the sheet in her typewriter, but the words would not make sense. It was an article on the changing beach scene that she had sold to *Los Angeles* magazine on the basis of a two-page outline. Now the whole thing seemed trite and overdone to her. She reread the sheaf of finished pages, trying to pick up the flow of ideas.

She raised her head at a soft sound at the front door.

Ivy cocked her head and listened. Sometimes the wind created odd noises here. The doorbell had never worked during her residence, and visitors had to knock.

It came again. Not exactly a knock, but more of a spongy thump. It was too soon for Mac to have made it all the way from Hollywood, but somebody was out there. She got up and went to look.

There were no close neighbors to hear Ivy Hurlbut scream.

Chapter 27

The beach town of Venice was striving to hold on to its reputation for funkiness—a laid-back community where nobody got hassled and everybody did his own thing. It was a losing battle. With Santa Monica in the grip of rent-control laws, developers and builders focused their attention on Venice, just to the south. High-rise, high-priced apartments and condos were rapidly pushing out the beach cottages and boardwalk hustlers.

Mac Fain drove past Violet Street the first time, missing the street sign in the lowering fog and under the old-fashioned incandescent streetlight. He found it on the way back and drove slowly up to the lone cottage.

He parked out in front, and his flesh tightened as he saw the lights on and the front door standing open. Not a good omen. He got out and looked around carefully. Nothing stirred in the misty night. Moving cautiously, he walked up the path to the front door and looked in.

Ivy Hurlbut, what was left of her, lay against the far wall. Her head was turned toward the door, giving Fain a look he would never forget. Her throat and the upper part of her body had been torn away. The tiny living room was awash with her blood.

Fain backed away from the scene, fighting down an

impulse to be sick. He stumbled back to his car, got in, slammed and locked the door.

It could have been some doped-up crazies. They were not unknown in the new Venice. Or a robbery. Sure. And it could have been a band of maurading nuns. Quit kidding, Fain told himself. He knew who had destroyed Ivy Hurlbut. He had been warned. It was his people. The terrible walking-dead ones he had brought back. Unable to reach him, they had struck out at someone they saw as his friend. Ivy had written about him; she had been present when he revived Miguel Ledo. Darcia's words—his mother's words—echoed in his head. "Your friends will suffer too."

He had to bring this to an end before someone else was struck down. Jillian. If they found Ivy, they could find Jillian. Maybe she had escaped tonight only because she was not home. Or was she lying there now, ripped apart like Ivy Hurlbut, her answering machine giving out its bland reassuring message? Fain got into his car and headed for Studio City, ignoring all speed limits.

It was after eleven when he pulled up in front of the building where Jillian had her studio apartment. He went in through the nonsecure entrance and thumped up the stairs. Jillian's door was locked. He banged on it until a woman came out of an apartment across the hall, wearing a chenille robe and a scowl.

"What the hell's the idea? You want to wake the whole building?"

"I've got to see Jillian Pappas. Family emergency."

The woman's scowl lightened up. "Oh. Well, she's out to rehearsal. Goes every night."

"Do you know where she's rehearsing?"

"No, I don't pay any attention. She'll prob'ly be home pretty soon, though."

"Thanks." At least she wasn't in there like Ivy.

Fain checked his watch. Eleven-thirty. He sat in his car out in front of the building and waited.

The shadows of the night seemed filled with moving shapes as Fain sat watching. He lit one cigarette after another and, coughing, snapped them though the window, sending little spinning red arcs to the asphalt.

He tried to make some sense out of what was happening and figure out a plan. So many questions. What were the chances that the dead ones were nearby? How quickly could they have got here from Ivy Hurlbut's cottage in Venice? They certainly couldn't have beaten him. But why couldn't they have split up?

He ticked them off on his fingers, beginning with Leanne Kruger and ending up with tragic Ada Dempsey, the hit-and-run victim. Nine. Nine dead people brought back to life. More accurately, brought part of the way back. Now existing in what Darcia called a "living hell." They might have split up. Some to Venice for Ivy, some here to Studio City. And the rest out in the night, looking for him.

He renewed his scrutiny of the block where Jillian lived. Apartment buildings. Quiet, innocent. Ordinary, comfortable lives going on behind their curtained windows. Would he, Fain wondered, ever live such a life again?

There were few cars and fewer pedestrians. Fain studied each of the passersby carefully. They appeared normal enough, but would he recognize the dead ones in the dark?

And what if they had already found Jillian, wherever she was? The vision of poor torn Ivy Hurlbut swam before him, with Jillian's face superimposed. The waiting became agony.

At a quarter to one a familiar little Mustang rounded the corner and parked across the street. When he saw Jillian get out, Fain all but collapsed with relief. He leaped from the car and sprinted across to reach her as she was locking the door. He swept her into his arms.

She gasped in surprise. "Mac? What are you doing here? What's wrong?"

He held her tight, and she yielded to the urgency of his embrace. All the things they had not said to each other for months were spoken through their bodies.

"Thank God you're all right."

"Sure I'm all right." She drew back enough to look up into his face. "But you're not, are you."

"Do you trust me, Jill?"

"Well . . ."

243

"I mean, if it were something really important."

"I guess so."

"Would you do something crazy if I told you it was a matter of life and death?"

"Is this a big joke of some kind?"

"Believe me, it is no joke."

"What crazy thing do you want me to do?"

"Come away with me right now."

"Come away with you? Wait a minute; you're not proposing marriage, are you?"

"Hell, I don't know. What difference does that make?"

"Quite a lot of difference, mister. I have a life of my own going, you know, and if you think I'm going to chuck everything and go bucketing off with you on a moment's notice, you can just fleeping forget it."

She turned and started toward the apartment building. He followed.

"Wait, Jill. I'll marry you in a minute if you'll have me. I love you, damn it."

She kept going. "Oh, sure, when all else fails, they offer marriage."

"Listen to me, Jill. Ivy Hurlbut's dead. You're in danger."

She whirled and faced him. "Ivy's dead? When?"

"Tonight. In a way it's my fault. I don't want it to happen to you."

Jillian looked up at him. Her tears glittered in the street lamps. "Darn it, Mac, I didn't want to have anything more to do with you. I don't know what you've got yourself into, but the things I've been reading are just terrible. I wish I knew what to do. I . . . I . . . oh, shoot!"

She pushed open the door to her building and walked in. Fain caught it before it closed and ran after her. She climbed quickly up the steps to her apartment, turning there to face him.

"You'd better leave now. I don't think I want to talk anymore."

"Jill, don't—"

She opened the door and reached in to flip the wall switch. As Fain put out a hand to stop her, she was jerked away from him and pulled into the darkened room.

Fain stumbled in after her. He groped for something to hang on to, found only air, staggered and barely kept his balance.

The door slammed shut behind him.

"Jill!" he called.

"Something grabbed me," she said out of the darkness.

He banged into the wall and scrabbled along it, looking for a light switch. He stumbled over an electric cord, followed it until he found a lamp, and switched it on.

Jillian was crouched against the far wall next to where the little kitchen alcove was. Standing in front of her was a tall figure, long arms outstretched to seize her. Its head turned to look at Fain.

"Holy Christ!"

Kevin Jackson was still recognizable, although the gleaming ebony skin was turned a mottled gray, with oozing cracks beginning to open. The eyes had a milky film, but there was a fire within. He took a step toward Fain.

"Stop!"

Kevin, or the thing he was now, shook his head. "Look what you done to me, man. Look what I am. This what you did to all of us. Now you gon' die."

He lunged forward and reached for Fain. Fain ducked and chopped at one of the outstretched arms. It was like slamming his hand into a tree branch. He staggered back; Kevin swiped at him with one hand and hit him a glancing blow. Fain went to his hands and knees on the floor. Fireflies buzzed around the darkness in his eyes. He wanted to go to sleep.

The crash of breaking glass brought him out of it. Jillian stood holding the handle of a heavy glass pitcher. The rest of it was on the floor in fragments. There was a dent in the side of Kevin's head, but he seemed otherwise unaffected by the blow. He came toward Fain.

Fain scrambled to his feet and backed toward the wall. He raised one hand above his head, looked up at it, and seemed to snatch something out of the air. For a second Kevin followed the misdirection. Fain opened the hand and a shower of coins spilled to the floor.

Using the distraction, he lowered his head and charged. The top of Fain's head hit Kevin Jackson just below the breastbone. The impact carried both of them across the room. A window shattered, and Fain clutched the sill for support as a cool wind blew in his face. Below him outside there was a soft thump, a grunt, and the scrape of feet on concrete.

Fain pushed himself back from the window and spoke to Jillian, still holding the glass pitcher handle. "What's down there?"

"Courtyard," she said. "He'll have to go out through the alley."

"Come on; we can get to the car."

He took Jillian's hand, and they ran together across the room to the door. Fain yanked it open and they took one step into the hallway. Then stopped. Standing between them and the stairway was what looked like a badly made female dummy. The shoulders were uneven, a hand was mashed into hamburger, and one leg hung useless. The face was a mass of old bruises and congealed blood. One eyes was closed, and the other blinked incessantly. From the mouth came a soft whimpering sound.

"Mac, what is it?" Jillian said.

He did not answer, but he recognized this ruin of a woman as Ada Dempsey.

"Go for the car," he said to Jillian, and used both his hands in an attempt to sweep the woman aside.

The broken body offered little resistance, but her one good hand fastened onto his forearm like a steel clamp. He tried to pry the fingers loose, but they would not give a millimeter. *Death grip* floated in and out of his mind as he clawed to free himself.

In desperation he reached into his pocket and pulled out the cheap butane lighter he had bought when he started smoking again. He flicked up the flame and held it under the wrist of the ruined woman. He smelled the flesh burning and heard the sizzle, but the twisted face of the woman showed nothing.

There was a sudden *pop* as a tendon in the wrist gave way. One of the clutching fingers went dead. Fain dropped the lighter, and using all the strength terror could summon, clawed free of the wounded hand.

He sprang for the stairway and went down it, barely touching the treads. He could hear the woman bumping and flopping down behind him. Out in the street he bolted across to his car where, thank God, Jillian was waiting for him. Someone else was running for it in long, loping strides from the end of the street. Kevin Jackson.

Jillian pushed open the door, and he jammed himself in behind the wheel. He fired the engine, and they peeled away. Fain did not slow down until many miles separated them from the ghoulish things back at Jillian's apartment.

The rest of the night they drove the freeways. It was said you could drive for weeks on the Los Angeles freeway system without ever driving over the same patch of pavement twice. Fain was ready to believe it.

Jillian dozed fitfully with her head on his shoulder while he worked out a plan. His overpowering instinct was to point the car in one direction, away from Los Angeles, and drive like hell. But you can't run forever, Darcia had said. And when he stopped, *they* would be there. These walking-dead things were his responsibility, and he had to deal with them here and now.

By the time the eastern sky faded from black to charcoal, he knew what he was going to do.

Jillian awoke and made little mewing sounds as the charcoal sky turned pearl gray.

"Where are we going?"

"I'm going to drop you somwhere where you'll be safe today; then I'm going to go and finish this business. Is there a friend you can stay with?"

"I don't want to stay with a friend. I'm with you."

"Come on, honey; you saw what we're fighting."

"You said 'we.' "

"Slip of the tongue."

"Phooey. Besides, I'm reponsible for you now."

He glanced over at her. "How do you figure that?"

"When I hit that mother with the pitcher, it might have slowed him down just enough to let you get out of the way. Saved your life. Now I'm responsible."

"Seems I heard that somewhere else not long ago. You can't fight Oriental philosophy."

"By the way, what was that business with the coins? I never saw you do that one."

"An improvised variation of the Miser's Dream. Old trick but effective."

"Thank goodness."

"And amen."

"So where are we going?"

"We've got several stops to make, and I want to have everything ready by nightfall. First, how would you like to go to a motel?"

"At a time like this?"

"That later," he said. "I've got some things in a place on Sunset I'm going to need."

He swung off the Hollywood Freeway on Sunset and turned toward Western. The sun was up now. Another beautiful California day.

Chapter 28

" 'Mid pleasures and palaces," Fain said, steering into the parking lot of the Horizon Motel, "there's no place like home."

"Golly, Toto," said Jillian, "I don't think we're in Kansas anymore."

As they walked past the office, the desk man tapped on the window with a quarter and beckoned Fain inside.

"With you in a minute," he told Jillian, and entered the office.

Through the grill in the Plexiglas shield the clerk said, "You didn't sleep here last night."

"So?"

"So that don't mean it was free. If you're stayin' another day, it's another thirty dollars."

Fain peeled the money off his thin sheaf of bills and paid.

The clerk rolled his eyes toward Jillian, who waited just outside. "You didn't like the local stuff?"

"Nothing personal," Fain said, "but I haven't had all my shots."

In the room Fain tested the window to be sure it could not be opened, then pointed out the bolt lock and chain to Jillian. "As soon as I'm out, lock everything. Don't open the door until you're sure it's me."

"How long will you be, Mac?" The artificial banter of the parking lot was gone now. "I'm scared."

"I'll be back as soon as I can." He kissed her. "And if you want to know the truth, I'm scared, too. But I'll get us out of this. You watch."

"By magic?"

"A little magic," he told her, "couldn't hurt."

The People's Sunshine Clinic looked exactly as it had on Fain's last visit. Fain did not bother with his disguise. No one here would be looking for him. The left-over hippies in the waiting room wore the same outdated sixties clothes and spaced-out expressions. Giving them a casual once-over, Fain diagnosed two drug overdoses, a probable herpes, and one case of what looked like terminal acne. He felt like an old-timer here as he walked on through the NO ADMITTANCE door to where the young woman with the enormous eyes worked at a makeshift desk.

"You're not supposed to come back here," she said.

"I'm not a patient," Fain told her. "I have business with Le Docteur."

Her eyes narrowed. She started to rise.

Fain held up his hands, palms out. "Please don't call the two goons this time. I've been all through it with them. Just tell Le Docteur that McAllister Fain is here."

The young woman looked him over carefully and apparently decided he was no immediate threat. She said, "I'll tell him, but he won't like it."

"Thank you," Fain said. "I'll risk it."

The woman went out the back way. Fain stood impatiently around the desk and listened to the howling of one of the ODs in the waiting room.

In a few minutes she came back, wearing a surprised look. "Le Docteur remembers you," she said. "He's out in the back. You know where that is?"

"I know," Fain told her. "Thanks."

He went out and picked his way through the weed-grown patch of dirt to the corrugated metal shed. The door was closed, but the padlock was hanging open. Fain knocked, bruising his knuckles.

"Come," said the high, clear voice he remembered.

Fain pulled open the door and stepped into the shed. The air was hot and humid. The enormous black man sat in the same chair he had taken before. He wore a tentlike caftan into which were woven geometric patterns. His body seemed to fill the cramped little building.

"Close the door," Le Docteur ordered.

Fain obeyed. A flickering illumination came from two sputtering candles on the rickety folding table. There was no visible opening for ventilation.

"Sit," the black man said.

Fain eased himself into the second chair across the table from Le Docteur.

"I was expecting you before this."

"Then you know why I'm here?" Fain said.

"It is not difficult to guess, but I would like you to tell me."

"I want to know how to send back the people I called up from the dead."

"Of course you do. The ceremony is very simple, but I told you the last time it would be costly."

"I haven't much money, but I can get more."

Le Docteur made a wheezing sound that might have been a laugh or a growl. "Keep your money. I told you it is of no use to me. Your cost for this secret will be something much dearer than money."

Fain waited. The huge black man sat motionless, watching him. Waiting for him to ask. So he did. "What is the cost?"

"Your life's blood," said Le Docteur.

The stale air in the shed seemed to thicken as they sat in silence for several seconds. As before, Fain had the sense of things mystical and forbidden writhing on the walls.

To break the spell, he said, "You don't mean that literally?"

"I do not speak in metaphors. Your blood is the essential ingredient in the formula I will give you." He reached into the folds of the caftan and brought out two crumpled slips of paper. "This," he said, handing Fain the first, "is the formula. And these are the words."

Fain squinted, trying to make out the smudged handwriting.

"The formula is not difficult. The ingredients are easily purchased except for the most essential one, which you must supply. The mixture is to be splashed on the dead ones as you say the words. In this way, and only in this way, will you send them back."

Fain looked up from the formula sheet. "Am I misreading this, or does it say here three liters of blood?"

"You read it correctly."

"If I remember my basic anatomy, a man my size has about twelve pints, or five-and-a-half liters, of blood in his body. You drain more than half of that away and the man dies."

"I told you the cost was high."

Fain's mind spun, searching for a way out. "What if I had the blood taken a little at a time and stored it?"

"Not acceptable. In combination with the formula and the words, the dead ones you would send back must see the blood flow from your body."

"I don't believe this."

"Then return my papers and go."

"No," Fain said quickly, "I didn't mean that the way it sounded. I guess I didn't expect the cost would be so . . . so final."

"No one ever does."

Fain peered at the two slips of paper again. "These words are French?"

"Mostly. You must say them exactly as written when you perform the ceremony."

"I see a flaw here," Fain said. "How am I supposed to be able to splash this mess around if I'm in a coma from blood loss?"

"That is a problem I cannot solve for you."

"And what's to keep these people from ripping me apart while I'm doing the mixing? I've met a couple of them recently, and they are not patient."

"That I can help you with." Le Docteur shifted his bulk and plucked something from a hook on the wall behind him. He handed it to Fain.

It was a coil of finely braided rope, silky soft to the touch.

"It feels like human hair," said Fain.

"Yes," said Le Docteur. "It is plucked from . . . special heads. Place it full length on the ground between you and the dead ones. They will be unable to cross it while you prepare the formula. But do not delay. The power of the rope is limited."

"Like my blood supply," said Fain, shivering despite the stifling heat.

"Just so." Le Docteur reached out with a sausage thumb and forefinger to snuff out one of the candles. "Now go. Because you carry the power of the *gangan* I have given you secrets beyond a man's rightful knowledge. My business with you is finished. Do not come back to me. Ever."

"No," said Fain, still reading the formula. "I don't suppose I will."

He stood up, feeling suddenly giddy in the airless shed. As he opened the door and went out, the last candle died.

Fain sat in his car out in front of the clinic, oblivious to the hostile stares from the patrons of Big Mary's and the motorcycle shop. He read and reread the two slips of paper Le Docteur had given him. He refigured the amount of his fresh blood called for in the formula against the quantity of his body and came out with the same deadly result.

What the hell good would it do him to dispatch the dead souls if it left him a dry, dead man? But was there another choice? Run. But there had to be an end to running. And there was Jillian to consider. Come on, magic man, he told himself. It's time to pull off your greatest escape ever.

He looked at his watch and was surprised to see it was already past noon. As on his first visit, the time he spent with Le Docteur was squeezed out of proportion. If he was to be ready by the time night came again, he had to move. He made his decision and drove away.

Before returning to Jillian at the motel, Fain made four stops: a big chain drugstore, a medical-supply house, a meat packer in Vernon, and the Bekins warehouse in downtown Los Angeles. At the warehouse he spent twenty more of his dwindling dollars to reclaim part of his property.

When he returned to the Horizon Motel, Jillian was in a high state of nerves, and the sun was low in the west.

Chapter 29

"Where did you get the neat coat?" Jillian asked.

Fain ran a hand over the down-padded jacket. "Thrift shop. You like it?"

"I guess it goes with the funky baseball cap and the cheap shades.

"Thank you. I figured it would come in handy."

"I saw your picture on television," she said.

He made a last sweep of the motel room to be sure they had left nothing. "How did I look?" he said.

"You looked like somebody in trouble. Do you know there are a lot of people after you?"

Fain lowered the drugstore sunglasses and peered at her over the lenses. "Tell me about it."

"Did you really try to rob a bank this morning?"

"That's an exaggeration. All I wanted to do was cash a check."

"Do you think you ought to explain that before the police blow you away?"

Fain put both his hands on her shoulders. "Honey, if you were somebody in authority and I walked in and gave you my explanation of what's been going on, would you believe me?"

She shook her head. "I'd lock you up."

"The defense rests." He pulled off the shades and got

serious. "Jill, are you sure you want to be a part of this?"

"Are we always going to be fugitives?"

He shrugged. "For a while, anyway. But after tonight we won't have to worry about the walking dead anymore."

"Can you guarantee that?"

"No, but I'm going to give it my best shot."

"Call me crazy, but that's good enough for me, Mac Fain. I'm in."

"I'm relieved to hear that," he said, "because what I have worked out couldn't be done without you."

"Are you saying you need me?"

"I need you."

"I've waited a long time to hear that. Lead on, O Master of the Occult."

He needed the headlights for the drive up into the Hollywood Hills. The sky was still light in the west, but the shadows were deepening. He pulled to a stop at the gate before the private road leading to Eagle's Roost.

"It looks locked," Jillian said.

"Did locks stop Houdini?"

Fain got out of the car and worked over the padlock with a slim, saw-toothed pick. In less than a minute the shackle popped free. He opened the gate and returned to the car with a triumphant grin.

They drove slowly up the narrow, twisting road. An errant wind rustled the tree branches above them.

Jillian said. "How can you be sure they'll come tonight? The dead ones?"

"Some things a man just knows," he said. "My mother could probably explain it."

She looked at him curiously but said nothing more.

Fain parked in front of the big stone house and had the front door open in a few seconds. He was relieved to find that Federated Artists had not turned off the electricity. The night's work would be unpleasant enough without having to do it in the dark.

He walked through the house, turning on lights in all the rooms that were unsealed. He made sure the floodlights in front illuminated the approach up the road through the trees.

"I'm cold," Jillian said.

"All the rooms have fireplaces," he said. "Pick one where you want to wait and I'll start a blaze."

"It doesn't matter to me," she said. "They all look like something from a Christopher Lee movie."

Fain chose a room on one side of the house that was smaller than the rest. It had a high black-beamed ceiling, a curtained French window, heavy plush furniture, and a walk-in fireplace. Using wood from a supply stacked on the hearth, he soon had a crackling fire going.

He carried in the plastic bucket and the rest of his paraphernalia from the car. "Okay," he said. "Let's go over what we're going to have to do tonight."

"Do we get a rehearsal?" Jillian asked.

"Sorry, but due to the nature of the performance, it's strictly a one-shot. Now listen carefully."

Twenty minutes later he concluded, "So that's it. Any questions?"

She stared at him for a moment, then said, "Are you out of your mind?"

"I won't count that one."

"Mac . . . all that *blood*!"

"Honey, there isn't any other way. If there were, believe me, I'd take it."

"Jeepers!"

Fain took her in his arms and hugged her tightly. "If there wasn't another reason in the world, I think I'd love you just because you can use an expression like 'Jeepers.' "

"Are you sure it will work?" she asked, her mouth against his.

"No, but when you consider the alternative, I'd say it's worth a try."

He took his other purchases from the plastic bucket and emptied the contents of several bottles back into it. The mixture bubbled and steamed.

"Is it all right to mix that up beforehand?" Jillian asked.

"Yeah, except for the bl—" He saw her shudder.

"The crucial ingredient. That's the one they have to see go in."

"Sounds crazy to me."

"The workings of the world of magic are not for mortals to understand."

"Phooey."

"Let's go pick a good spot out in front to set up the show," he said. "We want something where we can see in all directions, and with an emergency escape route down the hill."

They walked out together into the chill night.

Fain paced back and forth in front of the house until he found a location off to the left of the entrance that satisfied him. It afforded a good view of the floodlit road and the edge of the surrounding wood. An unbroken stone wall would protect their backs.

"This will get it," he said. "We'll lay the hair rope down here in a half circle to make us a little stage."

"I'll go in and get it," Jillian offered.

The wind shifted subtly. Both of them sniffed the air.

Jillian made a face. "Wow, is something dead?" She covered her mouth as she realized what she had said.

"We'd better hurry it up," Fain said quietly.

As Jillian hurried inside, Fain reached into one of the jacket's deep pockets and pulled out the package he bought at the medical supply house. He unwrapped the package and checked its contents. A scalpel, surgical clamp, two feet of clear plastic tubing . . .

Glass crashed inside the house.

Jillian screamed.

"Mac, they're in here!" she cried.

He started toward the door but pulled up suddenly when a figure stepped between him and the entrance. A big man with a terrible wound in the front of his head. John Corely, the murdered policeman. Fluids from the bullet wound oozed down his face. He reached out for Fain and started forward.

"Jill!" Fain shouted. "Use the rope. Block yourself in a corner. They can't cross it."

He held the scalpel before him and feinted from side to side as the hulk of a policeman advanced. At the edge of his vision he could see other figures moving out of the trees.

Nice going, Fain, he told himself grimly. Preparation is ninety percent of a performance.

He ducked suddenly and tried to dash by under the policeman's outstretched arm. He was too slow. A hand, cold and leathery, clamped onto his face. The grip was like steel, and Fain thought his cheekbones would crack at any moment.

Fain bit at one of the fingers that was fastened across his mouth. He gagged as dead flesh came away with his teeth.

Unable to see, he gripped the scalpel and slashed blindly at the arm. He prayed that he would sever some vital muscle before the others reached him or before this one cracked his skull like an egg.

The hand went limp for a moment as his blade found nerve tissue. The fingers flexed for a renewed purchase on his head. Jerking free, Fain broke past the policeman and into the house.

He found Jillian in the room where they had built the fire. God bless her, she had stretched the silvery rope across the floor as he had told her, closing in a safe corner on the side of the room away from the fireplace. Inside the rope with Jillian was one tall-backed chair and, bless her again, the bucket of formula.

Fain sprinted past two foul-smelling creatures and joined her in the corner.

"Are you all right?" he panted.

"For the moment. What happened to your face?"

"It'll heal. Let's get set up."

He took a moment to look at the menacing figures that faced them across the rope. One was, or had been, female. Thick blond hair, now matted and tangled, framed the face on which flesh sagged from the wide-spaced cheekbones. Paula Foster, the movie star, let a few wrinkles take her to surgery, and to death. The other was old friend Kevin Jackson, his black face mottled with something like gray mold.

One by one the others came in the door and approached. Barney Quail, the transient, his toothless mouth a black hole in the dead stubbly face. John Corely the

259

policeman, seemingly unaware that the flesh of his right arm hung in shreds. Glenn Meiner, the brave young fireman. One empty eye socket squirmed with maggots. Ada Dempsey, the shattered hit-and-run victim, flopping her pitiful remains across the floor. Sharon Isaacs, the teenage suicide, swollen tongue coming out of her mouth like a dead white sausage. And finally, the most ravaged of all—a mass of putrescent flesh hanging loose in spots to reveal greasy yellow fat and pale bones. Leanne Kruger.

The two living people in the room were almost relieved when the lights suddenly went out. In the glow of the fire across the room, shadows leaped and danced like tormented things, but the loathsome details of decay in the walking dead were mercifully blurred.

"Here goes," Fain muttered to Jillian. He extended his arms to the sides and faced the misshapen figures that crowded the rope barrier, chattering and hissing at him. In a voice as strong as he could muster, he commanded, *"Mauvais nâmes . . . m'ecoutez!"*

The restless movement of the dead ones slowed. Fain continued with the words he had memorized from Le Docteur's incantation. The pronunciation he entrusted to the memory of his high school French.

"Regardez! Ce soir je vous renvois. Je vous delivre. Regardez!"

The only sound now was the crackle of the flames and the sigh of wind through the broken window.

"What did you say?" Jillian asked in a whisper.

"I told them the show was about to begin," Fain whispered back. In truth, he had only a general idea of the words' meaning, but they had the desired effect of quieting the dead ones. At least temporarily.

"Now comes the hard part," he said through gritted teeth. "Look away if you feel faint."

"I can take it if you can," she said.

Fain sat down slowly in the heavy chair. He positioned himself facing his grisly audience, with the steaming bucket of formula at his feet. Moving deliberately, he drew the scalpel and held it poised in his right hand. He inserted the point of the blade in the fabric of his left

260

jacket sleeve, halfway between the shoulder and elbow, and slit the material cleanly all the way down through the cuff. Wisps of down floated in the air as the quilted fabric parted.

He pulled the sleeve apart, exposing his bare arm, and laid the scalpel blade across the median cephalic vein. He glanced up at Jillian. Her eyes were large and luminous in the firelight. Fain winked at her, then sliced into his vein with the scalpel.

Jillian quickly handed him the plastic tubing and clamp. He had some difficulty attaching the tube to the open vein, once dropping the clamp while the loose jacket sleeve flapped over the wound. When he had the tube properly inserted, he held the open end up for the watchers to see as the crimson liquid quickly filled it.

"Avec le sang de mon coeur je vous renvoie!"

He dipped the open end of the tube toward the bucket. The dark scarlet blood flowed out, making a soft splash in the silent room.

With Jillian at his side, watching anxiously, Fain settled slowly in the chair as blood drained steadily into the bucket. She laid a hand on his shoulder. From time to time he looked up at her with a shadowed smile.

After many minutes, Fain raised his right hand. The small gesture cost him an effort. In a voice that had lost its timbre he said, *"Mauvais nâmes! Ne marchez pas jamais! Avec le sang de ma vie je vous renvois à travers la barrière!"*

McAllister Fain's eyes slid out of focus, and his head dropped forward as the blood continued to dribble from the tube into the bucket. Jillian clamped her teeth together, dipped her hands into the viscous red mixture, and splashed it out at the dead creatures beyond the rope.

The effect was instantaneous. The scarlet fluid spattered across the decaying flesh with the hiss of a virulent acid. The moldering faces sizzled and smoked. The poor ruined bodies thrashed about in a grisly dance, their ruined mouths agape in screams long delayed.

Jillian dipped her hands again and threw the fluid outward, trying not to think about what was happening.

They writhed now on the floor, their cries growing fainter. And fainter. At last, at long, long last, they were still.

Jillian, her hands red and dripping, sank slowly to the floor beside Fain's chair.

Chapter 30

Although the city of Guayaquil on the western hump of Ecuador had a population of more than a million, it retained the flavor of a sleepy coastal town. Calle de Gaviotas was a street of small shops and cozy houses overlooking the Gulf of Guayaquil. The building was two stories, painted a soothing pastel pink. A new sign beside the entrance read:

SEÑOR FANTÁSTICO
MAESTRO DEL OCULTISMO

McAllister Fain came down the stairs to the doorway, wearing a flowered shirt and high-cut white peasant pants. He shook hands with a stout, dark-browed woman who had preceded him through the doorway.

The woman smiled at him. "You sure there will be a man? In my life? *De verdad?*"

"Absolutely, *señora*. And soon. Very soon."

He watched the woman walk happily up the street, then turned and climbed the stairs. He walked through the small room where the tarot deck lay spread on the table and into the living quarters with the airy rattan furniture. He went out through the French window onto the pink balcony.

Jillian Pappas reached up from her chair and handed him a frosty glass decorated with a pineapple slice.

Fain took an appreciative sip. "Delicious. What is it?"

"Mostly rum. Did you have good news for Mrs. Ycaza?"

"The cards, my dear, not I."

"Let me guess. A man is coming into her life."

"Amazing. I might dispense with the cards and just use you."

"Sounds like fun," she said.

"No more pupils today?"

"Nope. The English department is closed for the weekend."

He pulled a chair next to hers, and they sipped their drinks in comfortable silence, looking out over the water.

"It doesn't seem as hot as when we first came," Jillian said.

"We've had two months to get acclimated," Fain said. After a moment he added, "Ever miss the old life?"

"Nope. I was kidding myself that I actually enjoyed busting my behind for some little bitty part in a bad play in a crummy theater that would go to some big-chested eighteen-year-old, anyway. Down here I feel like I'm really helping people, teaching English to the poor kids. And learning Spanish from them while I'm at it. How about you, Señor Fantástico? Do you think about what you left behind?"

"Oh, yeah, I think about it. Mostly what I left was a tangle of civil and criminal charges that would take years to straighten out even if I didn't go to prison. I was a little crazy for a while up there, but now I finally know what I want." He leaned over and kissed her. "And I've got it."

"Did you have any doubts we'd make it that last night in Eagle's Roost?"

"Plenty," he admitted. "I wouldn't want to have to do that again."

"Amen," she said. "What made you so sure the beef blood would work? Didn't the formula call for human blood? Yours?"

"It's the nature of magic, darling," he said. "How

264

much is real, and how much is trickery? Who knows for sure? With the alternative being a messy suicide, I figured I wouldn't lose a whole lot by trying a variation of the Sultan's Wine Flask.''

"It sure looked real. I didn't even see you switch the tube from your vein to the plastic blood bag under your jacket.''

"Another basic principle of magic—misdirection. When I dropped the clamp, everybody looked down just long enough for me to make the switch and start the beef blood flowing.''

"Thank gosh it worked. I never want to do anything that icky again.''

This time Fain was the one to say, "Amen.''

There was a knock at their apartment door.

"Adelante!" Fain called from the balcony.

Mrs. Ruiz, the landlady, entered and came over to the French window. She was a stout, dignified woman in black taffeta. "There is a visitor for you. A boy.''

"I thought you had no more pupils today,'' Fain said to Jillian.

"He may be new,'' she said.

"I can send him away,'' said the landlady.

"No,'' Jillian said. "I don't like to do that. Send him up.''

Mrs. Ruiz nodded and went back down to the foot of the stairs where the door opened onto the street. The boy waited there, bundled from head to foot despite the heat. She motioned for him to go up, then fanned the air in front of her face. It would take more than a bath, she thought, to wash away that carrion smell.

Slowly, purposefully, Miguel Ledo climbed the stairs.

By the year 2000, 2 out of 3 Americans could be illiterate.

It's true.

Today, 75 million adults...about one American in three, can't read adequately. And by the year 2000, U.S. News & World Report envisions an America with a literacy rate of only 30%.

Before that America comes to be, you can stop it...by joining the fight against illiteracy today.

Call the Coalition for Literacy at toll-free **1-800-228-8813** and volunteer.

Volunteer Against Illiteracy. The only degree you need is a degree of caring.

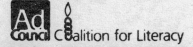

Ad Council · Coalition for Literacy

LV-2